In the Twilight

In the Twilight

Anton Chekhov

Translated by Hugh Aplin

ALMA CLASSICS

ALMA CLASSICS LTD
London House
243-253 Lower Mortlake Road
Richmond
Surrey TW9 2LL
United Kingdom
www.almaclassics.com

In the Twilight first published in Russian in 1887
This translation first published by Alma Classics Ltd in 2014

Translation and Notes © Hugh Aplin, 2014
Extra Material © Alma Classics Ltd

Cover image © Marina Rodrigues

Printed and bound by CPI Group (UK) Ltd, Croydon, CR0 4YY

ISBN: 978-1-84749-383-5

Contents

Anton Chekhov (1860–1904)

Anton Chekhov with his
brother Nikolai

Maria Chekhova,
Anton's sister

Yevgenia and Pavel, Chekhov's parents

The birthplace of Anton Chekhov
in Taganrog

The out-building to Chekhov's residence in Melikhovo,
where he wrote *The Seagull*

Olga Knipper as Mme Ranevskaya
in *The Cherry Orchard*

Olga Knipper as Masha
in *Three Sisters*

The House-Museum in Sadovo-Kudrinskaya Street, Moscow,
where Chekhov lived between 1886 and 1890

Introduction

The early part of Anton Chekhov's literary career was a period of frenzied writing. Working for periodicals to demanding deadlines, and generally within strictly defined limits on both the length and content of his stories, he was a literary journeyman receiving scant remuneration for what he considered the most arduous labour. There are some undeniably outstanding stories among the huge number he produced in those early years, yet there is equally undeniably a good deal of readily forgettable material too. The importance of this collection, *In the Twilight*, the third selection of stories compiled for publication in book form by the author himself, is that it can be seen as marking the watershed between that initial period and the subsequent one, the one which was to establish Anton Chekhov among the greatest exponents of the short story in any language and in any age.

This process was perhaps begun in mid-1885, when Chekhov started regularly contributing stories not only to his usual humorous publications, but also to a well-respected newspaper, *The Petersburg Gazette*. The very titles of some of the stories that followed this new departure – 'Grief' (November 1885), 'Misery' (January 1886) – are indicative of the changing nature of his work. But arguably even more significant in the process was the invitation received early in 1886 to write for Alexei Suvorin's newspaper *New Age*. The positive critical attention that Chekhov's work for *The Petersburg Gazette* had been attracting was doubtless influential in ensuring that the young writer was offered terms that substantially improved his working conditions. To illustrate the attraction of the new association, it need only be mentioned that, while a month's work for the comic press earned Chekhov 45–65 roubles, for 'The Witch' alone, his second story for Suvorin, he was paid a handsome 75 roubles. It comes as no surprise, then, that, while in 1886, as the changes in his career were taking place,

Chekhov wrote 113 stories, just a year later his annual output had dropped to 65. The improvement in remuneration with Suvorin meant that more time could be devoted to each work, and thus that the quality of the writing was likely to improve. This assumption would certainly appear to be borne out by the fact that, when selecting works for inclusion in a collected edition at the end of the century, Chekhov omitted 77 (a staggering 68 per cent) of the stories dating from 1886, as opposed to just 14 (21 per cent) of the works of the following year.

It is also worthy of note that it was when starting to write for Suvorin that Chekhov first used his true name to indicate his authorship. Prior to this, the pseudonym Antosha Chekhonte had masked the identity of the budding young doctor, who had intended to reserve the signature Anton Pavlovich Chekhov for works of a serious academic nature. But in February 1886, after his newspaper's staff had failed to obtain the author's permission, Suvorin himself prevailed upon his new contributor to allow 'The Requiem' to appear as the work of "An. Chekhov". The author had previously suggested that medicine was the field to which he had dedicated himself for life, while literature was merely a passing game, worthy only of a nom de plume. So the publication of 'The Requiem' can be regarded as a symbolic moment, when Chekhov's lasting significance in the world became primarily literary.

And it is Suvorin we also have to thank for the appearance in book form of the first stories written for *New Age*. On 13th March 1887, Chekhov wrote in a letter of having been lent 300 roubles by the publisher and asked to select material specifically from *New Age* for a volume scheduled to appear by the summer. A few days later he was writing again of the "very advantageous terms" he had been offered, and by 19th March he had already made all the decisions needed for the preparation of the volume to go ahead. As he was himself going south to his home town of Taganrog at the end of the month, he gave detailed instructions to his brother Alexander, who was to act for him in St Petersburg in ensuring that his wishes for the volume were met.

The one decision not yet taken at this point was what the title of the forthcoming book should be. Chekhov initially suggested either *Stories* or *My Stories*, telling Suvorin that "everything else that has occurred to me is either pretentious, or old, or silly". It was only at the beginning of June that the title *In the Twilight* was announced (Chekhov evidently being unaware that this too was "old", as a second-rank poet, Dmitry Minayev, had published a book of verse with the very same title almost twenty years earlier). The author explained his choice very clearly in a letter to his brother: "*In the Twilight* – there's an allegory here: life is twilight, and the reader who has bought the book should read it in the twilight, while resting after the day's labours." Alexander tried hard to persuade Anton that this title would not find favour with the book-buying public. "The reader," he wrote, "goes for a title that is either tendentious, or enticing, or else, more often than not, obscurely promising. But twilight melancholy isn't in fashion now." The author, however, was not to be moved. The word "twilight" occurs just six times in the sixteen stories, and is completely absent from twelve of them, yet Chekhov evidently believed that the overall tone of the stories was well represented by the unifying association with the crepuscular. Ten of them, for example, are set at least in part in the evening or night-time, three more at least in part in gloomy buildings, another in a mist; just two rely purely upon their subject matter to reflect the sombreness that is characteristic of the collection as a whole. Perhaps Chekhov was also seeking to draw a strong contrast between this and his previous collection, which had come out under the title *Motley Stories*: twilight may suggest a combination of light and shade – and there are certainly lighter moments in a number of the stories here – yet twilight is clearly distinct from the heterogeneity promised by the adjective "motley".

The choice of stories, and, indeed, the order in which they were to be printed, was, however, made at once, in March. And although the volume was meant to reflect Chekhov's work for *New Age*, he actually included three stories – 'A Restless Guest', 'An Event' and 'A Bad Business' – that had appeared in *The Petersburg Gazette*, demonstrating his intention to give the collection unity in the significant respect of its content, rather than merely by its source. He even took the precaution of suggesting which stories might be excluded from the book, should his selection prove too lengthy: 'An Event' and 'In Court' were first in the firing line, and then 'A Trivial Occurrence', but this only "as a last resort".

Critical responses to the collection, like the responses to the individual stories after their initial publication in the periodical press, were by no means universally positive. Professional reviewers and private readers alike expressed reservations about points of detail or, indeed, entire stories, but many also found a great deal to praise. Chekhov was, of course, still learning his craft at this stage, and his readiness to acknowledge the presence of imperfections in his work is illustrated by his exclusion from the text of 'The Witch' used in this translation of some so-called "naturalistic" detail that offended some readers of its first redaction in *New Age*. But the path to greatness that Chekhov was beginning to tread can be glimpsed in a comment made by Dmitry Grigorovich, to whom *In the Twilight* was dedicated. A famous chronicler of Russian rural life as early as the 1840s, and by the 1880s one of the grand old men of Russian literature, Grigorovich wrote to Chekhov that such mastery as his in the communication of his observations was otherwise encountered only in Turgenev and Tolstoy. This experienced and talented reader and writer could evidently foresee the potential stature of the young man he had been encouraging. And the reading public was sufficiently impressed with *In the Twilight* for Suvorin to be able to publish no fewer than twelve further editions of the collection between 1888 and 1899.

Less prescient, perhaps, than Grigorovich, but encouraging, nonetheless, were the judges of the fourth Pushkin Prize, awarded by the Academy of Sciences in 1888. After due deliberation and voting, they awarded a "full prize" of one thousand roubles to Leonid Maikov, soon to be elected an academician and shortly thereafter Vice-President of the Academy, for his new edition of the poetry of Konstantin Batyushkov, one of the most important mentors of Pushkin himself. To Chekhov, meanwhile, for the previous year's *In the Twilight*, they awarded a "half-prize" of five hundred roubles. Why not a full prize? One academician's review of the collection noted the author's "undoubted talent for drawing pictures of nature and scenes of everyday life", but regretted that "the author's gift was used for such insignificant little things, which bear, to a greater or lesser degree, traces of happenstance, in which one senses that he is relating things that have chanced to catch his eye". Thus the judges considered the stories incapable of "fully satisfying the demands of the highest artistic criticism", while deeming them nonetheless "an outstanding phenomenon in our contemporary belles-lettres, giving cause for hope that the author will, in the further development of his talent, be able to avoid the weak aspects noted in his work".

This translation offers today's Anglophone reader an opportunity to decide whether the academicians were justified in being cautious in their assessment of the developing Chekhov. But in any event, whether they were right or wrong, it was a remarkable achievement for a writer who had until but recently been labouring in the thankless sphere of hack comic literature for the periodical press to achieve recognition of any sort at all in the most exclusive and rarefied air of the Academy of Sciences. *In the Twilight* thus demonstrated how far Chekhov had come – and it also gave clear indications of how far he might yet go.

– Hugh Aplin

In the Twilight

Dreams

Dreams

Two village policemen – one black-bearded, stocky, on unusually short little legs, so that if you look at him from behind, it seems as if his legs start much lower down than anyone else's; the other lanky, thin and straight as a stick, with a straggly little beard, dark ginger in colour – are escorting a tramp with no recollection of his kin* to the District town. The first is waddling along, looking from side to side, chewing now on a piece of straw, now on his sleeve, slapping himself on the thighs and singing softly, and all in all has a carefree and frivolous air; while the other, despite his gaunt face and narrow shoulders, looks solid, serious and sound, reminiscent in the stamp and expression of his entire figure of Old Believer priests* or those warriors that are painted on antique icons. "God gave him some extra forehead for wisdom", i.e. he is bald, which increases still further the similarity mentioned. The first is called Andrei Ptakha, the second Nikandr Sapozhnikov.

The man under escort in no way corresponds to the idea that everyone has of tramps. He is a small, puny man, feeble and sickly, with tiny, colourless and extremely indefinite features. His eyebrows are sparse, his gaze humble and meek, his moustache scarcely shows, although the tramp has already turned thirty. He treads hesitantly, bent over and with his hands tucked into his sleeves. The collar of his little coat of thick woollen cloth with threadbare nap, not that of a peasant, is turned up to the very edge of his cap, so that just his small red nose alone dares to look out upon God's earth. He speaks in an ingratiating little tenor voice, and is forever coughing. It is hard, very hard to recognize in him a tramp concealing his name. He is more likely the impoverished, godforsaken, unfortunate son of a priest, a clerk dismissed for drunkenness, the son or nephew of a merchant who has been trying his feeble little powers in the world of acting and is now going

3

home to play out the final act of the parable of the Prodigal Son;*
perhaps, judging by the dull patience with which he does battle
with the impassable mud of autumn, he is a fanatical lay brother,
roaming around the monasteries of Russia, doggedly seeking "a
life peaceful and sinless" and failing to find it...

The travellers have been walking for a long time, but simply
cannot get away from one small plot of land. In front of them is
some five *sazhens** of muddy, black-brown road, behind is just the
same, and beyond, wherever you look, is an impenetrable wall of
white mist. They walk and walk, but the earth is still the same,
the wall is no closer and the plot remains a plot. There will be a
glimpse of white, angular cobblestones, or a gully, or an armful
of hay, dropped by a passer-by, or the short-lived glint of a big,
murky puddle, or else suddenly and unexpectedly there will appear
up ahead a shadow with indefinite outlines; the closer to it, the
smaller and darker it is, closer still – and in front of the travellers
there rises a crooked milepost bearing a worn number, or else a
wretched birch tree, wet and bare, like a roadside beggar. The
birch will babble something with the remains of its yellow leaves,
and one little leaf will fall and float lazily towards the ground...
And then again there is the mist, the mud and the brown grass
along the edges of the road. Upon the grass hang opaque, unkind
tears. These are not the tears of quiet joy the earth cries when
greeting and seeing off the summer sun and that provide water
at dawn and dusk for quails, corncrakes and elegant, long-nosed
curlews! The travellers' feet stick in the heavy, clinging mud. Every
step costs an effort.

Andrei Ptakha is somewhat excited. He examines the tramp and
endeavours to understand how it is a lively, sober man can fail to
remember his own name.

"Are you Orthodox?" he asks.

"Orthodox," the tramp replies meekly.

"Hm!... so you've been christened then?"

"What do you think? I'm not a Turk. And I go to church, and I
fast, and I don't eat meat and dairy when it's not allowed. I follow
lerigion to the letter..."

"So what on earth's your name, then?"

"You call me whatever you like, lad."

Ptakha shrugs his shoulders and slaps himself on the thighs in extreme perplexity. The other policeman, Nikandr Sapozhnikov, is solidly silent. He is not as naive as Ptakha and is evidently well aware of the reasons that prompt an Orthodox man to conceal his name from people. His expressive face is cold and stern. He strides along on his own and does not stoop to idle chatter with his comrades, as though trying to demonstrate to all, even the mist, his steadiness and good sense.

"God knows how you're to be understood," Ptakha continues to pester him. "Not really a peasant, not really a gentleman, but kind of something in between... T'other day I was washing sieves in the pond and I caught this little snake thing, the size of my finger, with gills and a tail. To begin with I thought it was a fish, then I look and – well I'll be damned – it's got feet. Maybe it's a fish, maybe it's a snake, maybe it's the devil knows what it is... And you're the same... What class are you from?"

"I'm a peasant, from peasant stock," sighs the tramp. "My mum was a house serf. I'm not like a peasant to look at, that's for sure, because that's the way my fate turned out, good man. My mum lived with her masters as a nanny and had every pleasure, well, and I'm her flesh and blood, so I was with her in the masters' house. They pampered me, spoilt me and hammered away at the task of pulling me out of my simple station and making a fine man of me. I slept on a bed, had a proper dinner every day, wore trousers and half-boots in the manner of some little nobleman. What Mum ate, I was fed the same; the masters would give her money for clothes, and she'd dress me with it... It was a good life! The number of sweets and spice cakes I got through in my childhood years, if you were to sell them now, you'd be able to buy a good horse. Mum taught me my letters, inspired the fear of God in me from an early age, and fashioned me in such a way that now I can't utter a single indelicate peasant's word. And I don't drink vodka, lad, and I dress cleanly, and I can keep myself in a respectable state in good society. If she's still alive, then God grant her good health, and if she's dead, then rest her soul, Lord, in Thy kingdom, where the righteous do rest!"

The tramp bares his head with its protruding sparse stubble, lifts up his eyes and makes the sign of the cross over himself twice.

"Send her, Lord, a place that's lush, a place that's peaceful!" he says, drawing out the words in a voice more like an old woman's than a man's. "Teach her, Lord, Thy servant Kseniya, by Thy justification! Were it not for my beloved mum, I'd be a simple peasant, without any understanding! Now, lad, whatever you ask me about, I understand it all: secular writing, and divine, and all sorts of prayers and the cattychism. And I live according to the scriptures... I do no one no ill, I keep my flesh in purity and chastity, I observe the fasts, I eat at the right time. The only pleasure another man has is vodka and bawling, but me, if there's time, I'll sit down in a corner and read a book. I read, and just keep crying and crying..."

"And what are you crying for?"

"The writing's piteous! There are some books you give five kopeks for, and you cry and moan in the extreme."

"Is your father dead?" asks Ptakha.

"I don't know, lad. I don't know my parent, it's no use denying it. The way I see myself is that I was my mum's illegitimate child. My mum lived all her life with her masters and didn't want to get wed to a simple peasant..."

"And jumped on her master," grins Ptakha.

"She didn't say no, that's for sure. She was devout and God-fearing, but didn't keep her virginity. It's a sin, of course, a great sin, no question about it, but then maybe I've got noble blood in me. Maybe I'm only a peasant in station, but in essence I'm a noble gentleman."

The "noble gentleman" says all this in his quiet, sugary tenor, wrinkling his narrow little brow and emitting squeaking sounds from his little red, frozen nose. Ptakha listens, casting sidelong glances at him, and does not stop shrugging his shoulders. After walking six versts* or so, the policemen and the tramp sit down on a little knoll for a rest.

"Even a dog remembers its name," mutters Ptakha. "My name's Andryushka, his is Nikandra, everyone has their own sacred name and it's just not possible to forget that name! It just isn't!"

6

"Who has any need to know my name?" sighs the tramp, leaning his cheek on his fist. "And what's the good of it to me? If they'd let me go where I wanted, but I'll be worse off than I am now, won't I? I know the law, Orthodox brothers. Now I'm a tramp with no recollection of his kin, and the worst that can happen is they'll sentence me to Eastern Siberia and give me thirty or forty lashes, but if I tell them my real name and station, they'll send me back to hard labour. I know it!"

"So you've done hard labour, have you?"

"I have, dear friend. I spent four years with a shaved head, carrying shackles."

"For doing what?"

"For murder, good man! When I was still a boy, around about eighteen, my mum accidentally poured some arsenic into the master's glass instead of bicarbonate of soda. There were lots of different boxes in the pantry, it wasn't hard to mix them up..."

The tramp sighs, shakes his head and says:

"She was devout, but who knows, another's soul is an impenetrable forest! Maybe it was accidentally, but maybe in her soul she couldn't bear the hurt of the master favouring a new servant... Maybe she poured it in for him on purpose, God knows! I was little then and didn't understand everything... Now I remember that the master did indeed get himself a new concubine, and Mum was sorely distressed. It must have been a couple of years they spent trying us after that... Mum was condemned to hard labour for twenty years; I, through being a minor, only to seven."

"You for what, though?"

"As an accomplice. It was me that gave the master the glass. That was always the way: Mum got the soda ready, and I served it. Only I'm telling you all this, brothers, as a Christian, as if before God, don't you go telling anyone..."

"Why, no one'll even think of asking us," says Ptakha. "So you escaped from hard labour, then, did you?"

"I did, dear friend. About fourteen of us did. God grant them health, these men escaped themselves and took me along with them. Now you judge for yourself, lad, in all conscience, what reason is there for me to reveal my station? Because they'll send me back to hard labour! And what sort of a convict am I? I'm a delicate man, sickly, I like to sleep and eat where it's clean. When I'm praying to God, I like to light a little icon lamp or candle, and to have no noise around me. When I'm making low bows, to have no mess or spittle on the floor. And I make forty bows for Mum morning and evening."

The tramp removes his cap and crosses himself.

"Let them exile me to Eastern Siberia," he says. "I'm not afraid!"

"Is that any better?"

"It's another thing altogether! In hard labour you're just the same as a crayfish in a bast basket: it's a squash, a crush, a scrum, nowhere to take a breather – absolute hell, such hell, may the Queen of Heaven preserve us! You're a villain, and you get the respect due a villain, worse than any dog. You can't eat, nor sleep, nor pray to God. But it's different when you're in a penal settlement. In a penal settlement, first of all, I'll be a part of society in the manner of other people. By law, the authorities have to give me my share… ye-es! Land there is dirt-cheap, they say, the same as snow: take as much as you want! They'll give me land, lad, for ploughing, for a kitchen garden, to build a home… I'll do the ploughing, sowing, like everyone else, I'll get some cattle and all sorts of livestock, bees, sheep, dogs… A Siberian tomcat, so the mice and rats don't eat my things… I'll put up a wooden house, brothers, buy lots of icons… God willing, I'll marry, I'll have some kids."

The tramp is murmuring and looking not at his listeners, but off to one side. However naive his dreams, they are uttered in such a sincere, heartfelt tone that it is hard not to believe in them. The tramp's little mouth is twisted in a smile, while the whole of his face, his eyes, his little nose have become fixed and dim in blissful anticipation of distant happiness. The policemen listen and gaze at him seriously, not without sympathy. They believe too.

"I'm not afraid of Siberia," the tramp continues to murmur. "Siberia's the same Russia, it's the same God and Tsar as here, they speak Orthodox there just the same as you and me. Only there's more free space there and people live richer lives. Everything's better there. The rivers there, to take an example, are far better than the ones here! The fish, that there game – there's no end of it! And for me, brothers, the very first pleasure is fishing. There's nothing I like doing better than sitting with a fishing rod. Honest to God. I fish with a rod, and with a line, and I put fish traps out, and when the ice is moving, I fish with a landing net. I don't have the strength to fish with a landing net, so for five kopeks I hire a peasant. And Lord, what a pleasure it is! You'll catch a burbot, or some chub or other, and it's as if you've just seen your brother. And how d'you like that, every kind of fish has its own way of thinking: one you catch with live bait, another with a worm, a third with a frog or a grasshopper. And all of it needs to be understood, you know! Take a burbot, for example. A burbot's an unfussy fish, it'll even take a ruff, a pike likes a gudgeon, an asp likes a moth. If you're in a fast-flowing spot, there's no greater pleasure than fishing for chub. You let your line out about ten *sazhens*, without a sinker, with a moth or a beetle, so that the bait's floating on the surface, you stand in the water with no trousers on and let it go with the current, and there's the chub tugging! Only now you have to try and make sure the damned thing doesn't pull the bait off. As soon as it's jerked on your line, go ahead and hook it, there's no point waiting. I've caught a terrific number of fish in my time! When we were on the run, the other prisoners are asleep in the wood, but I can't sleep, I aim for the river. And the rivers there are wide, fast, the banks steep – ever so! The woods along the bank are all dense. Such trees, that if you glance up at the crown, your head's spinning. If you take the prices here, then for every pine you could pay about ten roubles."

Under the disorderly pressure of his daydreams, artistic images of the past and a sweet presentiment of happiness, the wretched man falls silent and just moves his lips, as though whispering to himself. A dull, blissful smile never leaves his face. The policemen are silent. They have fallen deep in thought and let their heads droop. In the autumnal quiet, when a cold, stern mist from the earth lies upon your soul, when it stands like a prison wall before your eyes and bears testament to a man of the limitations of his will, it can be sweet to think about wide, fast rivers with free, steep banks, about impassable forests, boundless steppes. Slowly and calmly the imagination draws the little patch of a man stealing along an unpeopled, steep bank in the early morning, when the blush of dawn has yet to leave the sky; age-old, mast-like pines, towering in terraces on both sides of the torrent, gaze sternly at the free man and grumble gloomily; roots, huge rocks and prickly bushes bar his way, but he is strong in flesh and hale in spirit, he does not fear the pines, or the rocks, or his solitude, or the rolling echo that repeats his every step.

The policemen are drawing themselves pictures of a free life they have never lived; whether they are vaguely recalling images of something heard long ago, or whether, along with their flesh and blood, they have inherited conceptions of a free life from distant, free ancestors, God knows!

First to break the silence is Nikandr Sapozhnikov, who hereto has yet to utter a single word. Perhaps he has grown envious of the tramp's imagined happiness, or has maybe sensed in his soul that dreams of happiness are not in keeping with the grey mist and the black-brown mud, but he looks sternly at the tramp and says:

"That's as may be, that's all well and good, only you'll not reach those free parts, brother. You've got no chance! You'll go three hundred versts and then give up the ghost. Look how weedy you are! You've only gone six versts, but you can't get your breath back at all!"

The tramp turns slowly in Nikandr's direction and the blissful smile disappears from his face. He directs a frightened, guilty look at the policeman's steady face, evidently recalls something and lets his head droop. Again silence falls... All three are thinking. The policemen are straining their minds to grasp with their imagination what perhaps God alone can imagine, namely, the terrible expanse that separates them from the free land. Whereas the pictures crowding in the tramp's head are clear, distinct and more terrible than that expanse. Vividly before him rise the rigmarole of the court, transit and convict prisons, prisoners' barges, wearisome stops on the journey, freezing winters, illness, the death of comrades...

The tramp blinks guiltily, uses his sleeve to wipe his forehead, on which little drops are appearing, and he lets out a puff of air, as though he has just slipped out of a well-heated bathhouse, then wipes his forehead with the other sleeve and fearfully looks around.

"Dead right, you aren't gonna get there!" agrees Ptakha. "You're no walker! Take a look at yourself: skin and bone! You're going to die, brother!"

"Of course he is! He's got no chance!" says Nikandr. "They'll be putting him in the hospital right away... For sure!"

The man with no recollection of his kin looks in horror at the strict, impassive faces of his ominous travelling companions and, without removing his cap, with staring eyes, he quickly crosses himself... He is all atremble, he shakes his head, and his whole body becomes contorted, like a caterpillar someone has stepped on...

"Well, it's time to go," says Nikandr, rising. "We've had our rest!"

A minute later, the travellers are already striding down the muddy road. The tramp is even more bent, and has tucked his hands deeper into his sleeves. Ptakha is silent.

A Trivial Occurrence

I T WAS A SUNNY NOONTIME in August when, with an impoverished Russian princelet, I drove up to the enormous so-called
Shabelsky wood, where we intended to search for hazel grouse.
My princelet, in view of the role he plays in this story, would
deserve a detailed description. He is a tall, well-proportioned,
brown-haired man, not yet old, but already quite crumpled by
life, with the long moustaches of a chief of police, black, bulging
eyes and the ways of a retired soldier. He is a limited man of the
oriental school, but honest and straightforward, not a fight-picker,
not a fop, and not a carouser – virtues that in the eyes of people
generally award you a diploma in colourlessness and indigence.
People generally didn't like him (in his District he was never
called anything other than "his Highness the simpleton"), but
for me personally the princelet was likeable in the extreme for
the misfortunes and failures of which the whole of his life was
unendingly composed. First and foremost he was poor. He didn't
play cards, didn't go carousing, didn't do anything, didn't poke
his nose in anywhere and was eternally silent, yet somehow or
other he had managed to squander the thirty or forty thousand
left to him by his father. God alone knows where the money went;
I'm only aware that, for want of supervision, a lot was misap-
propriated by managers, stewards and even servants, and a lot
went on loans, tips and guarantees. Rare in the District was the
landowner who wasn't his debtor. He gave to all who asked, and
not so much out of kindness or trust in people as out of affected
gentlemanliness, as if to say "have this, and feel how *comme il
faut** I am!" I made his acquaintance when finally he got into debt
himself, learnt what a second mortgage tastes like, and became
so entangled that he found it impossible to disentangle himself.
There were days when he had no dinner and went around with
an empty cigarette case, but people always saw him nice and

clean and fashionably dressed, and he always gave off a strong scent of ylang-ylang.

The Prince's second misfortune was his utter solitude. He was unmarried and had no family or friends. His taciturn, reticent character, and the *comme il faut* behaviour which came into prominence all the sharper, the stronger his desire to conceal his poverty, prevented him from getting close to people. He was too sluggish, inert and cold for romance, and so he rarely became intimate with women...

Having driven up to the wood, this princelet and I climbed out of the britzka* and set off along a narrow woodland path, hiding in the shade of enormous fern fronds. But we hadn't gone as much as a hundred paces, when from behind a stand of young firs an *arshin** high there arose, as though springing out of the ground, a tall, lanky figure with a long, oval face, dressed in a worn jacket, a straw hat and patent-leather Hessian boots. In one of the stranger's hands was a basket of mushrooms, with the other he was pulling playfully at a cheap little chain on his waistcoat. On seeing us, he became embarrassed, straightened his waistcoat, cleared his throat politely and smiled pleasantly, as though glad to see such good people as us. Then, quite unexpectedly for us, shuffling his long feet across the grass, bending his entire body and without ceasing to smile pleasantly, he approached us, raised his hat and pronounced in a sugary voice, in which could be heard the intonations of a howling dog:

"Eh-eh-eh... gentlemen, however hard as it might be for me, I must warn you that hunting in this wood is forbidden. Excuse me for taking the liberty of troubling you when not acquainted, but... permit me to introduce myself: I'm Grontovsky, chief clerk on Mrs Kandurina's estate!"

"Pleased to meet you, but why ever can't we hunt?"

"That's the will of the owner of the wood!"

The Prince and I exchanged glances. A minute passed in silence. The Prince stood and gazed pensively at a large fly agaric at his feet that someone had toppled with a stick. Grontovsky continued smiling pleasantly. His whole face was blinking, oozing honey, and even the chain on his waistcoat seemed to be smiling and trying to amaze us with its delicacy. Silent embarrassment swept through the air; all three felt awkward.

"Nonsense!" I said. "I was hunting here no more than a week ago!"

"That may very well be!" Grontovsky giggled through his teeth. "In reality everyone hunts here, irrespective of the ban, but as I've come upon you, it's my responsibility... my sacred duty to warn you. I'm a dependent man. If the wood were mine, then, Grontovsky's word of honour, I wouldn't oppose your pleasant amusement. But who's to blame for Grontovsky being dependent?"

The lanky fellow sighed and shrugged his shoulders. I started to argue and get heated, trying to prove my point, but the louder and more persuasively I spoke, the more honeyed and sickly-sweet Grontovsky's face became. The consciousness of having a certain power over us evidently afforded him the greatest enjoyment. He was enjoying his condescending tone, cordiality and manners, and it was with particular relish that he pronounced his resonant surname, of which he was probably very fond. Standing before us, he felt more than in his element. And judging by the sidelong, embarrassed glances he occasionally threw at his basket, there was just the one thing that marred his mood, and that was the mushrooms, the prose of peasant men and women that insulted his greatness.

"We're not going to turn back!" I said. "We've travelled fifteen versts!"

"What can one do?" sighed Grontovsky. "If you'd been so good as to travel not fifteen, but a hundred thousand versts, if the King himself had come here from America or some other distant country, even then I would consider it my duty... my sacred, so to speak, responsibility..."

"Does this wood belong to Nadezhda Lvovna?" asked the Prince.

"Yes, sir, Nadezhda Lvovna."

"Is she at home now?"

"Yes, sir... I'll tell you what, you go and see her – it's half a verst from here, no more – and if she gives you a note, then I'll... of course! Ha-ha... he-he!"

"Very well," I agreed. "It's much closer going to see her than turning back... You go and see her, Sergei Ivanych," I turned to the Prince. "You're acquainted with her."

The Prince, who had all this time been gazing at the toppled fly agaric, raised his eyes to look at me, had a think and said:

"I was acquainted with her once, but... I don't feel entirely comfortable going to see her. And I'm badly dressed, what's more... You go – you're not acquainted with her... It's easier for you."

I agreed. We got into the wagon and, with Grontovsky's smiles seeing us off, we set about driving around the edge of the wood to the owner's house. I wasn't acquainted with Nadezhda Lvovna Kandurina, née Shabelskaya, I had never before seen her up close and knew of her only by hearsay. I knew she was wealthy beyond measure, like no one else in the Province... After the death of her father, Shabelsky, a landowner of whom she was the only daughter, she was left with several estates, a stud farm and a lot of money. I'd heard that, despite her age of twenty-five or twenty-six, she was unattractive, colourless and insignificant, just like everyone else, and stood out from the run of ordinary provincial gentlewomen only by virtue of her enormous fortune.

It has always seemed to me that wealth is something palpable, and that the wealthy must have their own special feeling, unknown to the poor. Often, when riding past Nadezhda Lvovna's big fruit orchard, out of which there rose the enormous, heavy house with the curtains at the windows constantly drawn, I would think: "What's she feeling at the present moment? Is there happiness there behind the blinds?" etc. Once, from a distance, I saw her coming back from somewhere in a nice, light cabriolet, driving a pretty white horse, and, sinner that I am, not only did I envy her, I even found that there was something special in her manner of sitting and in her movements, something that those who aren't wealthy don't have, in the same way that people by nature servile contrive at first sight to find breeding in the ordinary appearance of people whose station is slightly more exalted than their own. Nadezhda Lvovna's private life was known to me only from gossip. It was said in the District that five or six years earlier, before her marriage, in her father's lifetime, she had been passionately in love with Prince Sergei Ivanovich, who was now riding alongside me in the wagon. The Prince had enjoyed going to see the old man and had sometimes spent days on end in his billiards room, where he had tirelessly played pyramid until his arms and his legs ached, but six months before the old man's death he had suddenly stopped visiting the Shabelskys. Without having any positive data, District gossip explains such an abrupt change in relations in all sorts of ways. Some say that the Prince, having apparently noticed plain Nadenka's feelings and not being in a position to reciprocate, had considered it the duty of a decent man to discontinue his visits; others assert that old Shabelsky, upon learning why his daughter was wasting away, had suggested the poor Prince marry her, but the Prince, imagining in his dimness that people were trying to buy him, together with his title, became indignant, said a lot of silly things and fell out. What is true and what untrue in this nonsense is hard to say, but that there is an element of truth is clear from the fact that the Prince would always avoid conversations about Nadezhda Lvovna.

I know that soon after her father's death, Nadezhda Lvovna married a certain Kandurin, a visiting Doctor of Law, a man not rich, but canny. She didn't marry for love, but having been touched by the love of a Doctor of Law who, so they say, played a man enamoured splendidly. At the time I'm describing, her husband, Kandurin, was for some reason living in Cairo, and from there wrote "travel notes" to his friend, the District Marshal, while she, surrounded by parasitic, sponging women, languished behind lowered blinds and whiled away her dull days with minor acts of philanthropy.

On the way to the house the Prince got talking.

"It's three days now that I've not been home," he said in a half-whisper, with a sidelong look at the driver. "I think I'm already a grown-up, I'm not an old woman and I'm not prejudiced, only I can't stomach bailiffs. When I see a bailiff in my house, I go pale, I tremble, and I even get cramp in my calves. D'you know, Rogozhin rejected my promissory note!"

The Prince didn't generally like complaining about bad circumstances; where poverty was concerned, he was secretive, proud in the extreme and fastidious, and for that reason this announcement of his surprised me. He gazed for a long time at a yellow patch of ground, warmed by the sun, where some trees had been felled, let his eyes follow a long line of cranes, floating in the azure heavens, then turned his face to me:

"And by the sixth of September the money for the bank needs to be made ready... the interest on the estate!" he said out loud, no longer shy about the presence of the coachman. "But where am I to get it from? Things are tough all round, old chap! Oh, really tough!"

The Prince examined the cocking pieces of his rifle, for some reason blew on them, and began looking for the cranes, which had disappeared from view.

"Sergei Ivanych," I asked after a minute's silence, "if, say, they sell your place, Shatilovka, what are you going to do?"

"Me? I don't know! Shatilovka can't survive, that's as plain as twice two is four, but I can't imagine such a calamity. I can't imagine myself without a ready crust of bread. What am I going to do? I have almost no education, I've yet to try working, it's too late to start in the civil service... And what branch? Where might I be suited? Let's say it's no big deal being in the civil service, if only here in the Zemstvo,* for example, but I'm... the devil knows, kind of faint-hearted, not a grain of courage. I'll go into the civil service and I'll forever be thinking that I've bitten off more than I can chew. I'm no idealist, no Utopian, no special sort of man of principle, I must simply be stupid and have a few screws loose. A psychopath and a coward. Not like other people generally. Everyone else is a normal person; I'm the only one that makes himself out to be something... I don't know what... On Wednesday I met Naryagin. You know him, drunk, scruffy... Doesn't pay his debts, a bit stupid..." the Prince pulled a wry face and shook his head, "a dreadful fellow! He's staggering as he says to me: 'I'm standing for Justice of the Peace!' He won't be elected, of course, but he actually believes he's suitable to be a Justice of the Peace, considers himself up to the job. He's got courage and self-confidence. I drop in on our Investigator too. The man gets 250 a month, but has practically no work; all he ever does is pace from corner to corner for days on end in nothing but his underwear, but ask him, and he's sure he's doing a real job, honestly fulfilling his duty. I couldn't do that! I'd be ashamed to look the Treasurer in the eye."

At this point Grontovsky galloped past us ostentatiously on a little chestnut horse. Dangling at the elbow of his left arm was the basket, in which the boletuses were bouncing up and down. Drawing level with us, he bared his teeth and waved his hand as if to old acquaintances.

"Blockhead!" the Prince muttered through his teeth, gazing in his wake. "It's amazing how offensive it can sometimes be to see smug physiognomies. A silly, animal feeling, and probably the result of being hungry... Where was I? Oh yes, the civil service... I'd be ashamed to be receiving a salary, though really and truly it's silly. If you look at things more broadly, seriously, then I'm living at the expense of others even now. Isn't that so? But for some reason I'm not ashamed now... Maybe it's habit... or an inability to ponder on my true position... And that position is probably dreadful!"

I looked to see if the Prince was putting on an act. But his face was meek, and his eyes were sadly following the movements of the little chestnut horse as it receded, as though his happiness were receding with it.

He was evidently in that state of irritability and sadness in which women cry quietly without reason, while men feel the need to complain about life, about themselves, about God...

By the gates of the manor house, as I was climbing out of the wagon, the Prince said:

"A certain person who wanted to hurt me once said I had the physiognomy of a cheat. I've noticed myself that cheats are most commonly brown-haired. Listen, it seems to me that if I really had been born a cheat, I'd have still remained an honest man until the day I died, as I wouldn't have had the courage to do wrong. I tell you frankly, I've had the opportunity in my life to grow rich. If I'd lied just once in my life, lied only to myself and to one wo... and to one person, who I know would have forgiven me my lie, I'd have pocketed a million in cash. But I couldn't! Didn't have the heart!"

From the gates to the house you had to go down a long road through a grove, as even as a ruler and planted on both sides with dense, clipped lilac. The house was a heavy and tasteless thing with a façade resembling a theatre. It rose awkwardly out of a mass of greenery and was offensive to the eye, like a big cobblestone thrown onto velvet grass. I was met at the front entrance by a corpulent old servant in a green frock coat and large silver spectacles; without announcing me, after just a fastidious inspection of my dusty figure, he took me through to the private rooms. While I was going up the soft staircase there was for some reason a strong smell of rubber, but in the hall upstairs I was enveloped by an atmosphere characteristic only of archives, seigniorial mansions and the ancient houses of merchants: the smell seems to be of something long gone, that once lived and has died, leaving its soul in the rooms. From the hall to the drawing room I went through three or four rooms. I remember bright-yellow, shiny floors, chandeliers wrapped in cheesecloth, and narrow striped rugs that ran not as normal, directly from door to door, but alongside the walls, and so in every room, so as not to risk touching the bright floor with my rough waders, I was obliged to describe a rectangle. In the drawing room, where the servant left me, there stood, wrapped in twilight, antique, old-fashioned furniture in white covers. It gazed sternly, in the manner of old men, and, as if out of respect for its peace, not a single sound was to be heard.

Even the clock was silent... In a gold frame, Princess Tarakanova* seemed to have fallen asleep, and the water and rats had frozen at the behest of magic. The light of day, afraid of disturbing the general peace, was barely breaking through the lowered blinds and lay on the soft rugs in pale, slumbering strips.

Three minutes passed, and noiselessly into the drawing room came a large old woman in black with a bandaged cheek. She bowed to me and raised the blinds. Immediately, enveloped in bright light, the rats and the water in the picture came to life, Tarakanova woke up, and the old men-cum-armchairs screwed up their eyes.

"The mistress will be here in just a minute, sir..." said the old woman, screwing her eyes up too.

Another few minutes of waiting, and I saw Nadezhda Lvovna. What struck me first and foremost was the fact that she was, indeed, plain: small in stature, skinny, rather round-shouldered. Her hair, thick and auburn, was luxuriant, her face, clean and cultured, breathed youth, the look of her eyes was intelligent and clear, but all the charm of her head was lost thanks to large, plump lips and too sharp an angle to the face.

I gave my name and told her the aim of my visit.

"I truly don't know what I should do!" she said pensively, lowering her eyes and smiling. "I wouldn't want to refuse, but at the same time…"

"Please!" I begged.

Nadezhda Lvovna looked at me and burst out laughing. I did too. She was probably amused by what Grontovsky had enjoyed, i.e. the right to permit or forbid, while I had suddenly begun to find my visit curious and strange.

"I wouldn't want to upset a long-established order," said Kandurina. "Hunting on our land has been banned for six years now. No!" she shook her head decisively. "I'm sorry, I must refuse you. If I allow you, I shall have to allow others too. I don't like unfairness. Either everyone or no one."

"That's a pity!" I sighed. "It's particularly sad as we've travelled fifteen versts. I'm not alone here," I added. "Prince Sergei Ivanych is with me."

I uttered the Prince's name without any ulterior motive, prompted by no particular considerations or aims, I just blurted it out in my innocence without thinking. On hearing the familiar name, Kandurina gave a start and fixed a lengthy gaze upon me. I noticed that her nose had turned pale.

"It makes no difference…" she said, lowering her eyes.

While conversing with her, I had been standing by a window that looked out onto the grove. I could see the entire grove with its avenues and ponds, and the road down which I had just walked. At the end of the road, beyond the gates, was the black rear end of our wagon. Standing by the gates, with his back to the house and his legs apart, was the Prince, chatting with lanky Grontovsky.

All the time, Kandurina had been by the other window. She had been glancing occasionally at the grove, but after I had uttered the Prince's name, she no longer turned away from the window.

"Forgive me," she said, narrowing her eyes at the road and the gates, "but it would be unfair to allow only you to hunt... And to add to that, what's the pleasure in killing birds? What's it for? They bother you, do they?"

A solitary life, enclosed within four walls with the twilight of the rooms and the oppressive smell of rotting furniture, disposes you to sentimentality. The idea Kandurina had let drop was an honourable one, but I couldn't keep myself from saying:

"If you reason that way, then you ought to go bare-footed. Boots are made from the skin of animals that have been killed."

"One has to distinguish between necessity and whim," Kandurina replied indistinctly.

By now she had recognized the Prince and couldn't tear her eyes away from his figure. It's hard to describe the rapture and the suffering with which her plain face was lit up. Her eyes smiled and shone, her lips trembled and laughed, and her face stretched closer to the glass. Holding on with both hands to a flower pot, with one foot slightly raised and with bated breath, she was reminiscent of a dog, pointing and waiting with passionate impatience for "fetch"!

I looked at her and at the Prince, who had been unable to lie just once in his life, and I began to feel vexed and bitter about truth and lies, which play such an elemental role in people's personal happiness.

The Prince suddenly roused himself, took aim and fired. The hawk flying over him flapped its wings and shot off like an arrow far away to one side.

"Aimed too high!" I said. "So then, Nadezhda Lvovna," I sighed, moving away from the window, "you won't allow it..."

Kandurina was silent.

"Then I'll bid you farewell," I said, "and beg you to forgive me for troubling you..."

Kandurina wanted to turn and face me, and had already completed a quarter of the turn, but immediately hid her face behind a drape, as though she'd felt tears in her eyes and wanted to conceal them...

"Farewell... I'm sorry..." she said quietly.

I bowed to her back and, no longer bothering about the rugs, I strode off across the bright-yellow floors. I felt pleased to be leaving this little kingdom of gilded tedium and sorrow, and I hurried, as though wanting to rouse myself from an oppressive, fantastical dream, with its twilight, Tarakanova and chandeliers...

By the entrance a maid caught up with me and handed me a note, where I read: "The bearers are permitted to hunt. N.K."

A Bad Business

"WHO GOES THERE?"

No reply. The watchman can see nothing, but through the noise of the wind and the trees he can clearly hear that someone is walking down the tree-lined path ahead of him. The March night, cloudy and misty, has shrouded the earth, and it seems to the watchman that the earth, the sky and he himself with his thoughts have merged into some one enormous, impenetrably black thing. You can only walk by feeling your way.

"Who goes there?" the watchman repeats, and it begins to seem to him that he can hear both whispering and stifled laughter. "Who's there?"

"Me, old boy..." replies an old man's voice.

"And who are you?"

"I'm... a passer-by."

"What passer-by might that be?" the watchman shouts angrily, wanting to mask his fear by shouting. "What the hell are you doing here, you devil, hanging about a graveyard in the night!"

"Is this a graveyard, then?"

"What do you think it is? Of course it's a graveyard! Can't you see?"

"Oh dear me. Heavenly Queen!" an old man's sigh is heard. "I can't see a thing, old boy, not a thing... Look how dark it is, how dark. You can't see your hand in front of your face in this dark, old boy! Oh dear me..."

"So who are you?"

"I'm a wanderer, old boy, a wandering pilgrim."

"Blasted devils, nightbirds... Call yourselves wanderers! Drunkards..." the watchman mutters, reassured by the passer-by's tone, and sighs. "The trouble you cause! Drinking all day long, and in the night they're the devil knows where. But from what I could hear, you didn't seem to be here alone, there seemed to be two or three of you."

"I'm alone, old boy, alone. Quite alone... Oh dear me, our sins..."

The watchman bumps into someone and stops.

"How did you get here?" he asks.

"I got lost, good man. I was on my way to the Mitriyevo mill and got lost."

"What's that? As if the road to the Mitriyevo mill's here! You dimwit! To get to the Mitriyevo mill you have to go way to the left, straight out of town on the highway. Through being drunk, you've done an extra three versts. You must have had a skinful in town, eh?"

"I must confess, it's true, old boy, it is... It is, truly, old boy, there's no use denying it. So where do I need to go now?"

"Keep going straight ahead down this path until you hit a blind alley, and now there you bear to the left and walk until you've gone through the entire graveyard, right as far as the gate. There'll be a gate there... Open it up and off you go, Godspeed. Mind you don't fall in the ditch. And there beyond the graveyard keep going through fields, fields, fields, until you come out on the highway."

"God bless you, old boy. May the Heavenly Queen preserve and have mercy on you. Or else you could see me on my way, good man! Be so kind, walk me to the gate!"

"Why, as if I've got the time! Go by yourself!"

"Be so kind, make me pray to God for you. I can't see a thing, not my hand in front of my face, nothing at all, old boy... It's the darkness, the darkness! Show me the way, sir!"

"Oh yes, as if I've got the time to be showing the way! If you fussed over everyone, you'd soon get tired of showing them the way."

"Show me the way, for the love of God. I can't see, for one, and I'm afraid to go through the graveyard on my own. It's scary, old boy, scary, I'm afraid, it's scary, good man."

"So I'm stuck with you then," sighs the watchman. "Well, all right, let's go!"

The watchman and the passer-by move off. They walk next to one another, shoulder to shoulder, in silence. The damp, biting wind hits them right in the face, and invisible trees, rustling and cracking, sprinkle big splashes down on top of them. The path is almost completely covered in puddles.

"There's one thing I don't get," says the watchman after a long silence, "how did you find your way in here? I mean, the gates are locked. Climb over the railings, did you? If it was over the railings, doing that sort of thing's as bad as can be for an old man."

"I don't know, old boy, I don't know. How I found my way in here, I don't know myself. An enticement. The Lord's punishment. Truly, an enticement, the devil led me astray. And you must be the watchman here, old boy?"

"I am."

"Just one for the whole graveyard?"

The pressure of the wind is so strong that they both stop for a moment. The watchman, waiting for the gust of wind to abate, replies:

"There's three of us here, but one's lying in a fever, and the other's asleep. We're taking it in turns, me and him."

"Right, right, old boy, right. This wind, what a wind! I expect the dead can hear it! Yowling like a f'rocious beast, it is... Oh dear me..."

"And where are you from yourself?"

"A long way off, old boy. I'm a Vologda man, from a distance. I go visiting holy places and pray for good people. Save us and have mercy on us, Lord."

The watchman stops for a little while to light his pipe. He squats behind the passer-by's back and lights several matches. The flash of light of the first match illumines for an instant a bit of path to the right, a white gravestone with an angel and a dark cross; the light of the second match, flaring up strongly, but put out by the wind, slips like lightning over the left side of the path, and only the corner part of some railing stands out in the darkness; the third match illumines both to right and left the white gravestone, the dark cross and the railing around a child's little grave.

"The dead are asleep, the dear souls are asleep!" the passer-by murmurs with a loud sigh. "The rich are asleep, and the poor, and the wise, and the foolish, and the kind, and the f'rocious. They're all worth the same. And they'll be asleep until the last trump. May the Kingdom of Heaven be theirs, and eternal rest."

"Here we are now, walking, but there'll come a time, we'll be lying there too," says the watchman.

"Right, right. We all will, all of us. There's not a man that won't die. Oh dear me. Our f'rocious doings, our cunning designs! Sin, sin! My accursed, insatiable soul, my gluttonous belly! I've angered the Lord and shall have no salvation, not in this world nor the next. I'm stuck in sin, like a worm in the earth."

"Yes, but you've got to die."

"That's just it, you have."

"I expect dying's easier for a wanderer than the likes of me…" says the watchman.

"There are wanderers and wanderers. There are the genuine ones, who're pleasing to God and keep a watch on their soul, and then there are those that mooch about a graveyard in the night to keep the devils amused… ye-es! There's one sort of wanderer that'll crack you on the nut with a great big axe, if he wants, and that'll be the end of you."

"Why say such a thing?"

"No reason… Well, and here's the gate, it seems. So it is. Open up, then, dear fellow!"

The watchman feels for the gate to open it, leads the wanderer out by the sleeve and says:

"This here's the end of the graveyard. Now keep going through fields, fields, until you hit the highway. But there'll be a boundary ditch here now, don't fall… And when you come out onto the road, bear to the right and keep on all the way to the mill…"

"Oh dear me…" the wanderer sighs after a short silence. "The way I'm thinking now is there's no reason for me to be going to the Mitriyevo mill… What the devil should I be going there for? Better if I stand here with you for a bit, sir…"

"What do you want to stand with me for?"

"No reason... it's more cheerful with you..."

"I like that, he's found himself a cheer-bringer! Wanderer, I can see you like having a joke..."

"Indeed I do!" says the passer-by with a husky cackle. "Oh, my dear man, my dear fellow! I reckon you'll remember this wanderer for a long time now!"

"And why should I remember you?"

"Well, it's just that I've conned you so cleverly... Am I really a wanderer? I'm not a wanderer at all."

"So who are you?"

"A dead man. Just got out of the coffin... Remember the locksmith, Gubarev, who hanged himself at Shrovetide? Well, I'm that same Gubarev..."

"Tell me another one!"

The watchman does not believe it, but can feel such heavy, cold fear all through his body that he darts off and begins quickly fumbling for the gate.

"Hang on, where are you going?" says the passer-by, grabbing him by the arm. "Hey... how about you, then! And who are you leaving me to?"

"Let go!" shouts the watchman, trying to tear his arm away.

"Stand still! I'm telling you to stand still, so stand still... Stop struggling, you filthy dog! If you want to stay alive, then stand still and keep quiet till I tell you... I just don't feel like spilling any blood, otherwise I'd have had you dead ages ago, you louse... Stand still!"

The watchman's knees buckle. He shuts his eyes in terror and, his whole body trembling, presses up against the railing. He would like to cry out, but knows that his cry will not reach anyone's home... The passer-by is standing alongside him, holding him by the arm... Two or three minutes pass in silence.

"One's in a fever, another's asleep, and the third shows wanderers the way," mutters the passer-by. "Good watchmen, they can be paid their wages! No-o, friend, thieves have always been quicker than watchmen! Stand still, stand still, don't move..."

Five, ten minutes pass in silence. Suddenly the wind brings the sound of someone whistling.

"Right, off you go now," says the passer-by, releasing his arm. "Go and pray, thank God you're still alive."

The passer-by whistles too, runs away from the gate, and can be heard jumping over the ditch. With a presentiment of something very bad, and still trembling in fear, the watchman irresolutely opens the gate and, closing his eyes, runs back. At the turning onto the big, tree-lined path he hears someone's hurrying footsteps, and somebody asks him in a hissing voice:

"Is that you, Timofei? And where's Mitka?"

And having run the full length of the big path, he notices in the darkness a dim little light. The closer to the light, the more terrified he becomes, and the stronger is the presentiment of something bad.

"The light seems to be inside the church," he thinks. "How can it be there? Save us, Our Lady, and have mercy on us! And so it is!"

The watchman stands for a minute before the shattered window and gazes in horror at the sanctuary… A small wax candle the thieves forgot to put out flickers in the wind breaking into the window and throws dim red patches onto scattered chasubles, an overturned cupboard, onto numerous footprints beside the altar and the table of oblation…

A little more time passes, and the howling wind carries through the graveyard the hurried, uneven sounds of the tocsin…

At Home

"S OMEONE CAME FROM the Grigoryevs to fetch some book or other, but I said you weren't in. The postman brought the newspapers and two letters. By the way, Yevgeny Petrovich, might I ask you to turn your attention to Seryozha. Today and the day before yesterday I noticed he was smoking. When I started appealing to his conscience, he blocked up his ears, as usual, and broke into loud song to drown out my voice."

Yevgeny Petrovich Bykovsky, the Public Prosecutor of the District Court, who had just returned from a session and was taking off his gloves in his study, looked at the governess reporting to him and laughed.

"Seryozha's smoking…" he shrugged his shoulders. "I can just imagine that little shrimp with a cigarette! And how old is he?"

"Seven. It may not seem serious to you, but smoking at his age constitutes a harmful and bad habit, and bad habits should be eradicated at the very outset."

"Perfectly true. And where does he get the tobacco from?"

"From inside your desk."

"Really? In that case send him to me."

After the governess had gone, Bykovsky sat down in the armchair in front of his desk, closed his eyes and began thinking. In his imagination, he for some reason drew his Seryozha with a huge, great, long cigarette amid clouds of tobacco smoke, and this caricature made him smile; at the same time the serious, concerned face of the governess evoked in him memories of the time long past and half-forgotten when smoking at school and in the nursery had inspired in pedagogues and parents a strange, not entirely comprehensible horror. It really had been horror. Lads were flogged pitilessly, they were expelled from school, their lives were ruined, although not one of the pedagogues or fathers knew where precisely the harm and criminality of smoking lay.

Even very intelligent people had no difficulty waging war on a vice they did not understand. Yevgeny Petrovich recalled his headmaster, a highly educated and genial old man, who was so worried whenever he caught a boy from the school with a cigarette that he turned pale, immediately convened an emergency meeting of the pedagogical council and condemned the guilty party to expulsion. Such, no doubt, is the law of communal life: the more incomprehensible the evil, the more bitter and crude is the fight against it.

The Prosecutor recalled two or three of those who had been expelled and their subsequent lives, and could not help thinking that the punishment very often does much greater evil than the crime itself. A living organism has the capacity to adapt quickly, to become accustomed and acclimatized to absolutely any atmosphere, otherwise a man would have to sense at every moment what an unreasonable substratum there not infrequently was to his reasonable activity, and how little entirely meaningful truth and certainty there still was even in such responsible fields of activity, frightening in their consequences, as the pedagogical, the juridical, the literary...

And similar thoughts, light and diffuse, such as enter only an exhausted brain now relaxing, began drifting through Yevgeny Petrovich's head; they turn up who knows from where and why, stay in your head for not very long, and seem to creep over the surface of the brain without going very far inside it. For people obliged to think officially, in a straight line, for hours or even days on end, such private, domestic thoughts constitute a sort of comfort, pleasant ease.

It was after eight in the evening. Upstairs, beyond the ceiling, on the first floor, someone was walking from corner to corner of the room, and higher still, on the second floor, two people were playing scales together. The person pacing – who, to judge by the nervy gait, was agonizing about something or else suffering from toothache – and the monotonous scales imparted to the quiet of the evening something somnolent, conducive to idle thoughts. Two rooms away in the nursery the governess and Seryozha were talking.

"Pa-pa's here!" the boy sang. "Papa's he-e-re! Pa! Pa! Pa!"

"*Votre père vous appelle, allez vite!*"* cried the governess, squeaking like a frightened bird. "I've already told you!"

"What am I going to say to him, though?" thought Yevgeny Petrovich.

But before he had managed to think anything up, his son Seryozha, a boy of seven, was already coming into the study. This was someone whose sex could be guessed only from his clothing: he was puny, white-faced, delicate... He was limp in body like a hothouse vegetable, and everything about him seemed extraordinarily gentle and soft: his movements, his curly hair, his gaze, his velvet jacket.

"Hello, Papa!" he said in a soft voice, climbing onto his father's knees and kissing him quickly on the neck. "Did you send for me?"

"Excuse me, excuse me, Sergei Yevgenyich," replied the Prosecutor, pushing him away. "Before kissing, we need to have a talk, and a serious one... I'm cross with you and I don't love you any more. I mean it, my boy: I don't love you, and you're no son of mine... No."

Seryozha looked at his father intently, then shifted his gaze to the desk and shrugged his shoulders.

"What ever have I done to you?" he asked, blinking his eyes in bewilderment. "I haven't been in your study once today and I haven't touched anything."

"Natalya Semyonovna has just been complaining to me that you smoke... Is it true? Do you smoke?"

"Yes, I've smoked once... That's right!..."

"You see, on top of that you're lying as well," said the Prosecutor, frowning and thus masking his smile. "Natalya Semyonovna has seen you smoking twice. So you've been found guilty of three bad deeds: you smoke, you take somebody else's tobacco from his desk and you lie. Thrice guilty!"

"Oh, ye-es!" Seryozha remembered, and his eyes smiled. "That's right, that's right! I've smoked twice: today and before."

"There, you see, so not once, but twice... I'm very, very displeased with you! You used to be a good boy before, but now, I see, you've gone wrong and become bad."

Yevgeny Petrovich straightened Seryozha's collar and thought: "What else should I say to him?"

"Yes, this is bad," he continued. "I didn't expect this from you. Firstly, you have no right to take tobacco that doesn't belong to you. Everyone has the right to make use only of his own property, and if he takes somebody else's, then... he's a bad person!" ("I'm not saying the right things to him!" thought Yevgeny Petrovich.) "For example, Natalya Semyonovna has a trunk full of dresses. It's her trunk, and we, that's to say you and I, don't dare touch it, since it's not ours. That's right, isn't it? You have your toy horses and pictures... I don't take them, do I? Maybe I'd like to take them, but... they're not mine – are they? – they're yours!"

"Take them if you want!" said Seryozha, with raised eyebrows. "Please, don't be shy, Papa, take them! This little yellow dog that's on your desk is mine, but I don't care, do I?... Let it stand there!"

"You don't understand me," said Bykovsky. "You gave the dog to me, it's mine now, and I can do anything I want with it, but I didn't give you any tobacco, did I? The tobacco's mine!" ("I'm not explaining it to him right!" thought the Prosecutor. "This isn't right! Not right at all!") "If I want to smoke somebody else's tobacco, first of all I have to ask his permission..."

Lazily linking one phrase to another and imitating the language of a child, Bykovsky began explaining to his son what property meant. Seryozha gazed at his chest and listened carefully (he enjoyed conversing with his father in the evenings), then leant his elbows on the edge of the desk and began screwing up his short-sighted eyes to look at the papers and the inkstand. His gaze roamed over the desk for a while and came to rest on a bottle of gum arabic.

"Papa, what's glue made of?" he asked suddenly, bringing the bottle up close to his eyes.

Bykovsky took the bottle from his hands, put it back in its place and continued:

"Secondly, you smoke... That's very bad! If I smoke, it doesn't just follow that smoking's allowed. I smoke and know that it's foolish, I scold myself and don't like myself for it..." ("I'm a cunning pedagogue!" thought the Prosecutor.) "Tobacco does great harm to one's health, and someone who smokes dies sooner than he should. And smoking is especially harmful for such little ones as you. You have a weak chest, you've not grown strong yet, and in weak people tobacco smoke causes consumption and other illnesses. Uncle Ignaty, he died of consumption. If he hadn't smoked, perhaps he'd have been alive to this day."

Seryozha gazed pensively at the lamp, touched the shade with his finger and sighed.

"Uncle Ignaty was good at playing the violin!" he said. "The Grigoryevs have got his violin now!"

Seryozha leant his elbows on the edge of the desk again and fell into thought. An expression froze on his pale face as though he were listening intently or else following the development of his own thoughts; sorrow and something resembling fright appeared in his big, unblinking eyes. He was probably thinking about death now, which had so recently taken his mother and Uncle Ignaty. Death carries mothers and uncles off to the other world, while their children and violins remain on earth. Dead people live in the sky, somewhere near the stars, and gaze down from there at the earth. Can they bear the separation?

"What shall I say to him?" thought Yevgeny Petrovich. "He's not listening to me. He obviously doesn't consider either his misdemeanours or my arguments important. How can I make him understand?"

The Prosecutor rose and started walking around the study.

"Before, in my day, these questions were decided with wonderful ease," he reflected to himself. "Any young lad found guilty of smoking was flogged. The faint-hearted and cowardly did indeed give up smoking while, after a thrashing, anyone who was a little braver and cleverer began carrying his tobacco inside the top of his boot and smoking in the shed. After he'd been caught in the shed and thrashed again, he'd go off to the river to smoke... and so on, until the fellow had grown up. My mother used to bribe me not to smoke with money and sweets. But those methods seem worthless and immoral now. Adopting a position founded on logic, the modern pedagogue tries to get a child to grasp good principles not out of fear, not from a desire to stand out or receive a reward, but with awareness."

While he was walking about and thinking, Seryozha clambered up onto the chair to one side of the desk and began drawing. On the desk, so that he didn't make marks on the official papers and didn't touch the ink, there lay a pack of paper, specially cut into quarters for him, and a blue pencil.

"The cook was shredding some cabbage today and cut her finger," he said, drawing a house and moving his eyebrows up and down. "She let out such a cry that we all had a real fright and ran into the kitchen. She's so silly! Natalya Semyonovna tells her to dip her finger in cold water, but she goes and sucks it... And how can she put a dirty finger in her mouth! It's not the done thing, Papa, is it?"

Then he recounted how at lunchtime an organ-grinder had come into the yard with a little girl who had sung and danced to the music.

"He has his own train of thought!" the Prosecutor reflected. "He has his own little world in his head, and he has his own idea of what's important and what's not. To capture his attention and awareness, it's not enough to adapt your language to match his, you have to know how to think the way he does too. He'd have understood me very well if I'd really minded losing the tobacco, if I'd been upset and started crying... The reason why mothers are irreplaceable in their children's upbringing is that they know how to feel, how to cry, how to chuckle with them as one... You won't achieve anything with logic and moralizing. Well, what else shall I say to him? What else?"

And it seemed strange and ridiculous to Yevgeny Petrovich that he, an experienced jurist, who had spent half his life practising all sorts of prevention, warning and punishment, was quite at a loss and didn't know what to say to the boy.

"Listen, give me your word of honour that you won't smoke any more," he said.

"Wo-ord of honour!" sang Seryozha, pressing hard with the pencil and bending down towards the picture. "Wo-ord of honour! Nour! Nour!"

"But does he know what word of honour means?" Bykovsky wondered. "No, I'm a poor mentor! If some pedagogue or one of our court officers took a look inside my head now, they'd call me a wet rag and quite likely suspect me of trying to be too clever by far... But of course, in school and in court all these tricky questions are decided much more easily than at home; here you're dealing with people you love madly, and love is demanding and complicates the question. If this little boy weren't my son, but my pupil or a defendant, I wouldn't be getting cold feet like this and my thoughts wouldn't be scattered!..."

Yevgeny Petrovich sat down at the desk and pulled one of Seryozha's drawings towards him. The drawing was of a house with a crooked roof and smoke that zigzagged like lightning from the chimneys to the very edge of the paper; beside the house stood a soldier with dots for eyes and a bayonet that looked like the figure four.

"A man can't be taller than a house," said the Prosecutor. "Look: your roof only comes up to the soldier's shoulder."

Seryozha climbed onto his father's knees and spent a long time shifting around to find the most comfortable way to sit.

"No, Papa!" he said, after looking at his drawing. "If you draw the soldier small, then you won't be able to see his eyes."

Had he needed to challenge him? From daily observation of his son, the Prosecutor was convinced that children, like savages, have their own distinctive artistic views and demands which are beyond the comprehension of adults. Upon careful observation, Seryozha might seem abnormal to an adult. He found it admissible and reasonable to draw people taller than houses, and to convey with a pencil his sensations as well as objects. Thus the sounds of an orchestra he depicted in the form of spherical, smoky spots, and whistling – in the form of a spiral thread... In his conception, sound was closely contiguous to shape and colour, so that every time he was colouring in letters, he invariably coloured the sound L yellow, M red, A black, etc.

Leaving the drawing, Seryozha moved around once more, adopted a comfortable pose and busied himself with his father's beard. First he assiduously smoothed it out, then he divided it into two and began combing it back like side-whiskers.

"Now you look like Ivan Stepanovich," he murmured, "and in just a moment you'll look like... our porter. Papa, why do porters stand at doors? Is it to stop thieves going in?"

The Prosecutor could feel Seryozha's breath on his face, his cheek was forever touching Seryozha's hair, and his soul was beginning to feel warm and soft, so soft that it was as if not just his hands, but his entire soul were lying on the velvet of Seryozha's jacket. He kept glancing into the boy's big dark eyes, and it seemed to him that gazing at him from those wide pupils were his mother, and his wife, and all he had ever loved.

"And now give him a flogging..." he thought. "And now kindly think up a punishment. No, how on earth are we to try and become educators? People used to be straightforward, they thought less, and that's why they decided questions boldly. Whereas we think too much, we've been corroded by logic... The more mature a man is intellectually, and the more he reflects and splits hairs, the more indecisive and tentative he is, and the greater the timidity with which he sets about anything. Indeed, if you ponder on it a little more deeply, what boldness and belief in yourself must you have to undertake teaching, judging, writing a fat book..."

It struck ten o'clock.

"Well, my boy, it's time for bed," said the Prosecutor. "Say goodnight and go."

"No, Papa," Seryozha pulled a wry face, "I'll stay a bit longer. Tell me something! Tell me a story."

"Very well, only after the story – to bed at once."

On free evenings Yevgeny Petrovich was in the habit of telling Seryozha stories. Just like the majority of businessmen and officials, he didn't know a single poem by heart and didn't remember a single story, and so had to improvise every time. He usually began with the cliché "once upon a time, in a land far, far away"; thereafter he piled up all sorts of innocent nonsense and, as he was telling the beginning, had absolutely no idea what the middle or the ending would be. Scenes, characters and situations were picked at random, impromptu, and the plot and moral emerged somehow of their own accord, independently of the storyteller's will. Seryozha very much enjoyed such improvisations, and the Prosecutor noticed that the more modest and unelaborate the plot turned out to be, the more powerful its impact upon the boy.

"Listen," he began, raising his eyes to the ceiling. "Once upon a time, in a land far, far away, there lived an old, aged Tsar with a long grey beard and... and with this huge moustache. Well, and he lived in a glass palace, which sparkled and shone in the sun like a great big block of pure ice. And the palace, my boy, stood in an enormous garden where, do you know, there were orange trees... bergamots and cherries grew... tulips, roses, lily of the valley flowered, and many-coloured birds sang... Yes... On the trees there hung little glass bells, and when the wind blew, they rang so gently you could listen to them spellbound. Glass gives you a softer and gentler sound than metal... Well, and what else? In the garden there were fountains... Remember, you saw the fountain at Auntie Sonya's dacha? Well, fountains exactly like that stood in the Tsar's garden, only much greater in size, and the jets of water reached to the top of the tallest poplar."

Yevgeny Petrovich had a think and continued:

"The old Tsar had an only son, the heir to the kingdom – a boy just as little as you. He was a good boy. He never had tantrums, he went to bed early, he didn't touch anything on the desk and... and was generally good as gold. He had only one fault – he smoked..."

Seryozha was listening hard and gazing, unblinking, into his father's eyes. The Prosecutor carried on and thought: "And what next?" He spent a long time padding and spinning things out, as they say, and ended like this:

"Through smoking, the Tsarevich fell ill with consumption and died when he was twenty. The decrepit and sickly old man was left without any kind of help. There was no one to govern the state or defend the palace. Enemies came, killed the old man, destroyed the palace, and in the garden now there are no cherry trees, no birds, no little bells... And that's how it is, my boy..."

Such an ending seemed ridiculous and naive to Yevgeny Petrovich himself, but the whole story had made a powerful impression on Seryozha. Again his eyes were clouded with sorrow and something resembling fright; he gazed pensively at the dark window for a minute, shuddered and said in a low voice:

"I shan't smoke any more..."

When he had said goodnight and gone off to bed, his father walked quietly from corner to corner of the room and smiled.

"People might say that it was beauty, the artistic form that made the impact here," he reflected, "and it may be so, but it's no comfort. After all, that's not a genuine remedy... Why should morality and truth be presented not in raw form, but with additives, always without fail in a sugared and gilded form, like pills? It's abnormal... Falsification, deception... conjuring tricks..."

He recalled the jurors who simply have to have a "speech" made to them; the public, who assimilate history only through epic legends and historical novels; himself, who had derived the meaning of life not from sermons and laws, but from fables, novels, poetry...

"Medicine has to be sweet, the truth – beautiful... And man has affected this silliness since the time of Adam... Though... maybe it's all natural and that's the way it should be... In nature there are plenty of expedient deceptions, illusions..."

He set to work, but for a long time idle, domestic thoughts continued to drift through his head. Beyond the ceiling the scales were no longer to be heard, but the first-floor resident was still pacing from corner to corner of the room...

The Witch

IT WAS GETTING ON FOR NIGHT-TIME. The sexton Savely Gykin was lying on the huge bed in his church lodge and was still awake, though he was always in the habit of falling asleep at the same time as the chickens. Looking out from one edge of the soiled blanket, made up of multicoloured scraps of calico, was his coarse ginger hair, and sticking out from beneath another were his big, long-unwashed feet. He was listening... His lodge cut into the church railings, and its only window looked out into the fields. And in the fields there was a real war going on. It was hard to understand who was trying to be the death of whom or for the sake of whose destruction Nature had kicked up such a rumpus, but someone, to judge by the incessant, ominous rumbling, was having a very tough time of it. Some kind of conquering force was chasing someone across the fields, raging in the wood and on the church roof, banging angrily with its fists at the window, ranting and raving, while something conquered was howling and crying... Piteous weeping could be heard, now outside the window, now above the roof, now in the stove. It was no cry for help that was audible in it, but anguish, an awareness that it was already too late, there was no salvation. The snowdrifts were covered with a thin, icy crust; tears trembled on them and on the trees, and spilling down the roads and paths was a dark slush made up of mud and melting snow. In short, there was a thaw on the earth, but the sky could not see it through the dark night and, for all it was worth, was sprinkling flakes of new snow onto the melting earth. And the wind was wandering like a drunkard... It would not allow this snow to settle on the earth and was spinning it around in the darkness as it liked...

Gykin was listening closely to this music and frowning. The thing was that he knew, or at least could guess, where all this fuss outside the window was leading and whose handiwork it was.

"I kno-ow!" he muttered, wagging a finger under the blanket at someone. "I know everything!"

On a stool by the window sat the sexton's wife, Raisa Nilovna. A tin lamp standing on another stool, as if timid and not trusting in its strength, poured a weak, flickering light onto her broad shoulders, the pretty, appetizing contours of her body and the thick plait that was touching the ground. The sexton's wife was sewing sacks from coarse sackcloth. Her hands moved quickly, while the whole of her body, the expression of her eyes, her eyebrows, her plump lips, her white neck, all were frozen, immersed in the monotonous, mechanical work, and seemed to be asleep. Only occasionally did she raise her head to let her weary neck have a rest and glance briefly at the window, beyond which the blizzard was raging, before bending again over the sackcloth. Not desires, nor sorrow, nor joy – nothing did her pretty face with its snub nose and dimples on the cheeks express. In the same way, a pretty fountain expresses nothing when it is not working.

But then she finished a sack, threw it aside and, stretching pleasurably, fixed her dim, immobile gaze on the window... There were tears floating on the panes, and the whiteness of short-lived snowflakes. A snowflake would fall onto a pane, glance at the sexton's wife and melt...

"Come to bed!" growled the sexton.

His wife was silent. But suddenly her eyelashes stirred and there was a flash of attention in her eyes. Savely, who had all the time been observing the expression on her face from under the blanket, poked his head out and asked:

"What?"

"Nothing... There seems to be someone coming..." his wife replied quietly.

The sexton threw off the blanket with his arms and legs, knelt on the bed and gazed obtusely at his wife. The timid light of the lamp lit up his hairy, pockmarked face and slid across his dishevelled, wiry head of hair.

"Do you hear?" asked his wife.

Through the monotonous howl of the blizzard he caught a thin, ringing moan, barely perceptible to the ear, like the whining of a mosquito when it wants to settle on your cheek and gets cross at being hindered.

"It's the post..." growled Savely, resting on his heels.

Three versts from the church lay the post road. At times when the wind was blowing from the high road towards the church, the inhabitants of the lodge could hear sleigh bells.

"Lord, why should anyone want to be travelling in such weather?" sighed the sexton's wife.

"It's official business. Like it or not, off you go..."

The moan hung in the air and then died away.

"It's gone by!" said Savely, lying down.

But he had not managed to cover himself with the blanket before a distinct sound of bells reached his ears. The sexton glanced at his wife in alarm, jumped off the bed and, swaying from side to side, began walking up and down beside the stove. The sound of the bell was there for a little and then died away again, as though cut short.

"Nothing to be heard..." the sexton muttered, stopping and narrowing his eyes at his wife.

But at that point the wind banged at the window, bringing with it the thin, ringing moan... Savely turned pale, gave a croak and again began slapping his bare feet over the floor.

"The post's being blown off course!" he wheezed, throwing an angry sidelong glance at his wife. "D'you hear? The post's being blown off course!... I... I know! Do you really think I don't... don't understand?" he muttered. "I know everything, damn you!"

"What do you know?" asked the sexton's wife, without taking her eyes off the window.

"What I know is this is all your doing, you she-devil! Your doing, damn you! This blizzard, and the post being blown off course... it's all been done by you! You!"

"You're going crazy, you silly man..." the sexton's wife remarked calmly.

"I noticed it in you ages ago! When I married you, on the very first day I saw you had the blood of a bitch in you!"

"Pah!" exclaimed Raisa in surprise, shrugging her shoulders and crossing herself. "You cross yourself too, you idiot!"

"A witch is a witch," continued Savely in a muffled, plaintive voice, hastily blowing his nose on the hem of his shirt. "You may be my wife, you may be of clerical stock, but I'll go and say what you are, even at confession... I certainly will! Protect and have mercy upon us, Lord! Last year, just before the Prophet Daniel and the Three Youths, there was a blizzard and – what do you know? – a tradesman dropped in to get warm. Then on Alexei's Day,* the ice on the river broke up, and that brought the village constable... The whole night he was chattering here with you, curse him, and when he left in the morning and I took a look at him, he had rings under his eyes and his cheeks were all hollow! Eh? Twice during the Saviours* there were thunderstorms, and both times a huntsman came to spend the night here. I saw everything, damn him! Everything! Oh, redder than a lobster now! Aha!"

"You didn't see anything..."

"Oh, no! And before Christmas this year, at the Ten Martyrs of Crete,* when there was a blizzard blowing day and night – remember? – the Marshal's clerk lost his way and ended up here, the dog... And what a thing to be tempted by! Pah, a clerk! And was it really worth stirring up God's weather for him? The devil, the short-arse, knee-high to a grasshopper, his ugly mug covered in blackheads and his neck all crooked... All right, if he'd been handsome, but he was just – ugh! – Satan!"

The sexton drew breath, wiped his lips and listened intently. There was no bell to be heard, but then the wind tore up above the roof, and in the darkness outside the window the jingling began again.

"And now too!" Savely continued. "The post isn't being blown off course for nothing! Spit in my eyes if it's not you the post's looking for! Oh, the demon knows its business, he's a fine assistant! He'll blow it off course, blow it off course, and then lead it here! I kno-ow! I se-ee! You can't hide it, your pagan lust, you demon's magpie! As soon as the blizzard started, I could read your thoughts straight away."

"What an idiot!" grinned the sexton's wife. "So what, according to you and your idiotic mind, I can make bad weather?"

42

"Hm... You can grin! You or not you, only I notice the way as soon as your blood begins to boil, the weather turns bad, and as soon as the weather turns bad, some madman or other gets brought here. That's how it happens every time! So it must be you!"

For greater persuasiveness the sexton put a finger to his forehead, closed his left eye and said in a melodious voice:

"Oh, the madness! Oh, the sinfulness of Judas! If you are indeed a human and not a witch, you might have thought in your head: what if that wasn't a tradesman, not a huntsman, not a clerk, but a demon in their image? Eh? You might have thought!"

"You really are stupid, Savely!" sighed the sexton's wife, looking at her husband with pity. "When Daddy was alive and lived here, lots of different people came to him to get treatment for the shaking sickness: from the village, and from the hamlets, and from the Armenian farmsteads. They came nigh on every day, and no one called them demons. But if someone drops in on us once a year in bad weather to get warm, then it's a wonder for you, you silly man, and straight away you get all sorts of ideas."

Savely was touched by his wife's logic. He set his bare feet apart, bent his head and fell deep in thought. He was not yet firmly convinced by his suppositions, and his wife's sincere, indifferent tone had him quite nonplussed, but nonetheless, after a little thought, he shook his head and said:

"It's not as if it's old men or pigeon-toed types that ask to spend the night, it's always young ones... Why's that? And if they only got warm, all right, but they get up to the devil knows what, don't they? No, woman, there's no creature more cunning in this world than your woman's breed! Heavens, there's less real intelligence in you than a starling has, and yet demonic cunning – ooh! – Heavenly Queen, preserve us! There, it's the post sleigh ringing! The blizzard was still only starting, but I already knew your every thought! You've done your bewitchery, you spider!"

"What are you picking on me for, curse you?" said the sexton's wife, running out of patience. "What are you picking on me for, you pest?"

"Why I'm picking on you is that, if tonight, God forbid, anything happens... you listen!... if anything happens, then tomorrow, at first light, I'll go to Dyadkovo* to Father Nikodim and explain everything to him. This is what I'll say, I'll say, Father Nikodim, be generous and forgive me, but she's a witch. Why? Hm... you want to know why? As you wish... That's what I'll say. And woe is you, woman! Not just at the dread seat of Judgement, but in the earthly life too you'll be punished! Not for nothing are there prayers written in the Book of Needs* regarding the likes of you!"

Suddenly a knock rang out at the window, so loud and extraordinary that Savely turned pale and sat down in fright. The sexton's wife leapt up and turned pale too.

"For God's sake, let us in to get warm!" a resonant, rich bass was heard. "Who's there? Be so kind! We've lost our way!"

"And who are you?" asked the sexton's wife, afraid to glance at the window.

"The post!" replied another voice.

"Your devilizing wasn't in vain!" Savely waved an arm. "So it is! I'm right... Well, just you watch out!"

The sexton jumped up and down twice in front of the bed, toppled onto the mattress and, wheezing angrily through his nose, turned his face to the wall. Soon there was a blast of cold at his back. The door creaked, and on the threshold appeared a tall human figure, plastered from head to foot in snow. Behind it there was a glimpse of another figure, equally white...

"Are the postbags to be brought in too?" asked the second figure in a hoarse bass.

"Well they can't be left there!"

Saying this, the first man began untying his hood, and then, without waiting for it to be untied, tore it from his head, together with his cap, and flung it angrily towards the stove. Next, dragging off his coat, he threw it in the same direction and, without a word of greeting, began pacing around the lodge.

He was a young, fair-haired postman in a tatty, threadbare uniform frock coat and dirty, ginger-coloured boots. Having warmed himself with his walking, he sat down at the table, stretched his dirty boots out towards the sacks and propped his head up with his fist. His pale face with red blotches still bore traces of the pain and terror he had just experienced. Contorted with anger, with

44

the fresh traces of its recent physical and moral suffering, with melting snow on its brows, moustache and little rounded beard, it was handsome.

"A dog's life!" the postman growled, casting his eyes over the walls, and as though not believing he was in the warm. "Almost done for! If it hadn't been for your light, I just don't know what would have happened... And the devil knows when it's all going to stop! There's simply no end to this dog's life! Where is it we've driven off course to?" he asked, lowering his voice and looking up suddenly at the sexton's wife.

"Gulyaevsky Hill, General Kalinovsky's estate," replied the sexton's wife, rousing herself and blushing.

"Hear that, Stepan?" the postman turned to the driver, who was stuck in the door with a big leather postbag on his back. "We've ended up on Gulyaevsky Hill!"

"Yes... that's a long way off!"

Uttering these words in the form of a hoarse, intermittent sigh, the driver went out and, after a little while, brought in another, rather smaller postbag, then went out again, and this time brought in the postman's sabre on its broad belt, similar in fashion to the long, flat sword with which Judith is drawn at the bed of Holofernes* in cheap popular prints. Having stacked the postbags along the wall, he went out into the lobby, sat down there and lit his pipe.

"Perhaps you'll take some tea after your journey?" asked the sexton's wife.

"A fat chance we've got of drinking any tea!" the postman frowned. "We need to get warm quickly and go, or else we'll be late for the post train. We'll sit for ten minutes or so and be off. Only be so good as to show us the way..."

"The weather's God's punishment!" sighed the sexton's wife.

"Mm, yes... And who would you yourselves be here?"

"Us? We're here at the church... We're of the clergy... That's my husband lying there! Savely, do get up, come and say hello! There used to be a parish church here, but about a year and a half ago it was closed down. Of course, when the masters lived here there were people here too, and it was worth keeping the parish, but now, without the masters, judge for yourself, what are the clergy to live on, if the nearest village to here is Markovka, and even that's five versts away! Savely's not attached to any parish now and… he does the job of a watchman. He's entrusted with looking after the church…"

And here the postman also learnt that if Savely went to the general's widow and asked her for a note to the bishop, then he'd be given a good place, but that he didn't go to the General's widow because he was lazy and afraid of people.

"After all, we're of the clergy," added the sexton's wife.

"So what do you live on?" asked the postman.

"There's a hayfield and allotments belonging to the church. Only we don't make much out of that…" the sexton's wife sighed. "Father Nikodim from Dyadkino, the greedy guts, conducts one service here for the summer Nikola and one for the winter Nikola,* and in return takes almost everything for himself. There's no one to stick up for us!"

"You're telling lies!" wheezed Savely. "Father Nikodim's a saintly soul, a guiding light of the church, and if he takes, then it's according to the rule book!"

"That's a grumpy one you've got there!" the postman grinned. "Been married to him long?"

"More than three years since Forgiveness Sunday.* My Daddy was sexton here before, and then, when the time came for him to die, he went to the consistory and asked for an unmarried sexton to be sent to me as a bridegroom, so that I still had the place. And so I got married."

"Aha, and so *you* killed two flies with one swatter!" said the postman, looking at Savely's back. "Got a job, and took a wife."

Savely twitched his leg impatiently and moved closer to the wall. The postman got up from his seat at the table, stretched and sat down on a postbag. After a moment's thought, he kneaded the bags a little, moved the sabre elsewhere and stretched himself out, leaving one leg resting on the floor.

"A dog's life…" he muttered, putting his hands beneath his head and closing his eyes. "I wouldn't even wish such a life on a rotten Tatar."

It soon fell quiet. All that could be heard was Savely breathing noisily through his nose, and the sleeping postman, as he breathed regularly and slowly, emitting a deep, long-drawn-out "k-kh-kh-kh..." every time he exhaled. Occasionally some little wheel in his throat would squeak a bit, and his quivering leg would rustle against the postbag.

Savely began turning back and forth under the blanket and slowly looked around. His wife was sitting on the stool and, squeezing her cheeks with the palms of her hands, was gazing into the postman's face. Her gaze was motionless, like that of someone surprised, frightened.

"Well, what are you staring for?" Savely whispered angrily.

"What's it to you? Lie down!" his wife replied, without taking her eyes off the fair-haired head.

Savely angrily exhaled all the air from his chest and turned abruptly towards the wall. Two or three minutes later he again began turning back and forth restlessly, knelt up in bed and, propping himself up with his hands against the pillow, cast a sidelong look at his wife. She was still not moving and still gazing at the guest. Her cheeks had turned pale and her gaze burned with some strange light. The sexton let out a croak, slid down off the bed on his stomach and, going over to the postman, covered his face with a scarf.

"What's that for?" asked the sexton's wife.

"It's so the light doesn't get in his eyes."

"Put the light out completely!"

Savely looked at his wife mistrustfully, then stretched his lips out towards the lamp, but stopped himself straight away and clasped his hands together.

"Well, isn't that demonic cunning?" he exclaimed. "Eh? Why, is there any creature more cunning than womankind?"

"Oh, you long-skirted Satan!" hissed the sexton's wife, wrinkling her face in annoyance. "Just wait!"

And settling herself comfortably, she again fixed her gaze upon the postman.

It was all right that his face was covered. She wasn't so much interested in his face as in the overall look, the novelty of this person. His chest was broad, powerful, his arms beautiful, slender, yet muscular, his shapely legs were much more beautiful and manly than Savely's two "chicken drumsticks". There wasn't even any comparison.

"I may be long-skirted and an unclean spirit," said Savely, after standing for a while, "but they shouldn't be sleeping here... No... They're on official business, and we'll have to answer as to why they were held up here. If you're taking the post, then take it, and you shouldn't be sleeping... Hey, you!" Savely shouted into the lobby. "You, driver... what's your name? Show you the way, should I? Get up, you shouldn't be sleeping with the post!"

And Savely, losing all restraint, leapt up to the postman and tugged at his sleeve.

"Hey, Your Honour! If you're going, then go, and if you're not going, then... sleeping won't do."

The postman jerked up into a sitting position, inspected the lodge with a lacklustre gaze and then lay down again.

"And when will you be going?" Savely's tongue began gabbling as he tugged at his sleeve. "That's why it's the post, isn't it, so that it gets there in good time, you hear? I'll show you the way."

The postman opened his eyes. Warm and weak from the sweet beginnings of sleep, still not fully awake, he caught sight, as in a fog, of the white neck and the motionless, yearning gaze of the sexton's wife, closed his eyes and smiled, as if he were dreaming it all.

"Oh come on, where are they to go in such weather!" he heard a soft female voice. "They should be sleeping, sleeping to their hearts' content!"

"And what about the post?" said Savely in alarm. "Who's going to take the post? Are you going to take it? You?"

The postman opened his eyes again, glanced at the moving dimples on the face of the sexton's wife, remembered where he was and understood Savely. The idea that a journey in the cold darkness lay in store for him ran in cold goose bumps from his head down through his entire body, and he shivered.

"We could have another five short minutes of sleep..." he yawned. "We're late anyway..."

"Or maybe we'll arrive right on time!" came a voice from the lobby. "Hey, you never know, we may be lucky and the train'll be late too!"

The postman rose and, stretching pleasurably, started putting on his coat.

Seeing that the guests were preparing to leave, Savely even guffawed in pleasure.

"Help, would you!" the driver called to him, lifting a postbag from the floor.

The sexton leapt over to him and together they lugged the heap of post into the yard. The postman started untangling the knot on his hood. And the sexton's wife peered into his eyes and seemed intent on getting inside his soul.

"Won't you have some tea?..." she said.

"I wouldn't mind... but they're ready, aren't they!" Still he tried to agree: "We're late anyway."

"Stay, why don't you!" she whispered, lowering her eyes and touching his sleeve.

The postman finally untied the knot and, in indecision, threw the hood over his elbow. He felt warm standing beside the sexton's wife.

"What a... neck you have..."

And he touched her neck with two fingers. Seeing that he met with no resistance, he stroked the neck and the shoulder with his hand...

"Ugh, what a..."

"Won't you stay... won't you have some tea?"

"Where are you putting that? You boiled rice and treacle!" came the driver's voice from the yard. "Put it crosswise."

"Won't you stay?... Hark at the weather howling!"

And the postman, who was not yet fully awake and had not had time to shake off the charm of young, wearisome sleep, was suddenly gripped by a desire for whose sake postbags, post trains... everything in the world is forgotten. He threw a frightened glance at the door, as though wishing to flee or to hide, grabbed the sexton's wife by the waist, and had already bent over the lamp to put out the light when there was a clattering of boots in the lobby, and on the threshold appeared the driver... Looking out from behind his shoulder was Savely. The postman quickly lowered his hands and stopped as if in thought.

"Everything's ready!" said the driver.

The postman stood for a little, gave his head a sharp shake, like someone who has finally woken up, and went after the driver. The sexton's wife remained alone.

"Well then, get in, show us the road!" she heard.

One bell began to ring out lazily, then the other, and the little ringing sounds drifted in a long line away from the hut.

When, little by little, they had died away, the sexton's wife burst into motion and started walking nervously from corner to corner. At first she was pale, but then she went all red. Her face was contorted with hatred, her breathing began to quiver, her eyes began to shine with wild, ferocious malice and, pacing as if in a cage, she resembled a tigress being frightened with a heated iron poker. She stopped for a moment and looked at her home. Almost half the room was occupied by the bed, which stretched along an entire wall and consisted of a dirty mattress, rough, grey pillows, a blanket and various nameless bits of cloth. This bed was a formless, ugly lump, almost the same as the one that always stuck out on Savely's head when he felt a desire to grease his hair. From the bed to the door that went out into the cold lobby stretched the dark stove, with pots and hanging cloths. Everything, with Savely, who had just gone out, no exception, was dirty, covered in grease and blackened by smoke, so that it was strange to see in the midst of such surroundings the white neck and fine, delicate skin of a woman. The sexton's wife ran up to the bed, reached out her hands, as though wanting to scatter, trample, rip and reduce it all to dust, but then, as if frightened of touching the dirt, she leapt back and again began pacing...

When, after a couple of hours, Savely returned, plastered in snow and worn out, she was already lying undressed in bed. Her eyes were closed, but from the little spasms that ran across her face, he guessed she was awake. As he had been returning home, he had promised himself to keep quiet and not bother her until the next day, but now he could not resist being spiteful.

"Your sorcery was all in vain; he's gone!" he said with a gloating smirk.

His wife was silent, only her chin quivered. Savely slowly got undressed, climbed over his wife and lay down by the wall.

"And tomorrow I'm going to explain to Father Nikodim the sort of wife you are!" he muttered, curling up into a ball.

The sexton's wife quickly turned to face him and her eyes flashed at him.

"Your place here is what you deserve," she said, "but you can look for a wife for yourself in the wood! I'm not your wife! I wish you'd croak! Why do I have to put up with you all the time, you oaf, you lie-abed, God forgive me!"

"All right, all right... Go to sleep!"

"I'm wretched!" the sexton's wife began sobbing. "If it hadn't been for you, maybe I'd have married a merchant, or someone noble! If it hadn't been for you, I'd have loved my husband now! Why weren't you lost in a snowdrift, why weren't you frozen out there on the highway, you monster!"

The sexton's wife cried for a long time. In the end she heaved a deep sigh and fell quiet. Outside the window the blizzard was still raging. In the stove, in the chimney, behind every wall there was something crying, but it seemed to Savely that the crying was inside him and in his ears. This evening he had finally become convinced of his suppositions regarding his wife. That his wife, with the help of devilry, could control the winds and postal troikas, of that he was no longer in any doubt. But to his profound sorrow, this mysteriousness, this supernatural, wild power lent the woman lying beside him an incomprehensible charm, such as he had not even noticed before. Because, in his stupidity, without noticing it himself, he had poeticized her, it was as if she had become whiter, smoother, more inaccessible...

"Witch!" he fumed. "Ugh, disgusting!"

But at the same time, having waited for her to fall quiet and begin breathing evenly, he touched the back of her head with his fingers... held her thick plait in his hand. She did not feel it... Then he became bolder and stroked her neck.

"Leave me alone!" she cried, and hit him so hard on the bridge of the nose with her elbow that he saw stars.

The pain in the bridge of his nose soon passed, but the torture still went on.

Verochka

I VAN ALEXEYEVICH OGNEV remembers making the glass door ring as he opened it that August evening, and going out onto the terrace. At the time, he was wearing a light caped cloak and a wide-brimmed straw hat, the very one that now lies in the dust under the bed along with his Hessian boots. In one hand he was holding a large bundle of books and notebooks, in the other a thick, knotty stick.

Inside the door, lighting his way with a lamp, stood the master of the house, Kuznetsov, a bald old man with a long grey beard in a piqué jacket as white as snow. The old man was smiling genially and nodding his head.

"Farewell, old chap!" Ognev cried to him.

Kuznetsov put the lamp on a table and went out onto the terrace. Two long, narrow shadows strode down the steps towards the flower beds, began to sway, and then their heads ran up against the trunks of the lime trees.

"Farewell, and thank you once again, my dear fellow!" said Ivan Alexeyevich. "Thank you for your cordiality, for your kindness, for your love... Never ever will I forget your hospitality. You are good, and your daughter is good, and everyone here at your home is kind, cheery, cordial... Such a magnificent bunch, I don't even know how to say it!"

From the fullness of his heart, and under the influence of the fruit liqueur he had just drunk, Ognev spoke in the melodious voice of a seminarist, and was so moved that he expressed his feelings not so much in words as in the blinking of his eyes and the twitching of his shoulders. Kuznetsov, moved and a little tipsy too, reached out to the young man and exchanged kisses with him.

"I've grown accustomed to you like a hunting dog!" Ognev continued. "I've come wandering out here almost every day, I've stayed the night about a dozen times, and I've drunk so much of your fruit liqueur that it's frightful to think about it now. But the main thing I want to thank you for, Gavriil Petrovich, is your cooperation and help. Without you, I'd have been busy here with my statistics till October. That's exactly what I'll write in the foreword: I consider it my duty to express my gratitude to Kuznetsov, the chairman of the Zemstvo Board of the District of N., for his courteous cooperation. Statistics have a brilliant future! The deepest of bows to Vera Gavrilovna, and tell the doctors, both Investigators and your secretary that I shall never forget their help! And now, old man, let's embrace one another and perform one final osculation."

The wilting Ognev exchanged kisses with the old man once more and began going down the steps. On the last one he looked back and asked:

"Will we ever meet again?"

"God knows!" the old man replied. "Probably not!"

"No, that's right! You wouldn't come to Petersburg for love or money, and I'm unlikely ever to find myself in this district again. So then, farewell!"

"You should leave the books here!" Kuznetsov cried in his wake. "What makes you lug such a weight? I could send a man to you with them tomorrow."

But Ognev was no longer listening, and was moving quickly away from the house. His heart, heated by wine, was cheerful, and warm, and sad... As he walked, he thought of how often in life one comes to meet good people, and what a pity it is that nothing more remains of those meetings than memories. It can happen that you catch a glimpse of some cranes on the horizon, and a light wind brings you their plaintively rapturous cries, but a minute later, however avidly you peer into the blue distance, you can see not a dot, and nor can you hear a sound – in just the same way, people with their faces and speeches are glimpsed in life and then lost in our past, leaving nothing more than the paltry traces of memory. Living all the way through from the spring in the District of N. and spending time almost every day with the cordial Kuznetsovs, Ivan Alexeyich had grown accustomed, as to family, to the old man, his daughter, the servants, and he had studied the whole house to a nicety, the cosy terrace, the bends in the tree-lined paths, the silhouettes of the trees above the kitchen and bathhouse; but he would go out through the gate now, and it would all turn into a memory and would for ever lose its real meaning for him, and a year or two would pass, and all these dear images would tarnish in his consciousness on a par with fabrications and the fruits of fantasy.

"There is nothing in life more dear than people!" thought Ognev, deeply moved, as he strode down the path towards the gate. "Nothing!"

The garden was quiet and warm. There was the scent of the mignonette, tobacco plants and heliotropes, whose time to stop flowering in the beds had not yet come. The gaps between the bushes and the tree trunks were filled with mist, not dense, but delicate, impregnated through and through with moonlight; and, something that lingered long in Ognev's memory, wisps of mist resembling ghosts, gently, but still visibly to the eye, followed one another in cutting across the path. The moon hung high above the garden and, down below it, transparent patches of mist were hurrying away into the east. It seemed as if the whole world consisted only of black silhouettes and wandering white shadows, and Ognev, observing a mist on a moonlit evening in August for all but the first time in his life, thought he was seeing not nature, but a stage set, where unskilled pyrotechnicians, wanting to illumine the garden with white Bengal light, had ensconced themselves under the bushes and let white smoke off into the air as well as the light.

As Ognev was approaching the garden gate, a dark shadow detached itself from the low picket fence and started towards him.

"Vera Gavrilovna!" he said in delight. "So you're here? And I've been looking everywhere, wanting to say goodbye... Farewell, I'm off!"

"So soon? It's still only eleven, isn't it?"

"No, it's time! It's a walk of five versts, and I need to pack as well. I have to get up early tomorrow..."

In front of Ognev stood Kuznetsov's daughter, Vera, a girl of twenty-one, sad, carelessly dressed and striking, as usual. Girls who dream a lot, and spend days on end indolently lying reading everything that comes to hand, who are bored and sad, generally do dress carelessly. To those of them whom nature has endowed with taste and an instinct for beauty, this easy carelessness in dress imparts a particular charm. At least, remembering pretty Verochka subsequently, Ognev could not picture her without the roomy blouse which, though crumpled at the waist into deep folds, still did not touch her torso, nor without the lock of hair straying onto her forehead from her piled-up coiffure, nor without the red knitted shawl with fluffy little bobbles round the edges, which, in the evenings, hung dolefully on Verochka's shoulder like a flag in still weather, and in the daytime lay rumpled in the hall by the men's hats, or else on the trunk in the dining room, where the old cat unceremoniously slept on it. From that shawl and from the creases in the blouse there came an air of free indolence, a stay-at-home attitude and kindliness. Perhaps because Ognev liked Vera, he could read in every button and frill something warm, cosy, naive, something that was good and poetic, the very thing that is lacking in women who are insincere, devoid of a sense of beauty and cold.

Verochka had a good figure, a regular profile and beautiful wavy hair. To Ognev, who had seen few women in his lifetime, she seemed a beauty.

"I'm off!" he said, bidding her farewell by the gate. "Remember me kindly! Thank you for everything!"

In the same melodious, seminarist's voice in which he had conversed with the old man, and blinking and twitching his shoulders in just the same way, he began thanking Vera for her hospitality, kindness and cordiality.

"I wrote about you to my mother in every letter," he said. "If everyone were like you and your father, life on earth would be a bowl of cherries. The whole bunch here are magnificent! All straightforward, warm-hearted, sincere people."

"Where are you going now?" asked Vera.

"I'm going to see my mother in Oryol; I shall stay with her for a couple of weeks, and then – back to work in Petersburg."

"And after that?"

"After that? I shall work all through the winter, and in spring it's off again to some district or other to collect material. Well, be happy, live a hundred years... remember me kindly. We shan't meet again."

Ognev bent down and kissed Verochka's hand. Then, in silent agitation he straightened his cloak, took a comfortable hold of the bundle of books and was quiet for a moment before saying:

"What a lot of mist has come down!"

"Yes. You haven't forgotten anything at the house?"

"What's that? I don't think so..."

Ognev stood for several seconds in silence, then turned awkwardly towards the gate and went out of the garden.

"Wait, I'll go with you as far as our wood," said Vera, following him out.

They set off along the road. Now the trees no longer screened the open land, and it was possible to see the sky and into the distance. As though covered with a veil, the whole of nature was hiding behind a transparent, matt haze, with its beauty looking cheerfully through it; the mist, where denser and whiter, lay uneven by the stooks and the bushes or else wandered in wisps across the road; it pressed close to the ground and seemed to be trying not to screen the open land. The entire road was visible through the haze as far as the wood, with the dark ditches on either side of it, and the small bushes growing in the ditches that hindered the wandering of the wisps of mist. Half a verst from the gate was the black band of the Kuznetsovs' wood.

"Why has she come with me? I'll have to see her back again, won't I!" thought Ognev, but after looking at Vera's profile he smiled kindly and said:

"I'd rather not be leaving in such good weather! It's a really romantic evening, with the moon, the silence and all the trimmings. Do you know what, Vera Gavrilovna? I've been in this world for twenty-nine years, but not once in my life have I had a romance. Not a single romantic affair in my whole life, and so I'm familiar with rendezvous and avenues of sighs and kisses only by hearsay. It's not normal! In town, when you're sitting in your rented room, you don't notice the deficiency, but here, in the fresh air, it's very palpable... It makes you feel slighted somehow!"

"Why are you that way?"

"I don't know. I suppose I've had no time all my life, or perhaps I've simply not had occasion to meet the sort of women who... I have few acquaintances generally, and I don't go out anywhere."

The two young people walked three hundred paces in silence. Ognev threw glances at Verochka's uncovered head and shawl, and in his soul, one after another, the spring and summer days came back to life; it had been a time when, far from his grey rented room in St Petersburg, he had enjoyed the kindness of good people, nature and his beloved work, had had no time to notice how the glow of dawn was replaced by the glow of sunset or how, one after another, foretelling the summer's end, first the nightingale, then the quail and a little later the corncrake had stopped singing... Time had flown by unnoticed, meaning life had been good and easy... He began recalling out loud with what reluctance he, a man of no wealth, unaccustomed to movement and people, had come here at the end of April to the District of N., where he had expected to encounter boredom, loneliness and indifference to statistics, which, in his opinion, now occupied the most prominent place amongst the sciences. Arriving on an April morning in the poor little district town of N., he had put up at the coaching inn of the Old Believer Ryabukhin, where for twenty kopeks a day he had been given a light, clean room on condition that he smoked outside. After having a rest and enquiring who was chairman of the District's Zemstvo Board, he had set off without delay on foot to see Gavriil Petrovich. He had been obliged to walk four versts through luxuriant meadows and young groves of trees. Skylarks had been quivering beneath the clouds, spilling their silver sounds into the air, while rooks had been drifting above the greening plough land, flapping their wings in respectable, dignified fashion.

"Good Lord," Ognev had wondered then, "do they really breathe such air all the time here, or does it smell like this only today, just to mark my arrival?"

Expecting a dry, businesslike reception, he had entered the Kuznetsovs' house less than boldly, looking from under his brows and pulling shyly at his little beard. At first the old man had knitted his brow and not understood why this young man and his statistics might be needed by the Zemstvo Board, but when Ognev had explained to him at length what statistical material was and where it was gathered, Gavriil Petrovich had perked up, broken into smiles and started looking into his notebooks with childlike curiosity... On the evening of that same day, Ivan Alexeyich had already been sitting having dinner with the Kuznetsovs, quickly getting tipsy on the strong fruit liqueur and, looking at the placid faces and indolent movements of his new acquaintances, feeling throughout his body that sweet, drowsy indolence, when you want to sleep, stretch and smile. And his new acquaintances had looked him over genially and asked if his father and mother were alive, how much he earned in a month, whether he was often at the theatre...

Ognev recalled his travels around the *volosts*,* picnics, fishing, a trip made by the entire company to a convent to see Mother Superior Martha, who had presented each one of the guests with a purse decorated with beads; he recalled the heated, interminable, uniquely Russian debates, when the debaters, spluttering and banging their fists on the table, fail to understand one another and interrupt without noticing what they are doing, contradict themselves with every phrase, keep on changing the subject and, after two or three hours of debate, laugh:

"The devil only knows what started us arguing! We've gone from the sublime to the ridiculous!"

"And do you remember how you and I and the doctor went on horseback to Shestovo?" said Ivan Alexeyich to Vera, as they approached the wood together. "It was then that we met the holy fool.* I gave him five kopeks, and he crossed himself three times and threw my coin into the rye. Good Lord, I'm taking so many impressions away with me that, were it possible to gather them into a compact mass, the result would be a good bar of gold! I don't understand why it is that intelligent, sensitive people crowd together in the capitals and don't come here. Is there really more space and truth on Nevsky and in big, damp buildings than here? Truly, my furnished rooms, stuffed from top to bottom with artists, scholars and journalists, always seemed to me a prejudice."

Across the road twenty paces from the wood lay a small, narrow bridge with bollards at the corners, which always served the

Kuznetsovs and their guests as a little stopping point during evening walks. From here the wood's echo could be teased by those who wished, and the road could be seen disappearing in a black cutting.

"Well, and here's the bridge!" said Ognev. "This is where you turn back..."

Vera stopped and drew a deep breath.

"Let's sit down for a while," she said, taking a seat on one of the bollards. "Before a departure, when saying goodbye, everyone usually sits down." Ognev perched beside her on his bundle of books and carried on talking. She was breathing heavily after the walk and looked not at Ivan Alexeyich, but somewhere off to one side, and so he could not see her face.

"And what if we meet in ten years or so?" he said. "What will we be like then? You'll already be the venerable mother of a family, and I the author of some venerable collection of statistics that no one needs, the thickness of forty thousand such collections. We'll meet and remember old times... Now we can feel the present, it fills us and excites us, but then, when we meet, we'll no longer remember the date, the month, even the year when we last saw each other on this little bridge. Quite likely you'll have changed... Listen, are you going to change?"

Vera gave a start and turned to face him.

"What?" she asked.

"I was just asking you..."

"I'm sorry, I didn't hear what you were saying."

Only at this point did Ognev notice a change in Vera. She was pale, gasping for breath, and the tremor in her breathing was communicating itself to her hands, and her lips, and her head, and straying from her coiffure onto her forehead was not one lock of hair, as always, but two... She was evidently avoiding looking him straight in the eye and, trying to mask her agitation, she would now adjust her collar, which seemed to be cutting into her neck, now pull her red shawl from one shoulder to the other...

"You seem to be feeling cold," said Ognev. "Sitting in a mist isn't entirely healthy. Now, let me see you *nach Hause*."*

Vera was silent.

"What's wrong with you?" smiled Ivan Alexeyich. "You're silent and not answering any questions. Are you unwell, or cross? Eh?"

Vera pressed the palm of her hand tight against the cheek that was turned in Ognev's direction, but jerked it away abruptly at once.

"It's an awful situation..." she whispered, with an expression of great pain on her face. "Awful!"

"Why is it awful?" asked Ognev, shrugging his shoulders and not concealing his surprise. "What's the matter?"

Still breathing hard and with a shudder in her shoulders, Vera turned her back on him, gazed for half a minute at the sky and said:

"I need to have a talk with you, Ivan Alexeyich..."

"I'm listening."

"It may seem strange to you... you'll be surprised, but I don't care..."

Ognev shrugged his shoulders again and prepared to listen.

"The thing is this..." Vera began, bowing her head, and with her fingers pulling at a bobble on the shawl. "You see, this is what I... wanted to say... It'll seem strange to you and... silly, but I... I can't go on any longer."

Vera's speech became an indistinct murmuring, and suddenly stopped short in weeping. The girl covered her face with the shawl, bowed even lower and burst into bitter tears. Ivan Alexeyich gave a croak of embarrassment and, amazed, not knowing what to say or do, looked around despairingly. Unaccustomed to weeping and tears, he felt his own eyes begin to prick.

"Well, really!" he started mumbling in bewilderment. "Vera Gavrilovna, what's the point of this, one asks? My dear, are you... are you ill? Or has someone upset you? Tell me, perhaps I, er... might be able to help..."

When, in trying to comfort her, he allowed himself carefully to remove her hands from her face, she smiled at him through her tears and said:

"I... I love you!"

These words, plain and ordinary, were said in plain human language, but Ognev turned away from Vera in great confusion, rose and, following the confusion, felt fright.

The sadness, the warmth and the sentimental mood brought upon him by the leave-taking and the fruit liqueur suddenly disappeared, giving way to an acute, unpleasant feeling of awkwardness. It was as if his heart had been wrung, he cast sidelong glances at Vera, and now, having declared her love for him and cast off the unassailability which so beautifies a woman, she seemed to him somehow shorter in stature, plainer, darker.

"What ever is going on?" he said to himself, horrified. "But, I mean, I... do I love her or don't I? Now there's a question!"

She, meanwhile, now that the most important and difficult thing had finally been said, was already breathing easily and freely. She rose too and, looking Ivan Alexeyich straight in the face, began speaking quickly, ardently, without restraint.

Just as a person suddenly frightened cannot afterwards remember the order in which the sounds of the catastrophe that stunned them followed one another, neither does Ognev remember Vera's words and phrases. All that is memorable to him are the content of her speech, she herself and the sensation her speech produced in him. He remembers the voice sounding strangulated and somewhat hoarse with agitation, and the uncommon music and passion in its intonation. Crying, laughing, with the teardrops on her eyelashes sparkling, she told him that from the very first days of their acquaintanceship she had been struck by his originality, his intelligence, his kind, intelligent eyes, his tasks and aims in life, that she had come to love him passionately, madly and deeply; that whenever, during the summer, she had gone into the house from the garden and seen his cloak in the hall or heard his voice from afar, a chill had run though her heart, a presentiment of happiness; even his trivial jokes had made her chuckle, in every figure in his notebooks she had seen something extraordinary, judicious and grand, his knotty stick had seemed to her more beautiful than the trees.

The wood, the wisps of mist, the black ditches down the sides of the road all seemed to have fallen quiet listening to her, but in Ognev's soul something strange and not good was taking place... Declaring her love, Vera was captivatingly pretty, she spoke beautifully and passionately, yet he experienced not delight, not the joy of living, as he would have liked, but only a feeling of compassion for Vera, pain and regret that, because of him, a good person was suffering. God knows whether it was bookish reason that spoke up within him, or whether it was the effect of the insuperable habit of being objective, which so often stops people living, but Vera's raptures and suffering seemed to him cloying, not serious, and yet at the same time feeling rose indignantly within him and whispered that all he was seeing and hearing now was, from the point of view of nature and personal happiness, more serious than any statistics, books or truths... And he felt angry and blamed himself, although he did not really understand precisely what he was to blame for.

To make his awkwardness complete, he did not know what he should say at all, yet it was essential to say something. He lacked the strength to say outright: "I don't love you", but he was unable to say "yes", because, however much he rummaged, he could not find in his soul even one little spark...

He was silent, and in the meantime she was saying that there was no greater happiness for her than seeing him, following him, even now, wherever he wanted, being his wife and helpmeet, that if he left her she would die of anguish...

"I can't stay here," she said, wringing her hands. "The house, this wood, the air, they've all become hateful to me. I can't bear the continual peace and quiet and the aimless life, I can't bear the colourless, pale people here, who all resemble one another like peas in a pod! They're all good-hearted and genial because they're sated, they don't suffer, don't struggle... Whereas it's to big, damp buildings that I want to go, where people suffer and are hardened by toil and need..."

This too seemed to Ognev cloying and not serious. When Vera finished, he still did not know what to say, but he could not remain silent and began mumbling:

"I'm very grateful to you, Vera Gavrilovna, although I feel I've done nothing to deserve such... a feeling... on your part. Secondly, as an honest man, I ought to say that... happiness is founded on balance – that is, when both sides... love equally..."

But Ognev immediately felt ashamed of his mumbling and fell silent. He sensed that his face at this point was stupid, guilty and trite, that it was tense and strained... Vera must have been able to read the truth on his face, because she suddenly became serious, turned pale and hung her head.

"You must forgive me," Ognev mumbled, unable to bear the silence. "I respect you so much that... this is painful for me!"

Vera turned abruptly and set off quickly back towards the estate. Ognev followed after her.

"No, there's no need!" said Vera, waving her hand at him. "Don't come, I'll get there by myself..."

"No, all the same... I have to see you home..."

Whatever Ognev said, everything to the very last word seemed to him repulsive and trite. The feeling of guilt inside him grew with each step. He was angry, clenched his fists and cursed his coldness and his ignorance of how to behave with women. Trying to arouse himself, he looked at Verochka's beautiful figure, at her plait and at the prints her little feet left on the dusty road, he recalled her words and tears, but it all merely touched, rather than inflaming his soul.

"Ah, forcing yourself to fall in love is just not possible!" he tried to convince himself, but at the same time he was thinking: "And when *will* I fall in love without forcing myself? I mean, I'm nearly thirty already! I've never met any women better than Vera and I never will... Oh, damnable old age! Old age at thirty!"

Vera walked ahead of him quicker and quicker, without looking round and with her head hanging. It seemed to him as if grief had made her grow thinner, narrower in the shoulders...

"I can just imagine what's going on in her soul now!" he thought, gazing at her back. "She's probably both ashamed and hurt to the point of wanting to die! Good Lord, how much life, poetry, meaning there is in all this, enough for a stone to be moved, but I... I'm stupid and ridiculous!"

By the gate Vera threw him a cursory glance, then, hunched and bundling herself up in her shawl, she set off quickly down the tree-lined path.

Ivan Alexeyich remained alone. Returning towards the wood, he walked slowly and kept on stopping and looking round at the gate, with the expression of his entire figure seeming to suggest he did not believe himself. His eyes searched for Verochka's footprints along the road, and he could not believe that the girl he so liked had just declared her love for him and he had so clumsily and crudely "refused" her! For the first time in his life he was obliged to discover from experience how little a man depends upon his own free will, and to feel for himself the position of a decent and good-hearted man who, against his will, is the cause of cruel, undeserved suffering in someone close to him.

His conscience pained him, and when Vera disappeared, he began to think he had lost something very dear and personal that he would not find again. He felt that, along with Vera, a part of his youth had slipped away from him, and that the minutes he had lived through so fruitlessly would be repeated no more.

Reaching the little bridge, he stopped and fell into thought. He wanted to find the reason for his strange coldness. That it lay not outside, but within him himself was clear to him. He sincerely confessed to himself that this was not the rational coldness of which intelligent people so often boast, not the coldness of a self-obsessed fool, but simply feebleness of soul, an incapacity for a profound perception of beauty and premature old age, brought on by his upbringing, his disorderly struggle for a crust of bread and his life in rented rooms without a family.

From the bridge he set off slowly, as though reluctantly, into the wood. Here, where rays of moonlight appeared sporadically in harsh patches against the black, dense darkness, where he could sense nothing but his thoughts, he felt a passionate desire to retrieve what he had lost.

And Ivan Alexeyich remembers going back again. Spurring himself on with memories, forcing himself to draw Vera in his imagination, he strode quickly towards the garden. There was no longer any mist along the road or in the garden, and the clear moon gazed from the sky as if washed clean; only the east was enveloped in mist and gloomy... Ognev remembers his cautious steps, the dark windows, the heavy scent of heliotropes and mignonette. The familiar Karo came up to him, wagging his tail amiably, and sniffed at his hand... This was the only living creature that saw him as he walked around the house a couple of times, stood for a while by Vera's dark window, and then, with a deep sigh, giving up the struggle, set off out of the garden.

An hour later he was already in town and, exhausted, shattered, leaning his body and hot face against the gates of the inn, knocking with the catch. Somewhere in the town a dog, barely awake, was barking, and as if in reply to his knocking, someone by the church began clanging on a sheet of iron...

"You go prowling about in the night-time..." grumbled the Old Believer landlord, opening the gates for him in a long nightshirt like a woman's. "Rather than prowling, you'd be better off praying to God."

On entering his room, Ivan Alexeyich sank onto the bed and spent a long, long time gazing at the lamp, then shook his head and began to pack...

In Court

O
N AN OVERCAST AUTUMN DAY in the district town of N.,
in a brown public building where the Zemstvo Board, the
Assembly of Justices of the Peace, the Peasants', the Licensing,
the Military and many other governmental organizations take it
in turns to meet, the Department of the Circuit Court was making
a flying visit to hear its cases. Of the brown building in question
one local administrator had quipped:

"Here you have Iustitia, you have Politsia, you have Militsia – a
veritable Institute for Noble Girls."

But in line with the saying that too many cooks spoil the broth,
this building probably shocks and oppresses anyone fresh and not
in public service with its cheerless, barrack-like appearance, its
dilapidation and the complete absence of any kind of comfort
whatsoever, either outside or in. Even on the brightest spring days
it seems to be covered in dense shade, while on bright, moonlit
nights, when the trees and the little houses of the locals merge
into a single unbroken shadow and are sunk in quiet sleep, it
alone, all crushing stone, towers over the modest landscape in an
absurd and inappropriate sort of way, mars the general harmony
and stays awake, as though unable to rid itself of difficult memories of past, unforgiven sins. Inside, everything is barn-like and
extremely unattractive. It can be strange to see the way all those
elegant Procurators, Members and Marshals, who make a scene at
home over a few fumes or a little stain on the floor, easily reconcile
themselves here to buzzing ventilators, the odious smell of smoking candles and the dirty walls, eternally covered in condensation.

The session of the Circuit Court had begun before ten o'clock.
The process of hearing had been set about forthwith, with notice-
able haste. Cases began to be heard one after another and came to
an end quickly, like a Liturgy without choristers, so that no mind
could have constructed for itself a complete, pictorial impression

of the whole motley mass, racing like flood water, of faces, move-ment, speeches, misfortune, truth, deceit... By two o'clock much had been done: two men had been condemned to penal battalions, one man with privileges had been stripped of his rights and sent to prison, one man had been acquitted and one case adjourned...

At exactly two o'clock the presiding judge announced the hear-ing of the case of "the peasant Nikolai Kharlamov, accused of the murder of his wife". The composition of the court remained the same as it had been for the previous case, except that the place of the Defence Counsel was taken by a new individual, a young, beardless candidate for appointment to a judicial post wearing a frock coat with light-coloured buttons.

"Bring in the defendant!" ordered the President.

But the defendant, prepared in advance, was already walking towards the dock. He was a tall, stocky peasant of about fifty-five, entirely bald, with an apathetic, hairy face and a big, red beard. Following him was a puny little soldier with a rifle.

Almost right beside the dock the escort suffered a little unpleas-antness. He suddenly stumbled and dropped the rifle, but imme-diately caught it in mid-air, hitting his knee hard in so doing on the butt. A little laughter was heard amongst the public. From the pain, or perhaps out of embarrassment at his clumsiness, the soldier turned a deep shade of red.

After the usual questioning of the defendant, the shuffling of the jury, the calling and oath-taking of the witnesses, there began the reading of the indictment. The narrow-chested, pale-faced Secretary, who had become very thin for his uniform jacket and had a plaster on his cheek, read in a quiet, rich bass, quickly, like a sexton, neither raising nor lowering his voice, as though fear-ful of overworking his chest; he was echoed by the ventilator, buzzing indefatigably behind the judges' desk, and the result, all in all, was a sound that lent the quietness in the hall a soporific, narcotic character.

The President, not an old man, short-sighted and with extreme exhaustion written on his face, sat in his chair without stirring, holding the palm of his hand close to his forehead, as though shielding his eyes from the sun. To the accompaniment of the buzzing ventilator and the Secretary he was thinking about something. When the Secretary paused briefly to begin a new page, he suddenly roused himself and examined the public with drowsy eyes, then leant towards the ear of the Member of the Court next to him and asked with a sigh:

"Are you staying with Demyanov, Matvei Petrovich?"

"Yes, with Demyanov," replied the Member of the Court, rousing himself as well.

"I'll probably stay with him next time too. Forgive me, but staying with Tipyakov is quite impossible! Noise and uproar all night! Banging, coughing, children crying... It's insufferable!"

The Assistant Procurator, a plump, well-fed, dark-haired man in gold-rimmed spectacles, with a handsome, well-groomed beard, was sitting as still as a statue and, with his cheek propped up on his fist, was reading Byron's *Cain.*⁴ His eyes were filled with avid attention, and his brows rose ever higher and higher in surprise... Occasionally he would recline against the back of his chair, gaze out dispassionately into space for a minute, and then again immerse himself in his reading. The Defence Counsel was drawing the blunt end of a pencil over his desk and, with his head inclined to one side, was thinking... His young face did not express anything other than immobile, cold boredom, such as can be found on the faces of schoolchildren and office workers, obliged to sit, day in, day out, in one and the same place, to see always the same faces and the same walls. His forthcoming speech worried him not at all. For what, indeed, was that speech? By order of his superiors, to a long-established template, sensing that it was colourless and dull, he would blurt it out before the jurors without passion or fire, then after that – a gallop through the mud in the rain to the station, and thence to town, soon to get an order to travel out again to some district or other, to deliver another speech... how tedious!

The defendant coughed nervously into his sleeve at times and turned pale, but the quietness, the overall monotony and tedium communicated themselves to him too. He gazed with obtuse deference at the judges' uniforms and the exhausted faces of the jurors, blinking calmly. The court setting and procedure, waiting for which had so wearied his soul while he had been in jail, now had the most soothing effect upon him. Here he had encountered not at all what he might have expected. There hung over him a murder charge, and yet here he had encountered no stern faces, no indignant looks, no grand phrases about retribution, no sympathy for his uncommon fate; not one of those trying him had let a long, curious gaze rest upon him... The gloomy windows, the walls, the voice of the Secretary, the pose of the Procurator, all of it was steeped in official indifference and gave off an air of coldness, as though a murderer were a simple office accessory or he were being tried not by living men, but by some invisible machine, set in motion by God knows whom...

The soothed peasant did not realize that here they were just as accustomed and inured to everyday dramas and tragedies as they are in a hospital to deaths, and that it was in precisely this impassivity of the machine that all the horror and all the hopelessness of his position lay. It seemed that, were he not to sit quietly, but rather to get up and start imploring, to appeal tearfully for mercy, to repent bitterly, were he to die of despair, all of it would break on the deadened nerves and habitualness like a wave on a rock.

When the Secretary had finished, the President for some reason stroked the desk in front of him, looked at the defendant for a long time with narrowed eyes, and only then asked, moving his tongue indolently:

"Defendant, do you plead guilty to murdering your wife on the evening of the ninth of June?"

"No, sir," replied the defendant, rising and holding on to the breast of his prison robe.

After this, the court hurriedly got down to examining the witnesses. Two peasant women and five men were examined, and the village constable who had carried out the inquiry. All of them, spattered with mud, exhausted by their journey on foot and their wait in the witnesses' room, doleful and sullen, gave the same testimony. They testified that Kharlamov had "got on well" with his old woman, just like everyone else: he had beaten her only when drunk. On the ninth of June, when the sun had set, the old woman had been found in her lobby with a broken skull; beside her in a pool of blood lay an axe. When they had started hunting for Nikolai to let him know of the misfortune, he was neither in the hut, nor outside. They had begun running through the village looking for him, had run round to every tavern and hut, but had not found him. He had disappeared, and in a couple of days had come to the village office himself, pale and ragged and with his whole body shaking. He had been bound and put in the cooler.

"Defendant," the President addressed himself to Kharlamov, "can you explain to the court where you were during those two days after the murder?"

"I was wandering through the fields... With nothing to eat or drink,.."

"And why did you go into hiding if you were not the murderer?"

"I was affeared... Scared I'd be condemned,.."

"Aha... Very well, sit down!"

The last to be questioned was the district doctor who had carried out the post-mortem on the deceased woman. He told the court all he could remember of his report on the post-mortem and what he had had time to think up while walking that morning to court. The President narrowed his eyes at his new, glossy black suit, his foppish cravat, his moving lips; he listened, and inside his head, of its own accord somehow, there stirred the indolent thought: "Everyone goes around in short frock coats nowadays, so why has he got himself a long one? Why must his be a long one, and not a short one?"

Behind the President a cautious squeaking of boots was heard. It was the Assistant Procurator approaching the desk to get some document.

"Mikhail Vladimirovich," the Procurator leant towards the President's ear, "this Koreisky was incredibly slipshod in his conduct of the investigation. The brother wasn't questioned, the village headman wasn't questioned, you can't make head nor tail of the description of the hut..."

"What can one do... what can one do?" sighed the President, reclining against the back of his chair. "He's a wreck... the sands of time!"

"Incidentally," the Assistant Procurator continued to whisper, "turn your attention – in the public gallery, the front bench, third from the right... the physiognomy of an actor... That's the local financial bigwig. He has capital of some five hundred thousand in cash."

"Really? You couldn't tell from the look of him... Well, dear boy, shall we have a break?"

"Let's finish with the investigation, and then."

"As you wish... Well, sir?" the President raised his eyes to the doctor. "And so you find that death was instantaneous?"

"Yes, in consequence of significant damage to the brain tissue..."

When the doctor had finished, the President looked into the space between the Procurator and the Defence Counsel and enquired:

"Do you have anything to ask?"

Without tearing his eyes away from *Cain*, the Assistant gave a negative shake of the head; unexpectedly, though, the Defence Counsel stirred and, clearing his throat, asked:

"Tell me, Doctor, is it sometimes possible to judge from the size of the wound the... the mental state of the criminal? That is, I want to enquire whether the extent of the damage gives one the right to think that the defendant was in a state of temporary insanity?"

The President raised his sleepy, indifferent eyes to look at the Defence Counsel. The Procurator tore himself away from *Cain* and looked at the President. They merely looked, and no smile, no surprise, no perplexity, nothing did their faces express.

"It may be so," the doctor stumbled, "if one takes into account the force with which... er... the criminal strikes the blow... However... forgive me, I didn't quite understand your question..."

The Defence Counsel got no answer to his question, nor did he feel any need for one. It was clear to him that the question had popped into his head and escaped his lips only under the influence of the quietness, the tedium and the buzzing ventilation.

After letting the doctor stand down, the court set about examining the material evidence. First to be examined was a caftan, on the sleeve of which was the dark brown of a bloodstain. Asked about the origin of this stain, Kharlamov testified:

"About three days before the old woman's death, Penkov was letting his horse's blood... I was there, well, you know, helping, and... and got stained..."

"However, Penkov testified just now that he doesn't remember you being present at the blood-letting..."

"I wouldn't know."

"Sit down!"

They set about examining the axe with which the old woman was killed.

"It's not my axe," declared the defendant.

"Whose is it, then?"

"I wouldn't know... I didn't have an axe..."

"A peasant can't get by for a single day without an axe. And your neighbour, Ivan Timofeyich, with whom you repaired a sledge, testified that this is, indeed, *your* axe..."

"I wouldn't know, only I'm like before God," Kharlamov stretched a hand out in front of him and spread the fingers apart, "like before the true Creator. And I don't remember the time when I had my own axe. I did have one like that, I think it was smaller, though, but my son, Prokhor, lost it. A couple of years before he was to go and do his military service, he went out for firewood, started drinking with the lads and lost it..."

"Very well, sit down!"

This systematic mistrust and unwillingness to listen must have vexed and upset Kharlamov. He began blinking, and red blotches stood out on his cheekbones.

"Like before God!" he continued, stretching out his neck. "If you don't believe me, you ask my son, Prokhor. Proshka, where's the axe?" he suddenly asked in a rough voice, turning abruptly to his escort. "Where is it?"

This was a difficult moment! It was as if everyone sank lower in their seats or became shorter... Through every head, as many as there were in the courtroom, there flashed like lightning one and the same terrible, impossible idea, the idea of a fateful chance that had maybe occurred, and not one person ventured or dared to glance at the face of the soldier. Everyone wanted to disbelieve his idea and to think that he had misheard.

"Defendant, it is not permitted to speak to the guard..." the President hastened to say.

Nobody saw the face of the escort, and horror flew through the room like an invisible being, as if wearing a mask. The bailiff quietly rose from his seat and on tiptoe, using an arm to keep his balance, went out of the room. Half a minute later, muffled footsteps and sounds were heard, the sort there are when sentries are being changed.

Everyone raised their heads and, trying to look as though nothing had happened, got on with their business...

A Restless Guest

I N ARTYOM THE WOODMAN'S low, lopsided little hut, two men were sitting beneath a large, dark icon: Artyom himself, a stunted and skinny little peasant with the crumpled face of an old man and a little beard growing out of his neck, and a passing huntsman, a strapping young lad in a new red calico shirt and big waders. They were sitting on a bench at a small, three-legged table on which a tallow candle stuck into a bottle was burning lazily.

Outside the window in the nocturnal darkness was the noise of the sort of storm with which nature usually erupts before thunder and lightning. The wind was howling spitefully, and the bending trees were groaning painfully. One pane of the window had paper stuck over it, and the leaves that were being torn down could be heard knocking against the paper.

"I'll tell you this, good Christian…" Artyom was saying in a hoarse, half-whispered tenor, his eyes gazing at the huntsman unblinking, as if frightened. "I'm not scared of wolves, or of bears, or other sorts of beast, but I am scared of man. You can save yourself from beasts with a gun or some other weapon, but there's no salvation for you from a wicked man."

"That's right! You can shoot at a wild beast, but shoot at a robber and you'll answer for it yourself, you'll go to Siberia."

"I've been working here as a woodman, my friend, nigh on thirty years, and the amount of misfortune I've endured from wicked people can't be told. I've had loads of them here. The hut's in a cutting, it's a public road, well, so they keep on coming, the devils. In bursts some real villain or other, and without taking his hat off, without crossing himself, he goes straight for you: 'Give us some bread, you so-and-so!' And where am I to find you some bread? And what gives you the right? Am I a millionaire, to be feeding every passing drunk? And of course, he's got malice burning in his eyes… there's no fear of God in them, the devils… Without

75

too much thought he gives you a clip round the ear: 'Give us some bread!' So you give him some... You're not about to fight with that hard-bitten lot, are you? Some have got big broad shoulders, a huge great fist the size of your boot, and you can see for yourself the sort of build I've got. You can hurt me with your little finger... Well, you give him some bread, and he stuffs himself, sprawls all over the hut, and you don't get one word of thanks. And then there are some that ask for money: 'Speak up, where's the money?' And what money am I supposed to have? Where's it meant to come from?"

"As if a woodman might not have any money!" grinned the huntsman. "You get your salary every month, and I bet you sell some timber on the quiet."

Artyom threw a frightened sidelong glance at the huntsman and began twitching his beard like a magpie does its tail.

"You're young as yet to be saying such things to me," he said. "You'll be answering to God for them there words. What sort of family would you be from? Where d'you come from?"

"I'm from Vyazovka. Nefed the headman's son."

"You amuse yourself with a gun... When I was younger, I enjoyed that amusement too. Ye-es. Oh, our mortal sins!" Artyom sighed. "It's terrible! There are so few good people, but God alone knows how many villains and cut-throats there are!"

"It's as if you're afraid of me too..."

"What ever are you on about! Why should I be afraid of you? I can see... understand... You came in, and not just any old how, but you crossed yourself, bowed, all right and proper... I understand... You can be given some bread... I'm a widower, me, I don't heat the stove, sold the samovar... I don't have meat or anything else through poverty, but bread – be my guest."

At that moment something underneath the bench started growling, and after the growling a hissing was heard. Artyom winced, drew his legs in and looked questioningly at the huntsman.

"That's my dog giving your cat an 'ard time," said the huntsman. "You devils!" he shouted under the bench. "Down! You'll get a beating! That's a really thin cat you've got, friend! Just fur and bone."

"She's getting old, it's time she died. So you say you're from Vyazovka?"

"You don't feed her, I can see it. She may be a cat, but she's a creature all the same... everything that hath breath.* You ought to take pity!"

"It's unclean, that Vyazovka of yours," Artyom continued, as though not listening to the huntsman. "The church was robbed twice in one year... There are such darned beasts about, eh? So it's not just people they have no fear of, but even God! Stealing God's goods! Hanging's not enough for that! In days gone by, provincial governors used to put such scoundrels under the executioner's axe."

"However you punish them, giving them a damn good thrashing, giving them time, still nothing'll come of it. You can't beat the wickedness out of a wicked man with anything."

"Save us and have mercy upon us, Heavenly Queen!" sighed the woodman in a staccato. "Save us from every enemy and Satan. Last week in Volovyi Zaimisha one mower struck another in the chest with a scythe... Killed him dead! And why, O Lord, Thy will, did things turn out that way? This one mower comes out of the inn... he's been drinking. He comes upon the other, and he's been drinking too..."

The huntsman, who had been listening attentively, suddenly gave a start and stretched his face forward, cocking an ear.

"Hang on," he interrupted the woodman. "There seems to be someone shouting..."

Without taking their eyes off the dark window, the huntsman and woodman started listening. Through the noise of the wood could be heard the sounds that a straining ear can hear in any storm, so it was hard to make out whether it was people calling for assistance or else the bad weather crying in the chimney. But the wind tore at the roof, knocked on the paper at the window and bore a distinct cry of "help!".

"Talk of the devil – cut-throats!" said the huntsman, turning pale and rising. "Someone's being robbed!"

"Lord, have mercy upon us!" the woodman whispered, turning pale and rising too.

The huntsman had a pointless look out of the window and took a turn around the hut.

"Night, and what a night!" he muttered. "It's pitch-black. The very best time to be robbing. D'you hear? Another shout!"

The woodman looked at the icon, shifted his eyes from the icon to the huntsman and dropped onto the bench in the exhaustion of a man startled by sudden news.

"Good Christian!" he said in a plaintive voice. "You could go into the lobby and put the lock on the door! And the light ought to be put out!"

"On account of what?"

"Who knows, they might get in here… Oh, our sins!"

"We ought to be going out, and you want the doors locked! You're a bright one, you are! Are we going, then?"

The huntsman threw his gun up onto his shoulder and took hold of his hat.

"Put your things on, bring your gun! Hey, Flerka, *ici*!"* he called to his dog. "Flerka!"

Out from under the bench came a dog with long, chewed-up ears, a cross between a setter and a mongrel. It stretched at its master's feet and started wagging its tail.

"What are you sitting down for?" the huntsman shouted at the woodman. "Aren't you coming?"

"Where?"

"To help!"

"How am I to do that?" the woodman waved the idea away, his whole body cringing. "To hell with it all."

"Why is it you don't want to come?"

"After all that frightening talk I'm not about to take a single step in the dark now. To hell with it all! And there's nothing new for me to see in the wood!"

"What are you afraid of? Haven't you got a gun? Come on, be so kind! Going alone's scary, but it's merrier together! D'you hear? Another shout! Up you get!"

"Who d'you think I am, lad!" groaned the woodman. "Am I an idiot, that I'll go to my own death?"

"So you're not coming?"

The woodman was silent. The dog, probably having heard a human cry, started barking mournfully.

"Are you coming, I'm asking you?" shouted the huntsman, his eyes bulging angrily.

"What a pest, honest to God!" frowned the woodman. "Go yourself!"

"Ah… bastard!" growled the huntsman, turning to the door. "Flerka, *ici*!"

He went out, leaving the door wide open. Into the hut flew the wind. The candle flame flickered uneasily, flared up brightly and then went out.

As he shut the door after the huntsman, the woodman saw the puddles in the cutting, the nearest pines and the receding figure of his guest lit up by lightning. Thunder growled in the distance.

"Lord, Lord, Lord…" whispered the woodman, hurrying to push the thick lock into the big iron loops. "What weather God's sent!"

Going back inside the hut, he groped his way to the stove, lay down and covered himself up, head and all. Lying under his sheepskin coat and straining to listen, he could no longer hear any human cry, and yet at the same time the cracks of thunder were becoming more powerful and booming. He could hear the heavy rain, driven on by the wind, knocking angrily at the glass and the paper of the window.

"What the devil got into him?" he thought, imagining the huntsman getting wet in the rain and stumbling over tree stumps. "His teeth must be chattering in terror!"

Not more than ten minutes or so later, there was the sound of footsteps, and after them a loud knock on the door.

"Who is it?" shouted the woodman.

"It's me," came the huntsman's voice. "Open up!"

The woodman climbed down from the stove, felt for the candle and, having lit it, went to open up the door. The huntsman and his dog were soaked to the skin. They had been in the heaviest and fastest rain, and it was streaming off them now as if from cloths in need of wringing.

"What happened out there?" asked the woodman.

"A peasant woman driving a cart got onto the wrong road…" the huntsman replied, recovering his breath. "Ended up in a thicket."

"Cor, stupid woman! She got scared, then… So, did you take her back out onto the road?"

"I don't want to answer a swine like you."

The huntsman threw his wet hat onto the bench and continued:

"What I think of you now is you're a swine and the lowest of men. A watchman too, what's more, getting a salary! What a stinker…"

The woodman trudged guiltily over to the stove, let out a croak and lay down. The huntsman sat down on the bench, had a think, and then stretched himself out, wet, along the whole length of it. After a little while he rose, put out the candle and lay down again. During one especially loud crack of thunder he rolled over, spat and growled:

"He was frightened… And what if someone had been cutting the woman's throat? Whose business is it to stand up for her? An old man too – what's more, a Christian… A pig and nothing more."

The woodman let out a croak and a deep sigh. Somewhere in the darkness Flerka gave her wet body a violent shake, sprinkling splashes in all directions.

"So I suppose it wouldn't matter much to you if the woman had had her throat cut?" the huntsman continued. "May God strike me dead, I didn't know you were like that…"

Silence fell. The thunder cloud had already passed, and the cracks of thunder to be heard were from afar, but it was still raining.

"And if, let's say, it wasn't a peasant woman, but you shouting for help?" the huntsman broke the silence. "Would you feel good, you scum, if no one came running to the rescue? You've riled me with your rotten behaviour, damn you!"

Hereafter, following another long interval, the huntsman said:

"So I suppose you've got some money, if you're afraid of people! A man who's poor won't be afraid…"

"You'll have to answer to God for those words…" wheezed Artyom from the stove. "I don't have any money!"

"Oh, no! A swine always has some money... And why are you afraid of people? So I suppose you must have! I could up and rob you out of spite, so you understood!.."

Artyom climbed down noiselessly from the stove, lit the candle and sat beneath the icon. He was pale, and did not take his eyes off the huntsman.

"I'll up and rob you," continued the huntsman, rising. "What did you expect? The likes of you need to be given a lesson! Talk, where's the money hidden?"

Artyom drew his legs in tight beneath him and started blinking.

"What are you cringing for? Where's the money hidden? Lost your tongue, have you, you clown? Why don't you speak?"

The huntsman leapt up and went over to the woodman.

"Doesn't he look down in the mouth! Well? Hand over the money, or else I'll shoot you!"

"Why are you badgering me?" the woodman yelped, and big tears splashed from his eyes. "What's the reason? God sees everything! You'll have to answer to God for all those words. You don't have any right to demand money from me!"

The huntsman looked at Artyom's crying face, knitted his brows and started pacing around the hut, then he angrily pulled his hat down low onto his head and picked up his gun.

"Ah... ah... it disgusts me just looking at you!" he muttered through his teeth. "I can't stand the sight of you! I won't be sleeping in your hut anyway. Goodbye! Hey, Flerka!"

The door slammed – and the restless guest and his dog had gone... Artyom locked the door behind him, crossed himself and went to bed.

The Requiem

I N T H E C H U R C H of the Mother of God Who Shows the Way,* in the village of Verkhnie Zaprudy, the Liturgy has just ended. People have begun to move and are pouring out of the church. The only person not moving is the shopkeeper, Andrei Andreyich, one of Verkhnie Zaprudy's long-time inhabitants and intelligentsia. He is leaning on the rail of the left-hand choir place, waiting. His clean-shaven, flabby face, pitted by the spots it once had, expresses on this occasion two contrasting emotions: humility before the inscrutable fates, and obtuse, boundless arrogance before the rough peasant jackets and brightly coloured headscarves passing by. On account of the Sabbath day he is dressed like a dandy. He has on a cloth coat with yellow bone buttons, blue trousers hanging outside his boots and heavy galoshes, those huge, awkward ones found only on the feet of people who are positive, sober-minded and of religious convictions.

His swollen, indolent eyes are turned towards the iconostasis. He sees the long-familiar faces of the saints, the watchman Matvei puffing out his cheeks and extinguishing the candles, the darkened stands for the icons, the worn carpet, Lopukhov the sexton running swiftly out from the sanctuary and taking the communion bread to the churchwarden... All of this he has seen over and over again, like the palm of his own hand... There is just the one thing somewhat strange and out of the ordinary, though: standing by the northerly deacon's door* is Father Grigory, not yet out of his vestments, twitching his thick eyebrows angrily.

"Who is it he's twitching at, God bless him?" thinks the shopkeeper. "Ah, and now he's started beckoning with his finger! And he's stamped his foot, Good Heavens... What an odd thing, Holy Queen! Who's it at?"

Andrei Andreyich looks around and sees a church now completely deserted. A dozen or so people are crowded together by the doors, but even they have their backs to the sanctuary.

"Come here when you're called! What are you standing there like a statue for?" he hears Father Grigory's angry voice. "It's you I'm calling!"

The shopkeeper looks at Father Grigory's red, enraged face, and only now does he realize that the twitching of the eyebrows and the beckoning with the finger may actually have to do with him. He gives a start, detaches himself from the choir place and, making a clatter with his heavy galoshes, steps irresolutely towards the sanctuary.

"Andrei Andreyich, was it you that handed in a request for prayers for the repose of Mariya?" asks the priest, glancing up with angry eyes at his flabby, sweating face.

"That's right."

"So it was you, then, that wrote this? Was it?"

And Father Grigory angrily thrusts a note in front of his eyes. And on this note, which Andrei Andreyich had handed in along with the communion bread, is written in big letters that seem to be lurching:

For the repose of God's handmaid, the harlot Mariya.

"That's right... I did write it, sir..." replies the shopkeeper.

"And how did you dare to write that?" whispers the priest, drawing out the words, and audible in his hoarse whisper are rage and fright.

The shopkeeper looks at him in obtuse surprise, perplexed and frightened himself: never before in his life has Father Grigory spoken in such a tone to Verkhnie Zaprudy's intelligentsia! Both are silent for a moment and look one another in the eye. The shopkeeper's perplexity is so great that his flabby face spreads out in all directions like spilt batter.

"How did you dare?" the priest repeats.

"Wh... whom, sir?" asked Andrei Andreyich, perplexed.

"Don't you understand?" whispers Father Grigory, taking a step backwards in astonishment and clasping his hands together. "What have you got on your shoulders, a head or some other object? You hand in a note to the table of oblation, and on it you write a word that it's unseemly to utter even in the street! What are you goggling for? Do you really not know the meaning of the word?"

"Is it regarding 'harlot' you mean, sir?" mumbles the shopkeeper, flushing and blinking his eyes. "But I mean, the Lord, in His goodness, er... you know, forgave a harlot...* prepared a place for her, and from the life of the Venerable Mariya of Egypt* too you can see in what senses that there word, excuse me..."

The shopkeeper wants to bring forward some other argument in his justification, but gets muddled and wipes his lips with his sleeve.

"So that's the way you understand it!" Father Grigory clasps his hands together. "But, I mean, God forgave – do you understand? – forgave, but you condemn, revile, call by an unseemly name and, what's more, whom? Your own departed daughter! Even in secular, let alone in sacred writings you wouldn't find such a sin! I tell you again, Andrei: there's no need to try and be learned! No, there's no need, brother, to try and be learned! If God gave you an enquiring mind, but you can't control it, better not delve into things at all... Don't delve into things, and keep quiet!"

"But I mean, she was, er... forgive me, an actoress!" pronounces the stunned Andrei Andreyich.

"An actoress! Whatever she was, after her death you ought to forget everything, and not go writing things in notes!"

"That's so..." the shopkeeper agrees.

"If you had a penance imposed upon you," booms the deacon from the depths of the sanctuary, gazing scornfully at Andrei Andreyich's confused face, "you'd stop being so clever! Your daughter was a famous actress. They even wrote in the newspapers about her passing... Philosopher!"

"Well of course... truly..." mumbles the shopkeeper, "it wasn't a suitable word, but it wasn't meant to condemn, Father Grigory – I wanted it to sound godly... so it would be clearer for you who to pray for. After all, in lists of people to be prayed for they write various names, like the infant Ioánn, the drowned Pelageya, the

warrior Yegor, the slaughtered Pavel and various other things...
That's what I wanted."

"Unwise, Andrei! God will forgive you, but another time,
beware. The main thing is, don't try and be learned, and follow
the example of others in your thinking. Bow to the ground in
prayer ten times, then off you go."

"Very well," says the shopkeeper, glad that the lecture is now
over, and again adopting an expression of self-importance and
steadiness. "Ten times? Very good, sir, I understand. But now,
Father, may I make a request?... Since I am, after all, her father...
and, you know, she, whatever she may have been, is, after all, my
daughter, I, er... forgive me, mean to ask you to conduct a requiem
today. And permit me to ask you too, Father Deacon!"

"Now that's good!" says Father Grigory, taking off his vestments.
"I can praise you for that. That meets with my approval... Well,
off you go! We'll be out in a moment."

Andrei Andreyich paces heavily away from the sanctuary and
stops, red, and with a solemn expression befitting a requiem, right
in the middle of the church. The watchman Matvei sets down a
table with a bowl of boiled wheat and honey* before him, and
after a little while the requiem begins.

The church is quiet. All that can be heard is the metallic sound of
the censer and long-drawn-out singing... Beside Andrei Andreyich
stand the watchman Matvei, the midwife Makaryevna and her
little son, Mitka, with his withered arm. There is no one else. The
deacon sings badly, in an unpleasant, hollow bass, but the tune
and words are so sad that, little by little, the shopkeeper loses
his expression of steadiness and sinks into sorrow. He recalls his
Mashutka... He remembers she was born to him while he was
still working as a servant for the masters of Verkhnie Zaprudy.
The hectic life of a servant meant he did not even notice how his
little girl was growing. That long period when she was developing
into a graceful creature with fair hair and pensive eyes, as large
as copeck coins, went by for him unnoticed. She was raised, as
all the children of favoured servants always are, in some comfort,
alongside the young ladies. The masters, with nothing better to do,
taught her to read, write and dance, while he did not interfere in

her upbringing. Only perhaps occasionally, meeting her by chance somewhere by the gates, or on a staircase landing, would he recall that she was his daughter and start, so far as leisure time allowed, teaching her prayers and scriptural history. Oh, even then he was known as an expert on the canons and Holy Scripture! The little girl, no matter how gloomy and serious her father's face, listened to him willingly. She repeated the prayers after him with a yawn, yet when, faltering and trying to express himself more ornately, he began telling her stories, she became all ears. Esau's lentils, the punishment of Sodom and the calamities of the little boy Joseph* made her turn pale and open her blue eyes wide.

Later, when he gave up service and, with the money he had saved, opened a shop in the village, Mashutka went away with his masters to Moscow...

Three years before her death she came to visit her father. He barely recognized her. She was an elegant young woman with the manners of a lady, and dressed like a gentlewoman. She talked in a clever way, as if from a book, smoked tobacco and slept till noon. When Andrei Andreyich asked her what she did, she announced, looking him boldly straight in the eye: "I'm an actress!" Such candour seemed to the former servant the height of cynicism. Mashutka began to boast of her successes and her actor's life, but, seeing that her father was only turning crimson and spreading his hands in bewilderment, fell silent. And in silence, without looking at each other, they lived for a couple of weeks, right up until her departure. Just before her departure she prevailed upon her father to go for a walk with her along the riverbank. However horrific it was for him to go for a walk with his actress daughter in broad daylight, in full view of the whole world, still he yielded to her entreaties...

"What wonderful parts you have here!" she enthused as she walked. "What gullies and marshes! My God, how beautiful my homeland is!"

And she started to cry.

"Those parts only take up space..." Andrei Andreyich thought, gazing obtusely at the gullies and not understanding his daughter's rapture. "They yield as much profit as a billy goat does milk."

And she cried and cried, and breathed greedily, filling her breast, as though she sensed she had not much time left to breathe...

Andrei Andreyich shakes his head like a bitten horse and, to suppress the difficult memories, starts rapidly crossing himself...

"Remember, O Lord," he murmurs, "Thy departed hand-maid, the harlot Mariya, and pardon her sins, voluntary and involuntary..."

The unseemly word again escapes his lips, but he does not notice it: what has become firmly lodged in your consciousness, it seems, cannot be prised out even with a nail, let alone by Father Grigory's admonitions! Makaryevna is sighing and whispering something, drawing the air inside her; Mitka with the withered arm is deep in thought about something...

"...where there is no sickness, sorrow or groaning..." drones the deacon, covering his right cheek with his hand.

From the censer comes a stream of bluish smoke that bathes in a broad, oblique ray of light traversing the sombre, lifeless emptiness of the church. And it seems as if, along with the smoke, drifting in that ray of light is the soul of the departed herself. The streams of smoke, resembling the curls of a child, circle, drift up towards the window, and seem to be shunning the despondency and grief of which that poor soul is full.

On the Road

A little golden cloudlet spent the night
*On the breast of one giant of a crag...**
                                    – Lermontov

I N THE ROOM which the innkeeper himself, the Cossack Semyon Chistoplyui, calls "the travelling room", that is, the one set aside solely for passing travellers, at the large, plain wooden table there sat a tall, broad-shouldered man of about forty. With his elbows leaning on the table and his head propped on his fist, he was asleep. The stub of a tallow candle stuck into an empty pomade jar lit his brown beard, thick, broad nose, tanned cheeks and the dense black eyebrows overhanging his closed eyes... The nose, the cheeks, the eyebrows, all his features, each one individually, were crude and heavy, like the furniture and the stove in "the travelling room", yet in sum they produced something harmonious and even handsome. Such, as they say, is the lot of the Russian face: the larger and harsher its features, the softer and more genial it seems. The man was dressed in a gentleman's jacket, worn but trimmed with a broad strip of new ribbon, in a plush waistcoat and wide, black trousers tucked into big boots.

On one of the benches that stretched in an unbroken line along the wall, asleep on a fox-fur coat, was a little girl of about eight in a brown dress and long black stockings. Her face was pale, her hair blond, her shoulders narrow, her entire body thin and feeble, but her nose protruded in a lump just as thick and unappealing as the man's. She was fast asleep, and could not feel the semicircular comb that had fallen from her head and was cutting her cheek.

"The travelling room" had a festive look. There was a smell in the air of freshly washed floors, there were no cloths hanging, as there always were, on the line that stretched diagonally right across the room, and in the corner, above the table, throwing a red patch onto an image of St George, was a glimmering icon lamp. Observing the strictest and most cautious gradation in their transition from the sacred to the profane, there stretched from the icon, both left and right of the corner, a row of crude popular prints. In the dim light of the candle stub and the red icon lamp the pictures formed an unbroken band, covered in black smudges; but when, wanting to sing in unison with the weather, the tiled stove inhaled the air with a howl, and the logs, as though waking, flared up in bright flame and growled angrily, rosy patches would begin to dance on the wooden walls, and above the head of the sleeping man could be seen arising first the Elder Serafim, next Shah Nasr-Ed-Din,* then a plump, brown baby with bulging eyes, whispering something into the ear of a maiden with an unusually obtuse and indifferent face...

Outside, the weather was bad and noisy. Something furious and malicious, but deeply unhappy was tearing around the inn with the rage of a beast and trying to break inside it. Banging the doors, knocking on the windows and the roof, scratching the walls, it was now threatening, now imploring, or else it would quieten down for a while, and then with a joyful, treacherous howl would break into the chimney of the stove, but at that point the logs would flare up, and the fire, like a watchdog, would rush with malice to meet the enemy, and a struggle would begin, followed by sobbing, shrieking and an angry roaring. In all of it could be heard malevolent anguish, discontented hatred and the insulted impotence of one once accustomed to victories...

Spellbound by this wild, inhuman music, "the travelling room" seemed to have fallen still for good. But then the door creaked and into the room came a potboy wearing a new calico shirt. Limping a little and blinking sleepily, he snuffed the candle with his fingers, put some more logs into the stove and left. At once, in the church that was three hundred paces from the inn in Rogachi, they began striking midnight. The wind played with the chimes as if with snowflakes; chasing after the sounds of the bell, it spun them over an enormous expanse, so that some strokes were cut short, or else extended into a long, undulating sound, while others were completely lost in the general hubbub. One stroke resounded in the room as distinctly as if the ringing had been right outside the windows. The little girl sleeping on the fox fur gave a start and raised her head. For a minute she gazed senselessly at the dark window and at Nasr-Ed-Din, across whom the crimson light from the stove was at that moment sliding, then she transferred her gaze to the sleeping man.

"Papa!" she said.

But the man did not move. The girl knitted her brows angrily, lay down and drew her knees up. Beyond the door, someone in the inn let out a loud and protracted yawn. Soon after this were heard the squeal of the door block and some indistinct voices. Someone entered and, shaking off the snow, began a muffled stamping of felt boots.

"What is it?" a female voice enquired lazily.

"Miss Ilovaiskaya's here…" replied a bass.

The door block began squealing again. There was the noise of the wind breaking in. Someone, probably the lame boy, ran up to the door that led into "the travelling room", gave a deferential cough and touched the latch.

"This way, miss, if you please," said a melodious female voice, "it's clean in here, my beauty…"

The door swung open and there appeared on the threshold a bearded peasant in a coachman's caftan with a large suitcase on his shoulder, entirely plastered, from head to toe, in snow. In after him came a short female figure, little more than half the height of the coachman, faceless and handless, wrapped up, bound up, looking like a bundle, and covered in snow as well. The little girl was struck by a blast of damp, as though from a cellar, coming from the coachman and the bundle, and the flame of the candle began to dance.

"What nonsense!" said the bundle angrily. "It's quite all right to travel! There's only twelve versts left to go, for the most part through woodland, and we wouldn't lose our way…"

"We wouldn't lose our way, it's true, but the horses won't go on, miss!" answered the coachman. "And Lord above, it's as if I'd done it on purpose!"

"God knows where you've brought me… But quiet… There seem to be people sleeping here. Go away…"

The coachman put the suitcase down onto the floor, at which layers of snow fell from his shoulders; he let out a whimpering sound through his nose and left. Then the girl saw two little hands emerge from the middle of the bundle, stretch upwards and begin angrily disentangling a tangle of shawls, kerchiefs and scarves. First to fall to the floor was a large shawl, next a hood, and after that a white knitted kerchief. Having freed her head, the new arrival took off a topcoat and was immediately halved in width. Now she was wearing a long grey coat with big buttons and protruding pockets. From one pocket she pulled out a paper package of some sort, from the other a bunch of big, heavy keys, which she put down so incautiously that the sleeping man gave a start and opened his eyes. For some time he gazed around obtusely, as though not understanding where he was, then he shook his head, went into a corner and sat down... The new arrival took off her coat, which made her halve in width again, pulled off her velveteen boots and sat down too.

Now she no longer resembled a bundle. She was a small, slim brunette of about twenty, as slender as a snake, with an elongated white face and wavy hair. Her nose was long and sharp, and her chin too was long and sharp, her eyelashes long, the corners of her mouth sharp, and thanks to this general sharpness her facial expression seemed prickly. In a tight-fitting black dress with masses of lace on the neck and sleeves, with sharp elbows and long, pink fingers, she was reminiscent of portraits of medieval English ladies. A serious, concentrated expression increased this likeness still further...

The brunette examined the room, looked askance at the man and the girl and, with a shrug of her shoulders, moved to sit by the window. The dark windows shook in the damp, westerly wind. Large flakes of snow, sparklingly white, fell onto the panes but disappeared at once, carried away by the wind. The wild music was becoming ever more powerful...

After a long silence, the little girl suddenly began turning back and forth and, rapping every word out angrily, said:

"O Lord! O Lord! How wretched I am! More wretched than anyone!"

The man rose and, with a sheepish gait that did not at all suit his enormous height and big beard, went pattering towards the girl.

"Are you awake, my little friend?" he asked in an apologetic voice. "What do you want?"

"I don't want anything! My shoulder hurts! You're a bad man, Papa, and God is going to punish you! You see if He doesn't!"

"My darling, I know your shoulder hurts, but what can I do, my little friend?" said the man, using the tone in which tipsy husbands apologize to their stern spouses. "It's the travelling, Sasha, that's made your shoulder hurt. Tomorrow we'll reach our destination; have a rest, and it'll pass."

"Tomorrow, tomorrow... Every day you tell me 'tomorrow'. We'll be travelling for twenty days yet!"

"But my little friend, you have my word as a father, we'll be there tomorrow. I never lie, and if we've been delayed by a blizzard, I'm not to blame."

"I can't bear it any more! I can't, I can't!"

Sasha jerked her leg abruptly and filled the room with unpleasant, shrill crying. Her father gave up and threw a perplexed look at the brunette. She shrugged her shoulders and irresolutely went over to Sasha.

"Listen, dear," she said, "what's the good of crying? True, it's not nice if your shoulder hurts, but what's to be done?"

"You see, madam," the man quickly began, as though trying to justify himself, "we haven't slept for two nights and have been riding in an abominable carriage. Well of course, it's natural that she's ill and miserable... And then, what's more, we found ourselves with a drunken driver, don't you know, and had our suitcase stolen... and all the time there's the snowstorm, but what's the point, madam, of crying? I'm exhausted too from all this sleeping in a sitting position, and it's as if I were drunk. Honestly, Sasha, it's nauseating enough here as it is, and then here you are crying!"

The man shook his head, flapped his arm and sat down.

"Of course, one shouldn't cry," said the brunette. "It's only babes in arms that cry. If you're ill, dear, you need to get undressed and sleep... Come on, let's get you undressed!"

When the girl was undressed and calmed, silence fell once more. The brunette sat by the window and examined the inn room – the icon, the stove – in bewilderment... She evidently thought the room, the girl with her fat nose in a boy's short nightshirt and the girl's father strange. This strange man sat in the corner, looking around from time to time in perplexity like a drunk, kneading his face with the palm of his hand. He blinked his eyes in silence, and looking at his sheepish figure, it was hard to suppose he would start speaking soon. But he *was* the first to start speaking. Rubbing his knees and clearing his throat, he grinned and said:

"It's a comedy, honestly... I look and I don't believe my eyes: why the devil did fate drive us to this filthy inn? What did it want to say in doing so? Life sometimes performs such *salto mortale** that you can only look on and blink in bewilderment. And you, madam, are you travelling far?"

"No, not far," the brunette replied. "I'm travelling from our estate, some twenty versts from here, to our village, to be with my father and brother. I'm Ilovaiskaya myself, and the village is called Ilovaiskoye too, twelve versts from here. What unpleasant weather!"

"It couldn't be worse!"

The lame boy came in and put a new candle stub into the empty pomade jar.

"You could bring us the samovar, lad!" the man addressed him.

"Who drinks tea at this hour?" grinned the lame boy. "It's a sin to drink before the Liturgy."

"That's all right, lad, it won't be you burning in hell, but us..."

Over tea the new acquaintances got talking. Ilovaiskaya learnt that her interlocutor was called Grigory Petrovich Likharyov, that he was the brother of the Likharyov who was Marshal of the Nobility in one of the neighbouring districts, and had himself once been a landowner, but "went bust good and early". And Likharyov learnt that Ilovaiskaya was called Marya Mikhailovna, that her father's estate was enormous, but that she was obliged to manage things on her own, as her father and brother turned a blind eye to life, were heedless and too fond of borzois.

"My father and brother are all on their own in the village," said Ilovaiskaya, moving her fingers about (in conversation she was in the habit of moving her fingers about in front of her prickly face and, after every phrase, licking her lips with her sharp little tongue). "They're a heedless lot, men, and they won't lift a finger for themselves. I can just see somebody giving them something to break their fast! We have no mother, and the servants are the kind who can't even put a cloth on a table properly without me. Now you can picture their situation! *They'll* be left with nothing to break their fast with, while *I* have to sit here all night. How strange it all is!"

Ilovaiskaya shrugged her shoulders, took a sip from her cup and said:

"There are some holidays that have their own smell. At Easter, Whitsun and Christmas there's a special sort of smell in the air. Even unbelievers enjoy those holidays. My brother, for example, argues that there's no God, but at Easter he's the first to run off to matins."

Likharyov raised his eyes to look at Ilovaiskaya and laughed.

"They argue that there's no God," Ilovaiskaya continued, laughing too, "but why is it, tell me, that towards the end of their lives all the famous writers, scholars, clever people generally, are believers?"

"Someone, madam, who in his youth couldn't believe, won't come to do so in old age either, even if he's the writer to end all writers."

Judging by his cough, Likharyov had a bass voice, but probably from fear of speaking too loudly, or else through excessive shyness, he spoke in a tenor. After a short silence, he sighed and said:

"My understanding is that faith is a capacity of spirit. It's just the same as talent: you have to be born with it. So far as I can judge from myself and from the people I've seen in my life, from all that's happened around me, that capacity is inherent in Russian people in the highest degree. Russian life is an unbroken series of beliefs and passions, while of unbelief or denial, if you want to know, it doesn't yet have even an inkling. If a Russian doesn't believe in God, that means his faith lies in something else."

Likharyov took a cup of tea from Ilovaiskaya, drank half of it down at once and continued:

"I'll tell you about myself. Nature put an unusual capacity for belief into my soul. I've spent half my life, though it would be better left unsaid, in the ranks of the atheists and nihilists, but there hasn't been a single hour in my life when I haven't believed. Talents normally all come to light in early childhood, and my capacity too was already letting itself be known when I was still walking about under the table. My mother liked children to eat a lot, and there were times when she was feeding me and she'd say: "Eat! The most important thing in life is soup!" I believed it and ate that soup ten times a day, ate it like a shark, to the point where it revolted me and made me faint. My nanny would tell me fairy tales, and I believed in house sprites, wood demons, all sorts of devilry. There were times when I'd steal mercuric chloride from my father, sprinkle it on spice cakes and take them to the attic so the house sprites, you see, would eat them and die. And when I learnt to read and to understand what I'd read, then I really went to town! I ran away to America, left to join a band of robbers, wanted to enter a monastery, hired boys to torment me like Christ. And note that my belief was always active, not dead. If I was running away to America, it wasn't alone, I'd lead someone else astray with me, just as big a fool as I, and I was glad when I was freezing outside the town gate and when I was being flogged; if I was joining a band of robbers, I'd be certain to come back with my face all beaten. The most restless childhood, I can tell you! And when I was sent to grammar school and showered there with all sorts of truths, such as the fact that the earth goes round the sun, or that white light isn't white, but composed of seven colours, my little head began reeling! I had everything flying into a spin: Joshua, who stopped the sun, and my mother, who in the name of the Prophet Elijah rejected lightning conductors,* and my father, indifferent to the truths I'd learnt. My new vision inspired me. I went around the house and the stables like a madman, preaching my truths; I was horrified by ignorance, burned with hatred for all who could see only white in the colour white... That's all trivial and childish, though. The serious, manly, so to speak, passions began for me at university. Have you, madam, completed a course anywhere?"

"At Novocherkassk, at the Don Institute."*

"But you haven't been on any of the women's courses?* So you don't know what the sciences are. All the sciences, as many of them as there are in the world, have one and the same passport, without which they consider themselves unthinkable: the aspiration to truth! Each one of them, even pharmacognosy or something, has as its objective not benefit, not convenience in life, but a truth. Marvellous! When you set about studying some science or other, you're struck first and foremost by its starting point. I can tell you, there's nothing more fascinating or grandiose, nothing stuns or grips the human spirit so, as the starting point of some science or other. From the very first five or six lectures you're already exhilarated by the brightest hopes, you already seem to yourself the master of truth. And I gave myself to the sciences selflessly, passionately, as to a woman I loved. I was their slave and wanted to know no other sun but them. Night and day, without a let-up, I swotted, spent all my money on books, cried when before my eyes people exploited science for personal ends. But I wasn't fascinated for long. The thing is that every science has a beginning, but has no end at all, the same as a recurring decimal. Zoology has discovered 35,000 species of insect, chemistry numbers sixty elements. If in time ten zeros are added to the right of those numbers, zoology and chemistry will be just as far from their ends as they are now, and all modern scientific work is precisely that, the augmentation of figures. I comprehended this secret when I discovered the 35,001st species and felt no satisfaction. Still, I didn't have time to experience disenchantment, as I was soon gripped by a new belief. I became obsessed with nihilism, with its proclamations, black partitions and all sorts of other things. I went to the people,* worked in factories, oiled machines, was a barge-hauler. Then, when, roaming through Holy Russia, I got an inkling of Russian life, I turned into an ardent admirer of that life. I loved the Russian people to the point of suffering, I loved and believed in its God, its language, its works... And so on, and so forth... In my time I've been a Slavophile, plaguing Aksakov with letters,⁴ and a Ukrainophile, and an archaeologist, and a collector of examples of folk art... I've been fascinated by ideas, people, events, places... fascinated without a break! Five years ago I was serving the rejection of property; my last belief was non-resistance to evil."*

Sasha emitted a broken sigh and started shifting around. Likharyov rose and went over to her.

"My little friend, would you like some tea?" he asked tenderly.

"Drink it yourself!" the girl replied rudely.

Likharyov was embarrassed and returned with a sheepish step to the table.

"So you've led a jolly life," said Ilovaiskaya. "There are things for you to remember."

"Well, yes, it's all jolly when you're sitting having tea and a chat with a kind woman, but you might ask how much the jollity has come to? What has the variety of my life cost me? After all, madam, I haven't believed like a German doctor of philosophy, not *zierlich-manierlich*,* I haven't lived in a wilderness, each of my beliefs has ridden roughshod over me, has torn my body to pieces. You judge for yourself. I was rich, like my brothers, but now I'm a pauper. In the delirium of my passions I squandered both my own fortune and my wife's – masses of money not my own. I'm now forty-two, old age is just around the corner and I'm as homeless as a dog that's fallen behind its wagon train in the night. In the whole of my life I've not known what peace is. My soul has pined endlessly, suffering even in its hopes... I've been exhausted by hard, disorderly labour, suffered deprivation, I've been in prison half a dozen times, dragged around the provinces of Arkhangelsk and Tobolsk... it's a painful memory! I've lived, but in the delirium I've not sensed the actual process of life. Can you believe it, I don't remember a single springtime, I didn't notice my wife loved me, or my children being born. What more can I tell you? For all who've loved me, I've meant misfortune... My mother's been in mourning for me for fifteen years now, while my proud brothers, who've had to agonize, blush, break their backs and throw their money about because of me, have come in the end to hate me like poison."

Likharyov rose, then sat back down again.

"If I were merely unhappy, I'd give thanks to God," he continued, not looking at Ilovaiskaya. "My personal unhappiness recedes into the background when I remember how often in my passions I've been absurd, far from the truth, unfair, cruel, dangerous! How often I've hated and despised with all my soul those I ought to have loved – and vice-versa. I've been guilty of betrayal a thousand times. Today I believe, prostrate myself, and then tomorrow I flee like a coward from my gods and friends of today, and silently swallow the 'scoundrel' they shout after me. God alone has seen how often I've cried and bitten my pillow in shame over my passions. Not once in my life have I intentionally lied or done evil, but my conscience isn't clear! Madam, I can't even boast that I have no one's life on my conscience, since my wife died before my very eyes, worn out by my recklessness. Yes, my wife! Listen, in our society now there are two prevailing attitudes to women. Some measure female skulls to prove that a woman is inferior to a man, they seek her deficiencies in order to mock her, to try and wave their cleverness in her face and to vindicate their animalism. And others try with all their might to raise woman to their own level, i.e. to force her to learn the 35,000 species by rote, to talk and write the same nonsense as they themselves talk and write…"

Likharyov's face darkened.

"But I can tell you," he said in a bass voice, banging his fist on the table, "that woman always has been and always will be the slave of man. She is delicate, soft wax, from which man has always fashioned whatever he wanted. Good Lord, for a shoddy male passion she's cut off her hair, abandoned her family, died on foreign soil… Amongst the ideas for which she's sacrificed herself, there isn't a single woman's one… A selfless, devoted slave! I haven't measured any skulls, but I can say this from hard, bitter experience. The proudest independent women, if I've managed to communicate my inspiration to them, have followed me, without discussion, without questioning, and doing all I've wanted; I made a nihilist of a nun, who, as I heard later on, took a shot at a gendarme; my wife never left me for one moment in my wanderings and, like a weathervane, changed her belief in line with the way I changed my passions."

Likharyov leapt up and began walking around the room.

"Noble, exalted slavery!" he said, clasping his hands together. "Precisely therein lies the lofty meaning of a woman's life! Out of the dreadful chaos that has accumulated in my head over all the time I've been associated with women, there have remained intact in my memory, as in a filter, not ideas, not clever words, not philosophy, but this extraordinary submissiveness to fate, this exceptional mercy and capacity to forgive anything..."

Likharyov clenched his fists, fixed his gaze on a point in space, and with a kind of passionate exertion, as though chewing over every word, through clenched teeth he murmured:

"This... this magnanimous endurance, fidelity to the grave, poetry of the heart... The meaning of life lies precisely in this uncomplaining martyrdom, in the tears that soften stone, in the boundless, all-forgiving love that brings light and warmth into the chaos of life..."

Ilovaiskaya slowly rose, took a step towards Likharyov and fixed her eyes upon his face. From the tears that glistened on his eyelashes, from his quavering, passionate voice, from the flush on his cheeks, it was clear to her that women were no chance, no simple topic of conversation. They were the object of his new passion or, as he himself put it, his new belief! For the first time in her life Ilovaiskaya saw before her a man impassioned, an ardent believer. Gesticulating, and with eyes flashing, he seemed to her mad, frenzied, but in the fire of his eyes, in his speech, in the movements of his big body as a whole could be sensed so much beauty that, without noticing it herself, she stood rooted to the ground before him, gazing rapturously into his face.

"Just take my mother!" he said, reaching his hands out to her and pulling an imploring face. "I've poisoned her existence, I've defamed, according to her notions, the Likharyov family, caused her as much trouble as the most bitter enemy might, and what? My brothers let her have a few coppers for communion bread and prayer requests, and she, violating her religious feeling, saves the money up and sends it in secret to her dissolute Grigory! That small change alone can educate and ennoble one's soul much more powerfully than any theories, clever words or 35,000 species! I can give you a thousand examples. Let's take you, if you will! There's a blizzard outside, it's night-time, but you're going to your brother and father to warm them with kindness on a holiday, though they may not be thinking about, may have forgotten about you. And just wait, when you fall in love with a man, you'll follow him to the North Pole. You will, won't you?"

"Yes, if I... do fall in love."

"There, you see!" said Likharyov in delight, even stamping his foot. "Honestly, I'm so glad to have made your acquaintance! It's my good fortune that I'm always meeting splendid people. Never a day goes by without getting acquainted with someone for whom I'd simply give up my soul. There are far more good people in the world than bad. Just imagine, you and I have had a candid, heart-to-heart talk, as if we've known one another for ages. Sometimes, I can tell you, you hold out for ten years, you stay silent, keep things hidden from your friends and wife, then you meet a cadet in a train carriage and blurt your entire soul out to him. I have the honour of seeing you for the very first time, but I've confessed to you as never before. Why is that?"

Rubbing his hands and smiling cheerfully, Likharyov took a turn around the room and again began speaking of women. At the same time, the bell began to sound for matins.

"Oh Lord!" Sasha burst into tears. "He won't let me sleep with his talking!"

"Ah, yes!" Likharyov suddenly remembered. "Sorry, my little friend. You sleep, sleep... I've got two boys besides her," he began whispering. "They, madam, are staying with their uncle, but this one can't get through so much as a day without her father. She suffers and grumbles, but sticks to me like a fly to honey. Madam, I've let my tongue run away with me, and you could have done with a rest too. Would you like me to make up a bed for you?"

Without waiting for permission, he gave the wet topcoat a shake and stretched it out on a bench, the fur uppermost, picked up the scattered kerchiefs and shawls, rolled her coat up and put it at the head of the bed, and all this in silence, with an expression of servile reverence on his face, as though he were busy not with bits of women's clothing, but with broken fragments of holy vessels. In his figure as a whole there was something sheepish, bashful, as though in the presence of a weak creature he was ashamed of his height and strength...

When Ilovaiskaya had lain down, he extinguished the candle and sat on a stool by the stove.

"So, madam," he whispered, lighting up a fat cigarette and blowing the smoke into the stove. "Nature has put into Russian man an extraordinary capacity for belief, an inquisitive mind and a gift for thought, but it's all reduced to dust by heedlessness, indolence and frivolous dreams... Yes indeed..."

Ilovaiskaya peered in surprise into the darkness and saw only a red patch on the icon and the glimmering light from the stove on Likharyov's face. The darkness, the ringing bell, the roar of the snowstorm, the lame boy, grumbling Sasha, unhappy Likharyov and his speeches – it was all mixing together, growing into one enormous impression, and God's earth seemed to her fantastic, full of wonders and enchanting forces. All she had just heard rang in her ears, and human life seemed to her a fine, poetic fairy tale with no end.

The enormous impression grew and grew, it obscured consciousness and turned into sweet sleep. Ilovaiskaya slept, but saw the icon lamp and the fat nose on which the red light danced.

She heard crying.

"Dear Papa," a child's voice implored tenderly, "let's go back to Uncle! The Christmas tree's there! Styopa and Kolya are there!"

"My little friend, what can I do?" said a man's persuasive, quiet bass. "You must understand me! Do understand!"

And the child's crying was joined by a man's. This voice of human grief amidst the howling storm touched the young woman's ear with such sweet human music that she could not bear the delight and started to cry as well. Later she heard a large, black shadow quietly approach her, pick a fallen shawl up from the floor and cover her feet.

Ilovaiskaya was woken by a strange roaring. She leapt up and looked around in surprise. In through the windows, half-covered in snow, looked the blue of the dawn. Inside the room there was grey twilight, through which the stove and the sleeping girl and Nasr-Ed-Din were clearly outlined. The stove and the icon lamp had already gone out. Visible through the wide-open door was the big room of the inn with a counter and tables. Some man with an obtuse, gypsy face and startled eyes was standing in the middle of the room in a puddle of melted snow and holding a large red star on a pole.* He was surrounded by a crowd of little boys, as motionless as statues and plastered in snow. The light of the star, passing through red paper, made their wet faces glow. The crowd was roaring in a disorderly fashion, and from its roaring Ilovaiskaya could understand just the one verse:

> Hey, you, little fellow,
> Take a slender knife now,
> We'll kill the Jew, we'll kill
> The son who brought such ill…*

By the counter stood Likharyov, gazing emotionally at the singers and tapping his foot in time. On seeing Ilovaiskaya he grinned from ear to ear and went over to her. She smiled too.

"Happy Christmas!" he said. "I saw you were sleeping well."

Ilovaiskaya looked at him, was silent and continued to smile.

After the night's conversation he no longer seemed to her tall, or broad-shouldered, but small, in the way the biggest steamship seems small to us when it is said to have sailed across an ocean.

"Well, it's time for me to go," she said. "I must put my things on. Tell me, where is it you're heading now?"

"Me? To the station at Klinushki, from there to Sergiyevo, and from Sergiyevo forty versts by horse to the coal mines of some dimwit, one General Shashkovsky. My brothers found me a job as manager there… I'm going to be digging coal."

"Forgive me, I know those mines. Shashkovsky's my uncle, you know. But… what are you going there for?" asked Ilovaiskaya, examining Likharyov in surprise.

"As manager. To manage the mines."

"I don't understand!" Ilovaiskaya shrugged her shoulders. "You're going to the mines. But it's bare steppe there, you know, no people, so boring that you won't last a day! The coal's appalling, nobody buys it, and my uncle's a maniac, a despot, a bankrupt... You won't even get any wages!"

"It's all the same," said Likharyov indifferently. "I have to be grateful even for the mines."

Ilovaiskaya shrugged her shoulders and began walking around the room in agitation.

"I don't understand, I don't understand!" she said, moving her fingers about in front of her face. "It's not possible and... and not sensible! You must understand that it's... it's worse than exile, it's a grave for a living man! Ah, Lord," she said fervently, going over to Likharyov and moving her fingers about in front of his smiling face; her upper lip was trembling and her prickly face had turned pale. "Why, just imagine the bare steppe, the loneliness. There's no one to exchange a word with there, and you're... fascinated by women! Mines and women!"

Ilovaiskaya suddenly felt embarrassed by her fervour and, turning away from Likharyov, she moved off towards the window.

"No, no, you mustn't go there!" she said, drawing a finger rapidly over the glass.

She sensed not merely with her soul, but even with her back that behind her stood an endlessly unhappy, hopeless, desolate man, while he, as though unconscious of his unhappiness, as though it had not been him crying in the night, gazed at her with a good-natured smile. Better if he had carried on crying! In agitation, she took several turns around the room, then stopped in a corner and fell into thought. Likharyov was saying something, but she did not hear him. Turning her back to him, she took a twenty-five rouble note from her purse, crumpled it in her hands for a long time, and then, looking round at Likharyov, she blushed and stuffed the note into her pocket.

From outside the door came the voice of the coachman. In silence, with a stern, focused face, Ilovaiskaya began putting her things on. Likharyov wrapped her up, while chatting cheerfully, but every one of his words fell upon her soul like deadweight. It's no fun listening to the banter of the unhappy or the dying.

When the transformation of a living person into a formless bundle was complete, Ilovaiskaya surveyed "the travelling room" one last time, stood for a moment in silence and slowly went out. Likharyov went to see her off…

And outside, God knows why, winter was still in a rage. Whole clouds of big, soft snowflakes spun restlessly over the earth and could find no peace. Horses, sleigh, trees, the bull tied to a post, all was white and seemed soft and fluffy.

"Well, God bless," murmured Likharyov, helping Ilovaiskaya into the sleigh. "Remember me kindly…"

Ilovaiskaya was silent. When the sleigh had moved off and begun to skirt a large snowdrift, she turned to look back at Likharyov with an expression that suggested she wanted to say something to him. He ran over to her, yet she said not a word to him, but only glanced at him through long eyelashes on which hung flakes of snow…

Was his sensitive soul truly able to read that glance, or did his imagination perhaps deceive him? Only it suddenly began to seem to him that two or three more good, strong brushstrokes, and this girl would have forgiven him his failures, old age and ill fortune, and would have followed him, without questioning, without discussion. He stood for a long time, rooted to the ground, and gazed at the tracks left by the sleigh runners. Snowflakes were falling avidly onto his hair, his beard, his shoulders… Soon the tracks of the runners had disappeared, and he himself, covered in snow, had begun to resemble a white crag, but still his eyes searched for something amid the clouds of snow.

Misfortune

S OFYA PETROVNA, the wife of the notary Lubyantsev, a pretty young woman of about twenty-five, was walking quietly down a forest cutting with the man from the neighbouring dacha, the barrister Ilyin. It was getting on for five in the evening. Thick above the cutting were white, fluffy clouds; peeping through in places from behind them were bright-blue patches of sky. The clouds hung motionless, as if caught on the tops of the tall old pines. It was quiet and sultry.

In the distance, the cutting was broken by a low railway embankment, along which for some reason on this occasion there strode a sentry with a rifle. Immediately behind the embankment was a large, white, six-domed church with a rusty roof...

"I didn't expect to meet you here," Sofya Petrovna was saying, looking at the ground and touching last year's leaves with the tip of her parasol, "but now I'm glad that I have. I need to have a serious and definitive talk with you. Please, Ivan Mikhailovich, if you really do love and respect me, then stop your pursuit! You follow me like a shadow, you're forever looking at me with no good in your eyes, you declare your love, write strange letters and... and I don't know when it's all going to end! Good Lord, now where's it all going to lead?"

Ilyin was silent. Sofya Petrovna walked on a few paces and continued:

"And this marked change in you has taken place in just some two or three weeks, after a five-year acquaintanceship. I don't recognize you, Ivan Mikhailovich!"

Sofya Petrovna threw a sidelong glance at her companion. He was gazing intently, with his eyes narrowed, at the fluffy clouds. The expression on his face was cross, capricious and absent-minded, like that of a man who is suffering and is at the same time obliged to listen to nonsense.

"It's amazing how it is you can't understand it for yourself!" Lubyantseva continued, shrugging her shoulders. "You must realize you're undertaking a rather unlovely game. I'm married, I love and respect my husband... I have a daughter... Do you really not set any store by that? And besides, as an old friend of mine, you know my views on the family... on the fundamentals of the family generally..."

Ilyin let out an irritable croak and sighed.

"The fundamentals of the family..." he muttered. "Oh Lord!"

"Yes, yes... I love my husband, I respect him, and in any event hold the peace of the family dear. I'd more likely let myself be killed than be the cause of unhappiness for Andrei and his daughter... So please, Ivan Mikhailovich, for God's sake leave me in peace. Let's be good, kind friends as before, and stop this sighing and moaning, which doesn't suit you. It's settled, over and done with! Not a word more about it. Let's talk about something else."

Again Sofya Petrovna looked sidelong at Ilyin's face. Ilyin was gazing up into the air; he was pale and was angrily biting his trembling lips. Lubyantseva could not understand what he was cross and exasperated about, but his pallor touched her.

"Don't be angry, now, let's be friends..." she said affectionately. "Agreed? Here's my hand."

Ilyin took her small, plump hand in both of his, squeezed it and lifted it slowly to his lips.

"I'm not a schoolboy," he muttered. "I'm not tempted one bit by friendship with the woman I love."

"Enough, enough. It's settled, over and done with. We've reached the bench, let's sit down..."

Sofya Petrovna's soul was filled with a sweet sense of relaxation: the most difficult and ticklish thing had now been said, the agonizing question was settled, over and done with. Now she could breathe easily and look Ilyin straight in the face. She did look at him, and a beloved woman's egotistical feeling of superiority over the one who loves her comforted her pleasantly. She liked the way this strong, enormous man, with a manly, cross face and a big black beard, clever, educated and, so they said, talented, obediently sat down next to her and hung his head. They sat for two or three minutes in silence.

"Nothing is settled or over and done with yet..." Ilyin began. "It's as if you're reading to me from a copy book: 'I love and respect my husband... the fundamentals of the family...' I know it all without your telling me, and I can tell you more. I say to you sincerely and honestly that I consider this behaviour of mine criminal and immoral. What more, you might think? But what's the point of saying what everyone already knows? Instead of buttering parsnips with pathetic words, you'd do better to teach me what I should do."

"I've already told you: leave!"

"I've left – and you know this very well – five times already, and every time I've got halfway and then come back! I can show you the through tickets – I've kept them all. I haven't the will to run away from you! I struggle, I struggle terribly, but what the hell am I any good for if I've got no backbone, if I'm weak and pusillanimous! I can't struggle with nature! Do you understand? I can't! I run away from here, but it holds me by my coat-tails. Base, vile feebleness!"

Ilyin flushed, stood up and began walking about beside the bench.

"I'm angry as a dog!" he growled, clenching his fists. "I hate and despise myself! My God, I'm running after another man's wife like a depraved kid, writing idiotic letters, demeaning myself... argh!"

Ilyin took his head in his hands, let out a croak and sat down.

"And then there's your insincerity too!" he continued bitterly. "If you're against my unlovely game, why ever did you come here? What drew you here? In my letters I ask you only for a categorical, straight answer – yes or no, but instead of a straight answer you strive to meet with me 'accidentally' every day and treat me to quotations from copybooks!"

Lubyantseva took fright and blushed crimson. She suddenly felt the discomfort that respectable women are obliged to experience when accidentally caught undressed.

"You seem to suspect a game on my part..." she began mumbling. "I've always given you a straight answer, and... and today I've made a request of you!"

"Ah, do people really make requests in such matters? If you'd said 'go away' at once, I'd have been long gone, but you didn't say that to me. Not once have you given me a straight answer. Strange indecisiveness! I swear you're either playing with me, or else..."

Ilyin did not finish his sentence and propped his head up with his fists. Sofya Petrovna began to recall her behaviour from beginning to end. She remembered that every day, not only in deed, but even in her innermost thoughts, she had been against Ilyin's advances, but at the same time she felt that there was a grain of truth in the barrister's words. And not knowing what that truth was, however hard she thought, she was at a loss what to say to Ilyin in reply to his complaint. She felt awkward remaining silent, and said with a shrug of her shoulders:

"So what's more, I'm to blame."

"I'm not blaming you for your insincerity," Ilyin sighed. "I just said it because it happened to come up... Your insincerity is both natural and in the order of things. If everybody came to an agreement and suddenly became sincere, they'd find everything damned well going to the dogs."

Sofya Petrovna was in no mood for philosophy, but she was glad of an opportunity to change the subject and asked:

"Why's that, then?"

"Because only savages and animals are sincere. Since civilization brought into life the requirement for such a comfort as, for example, feminine virtue, sincerity has no longer been appropriate..."

Ilyin poked angrily at the sand with his cane. Lubyantseva listened to him, and there was a lot she did not understand, but she liked his conversation. First and foremost she liked the fact that a talented man was talking to her, an ordinary woman, "about brainy things"; and then it gave her great pleasure to watch the way his pale, animated and still angry young face moved. There was a lot she did not understand, but clear to her was that beautiful boldness of the modern man, by means of which, without pausing for thought and without a moment's hesitation, he decides big questions and draws definitive conclusions.

She suddenly caught herself admiring him and took fright.

"Forgive me, but I don't understand," she said hurriedly. "Why did you start talking about insincerity? Once again I'm repeating my request: be a good, kind friend, leave me in peace! I'm asking you sincerely!"

"Very well, I shall struggle some more!" Ilyin sighed. "I'll do my best... Only it's unlikely anything will come of my struggle. Either I'll put a bullet through my head, or else... I'll hit the bottle in the most idiotic way. It'll be a bad lookout for me! Everything has its limit, struggling with nature too. Tell me, how can one struggle with madness? How do you overcome excitement by drinking wine? What can I do if your image has become grafted onto my soul and stands importunately, day and night, before my eyes, as this pine tree here does now? Come on, teach me what feat I have to perform to rid myself of this loathsome, unhappy condition, when all my thoughts, desires and dreams belong not to me, but to some demon that has got inside me? I love you, love you to the point where I've been thrown out of joint, I've abandoned my work and everyone I'm close to, forgotten my God! Never in my life have I loved like this!"

Sofya Petrovna, who had not expected such a shift, leant back from Ilyin and looked at his face in fright. He had tears in his eyes, his lips were trembling, and spread across the whole of his face was a hungry, imploring sort of expression.

"I love you!" he murmured, moving his eyes up close to her big, frightened ones. "You're so beautiful! I'm suffering now, yet I swear I'd sit my whole life through like this, suffering and gazing into your eyes. But... stay silent, I implore you!"

Sofya Petrovna, as if taken unawares, began ever so quickly thinking up words with which she could stop Ilyin. "I'll go!" she decided, but she had not had time to make a movement to rise before Ilyin was already kneeling at her feet... He was hugging her knees, gazing into her face and talking passionately, ardently, beautifully. In terror and intoxication she did not hear his words; now, for some reason, at this dangerous moment, when her knees were squeezed together pleasantly as if in a hot bath, she sought with a kind of angry spite for some sense in her feelings. She was angry that she was completely filled not with protesting virtue, but rather with feebleness, indolence and emptiness, like a drunk knee-deep in the sea; only in the depths of her soul was some distant little part teasing in malicious delight: "Why ever don't you go? So this is how it should be, then? Yes?"

Seeking for some sense inside her, she could not understand how it was that she did not pull away the hand to which Ilyin had attached himself like a leech, nor why she glanced hurriedly left and right at the same time as Ilyin, to see whether anyone was looking. The pines and the clouds were motionless and looked on sternly, in the manner of old tutors who see mischief, but in return for some money have undertaken not to report it to their superiors. The sentry was standing stock-still on the embankment and seemed to be looking at the bench.

"Let him look!" thought Sofya Petrovna.

"But... but listen!" she said finally, with despair in her voice. "Where is this going to lead? What will happen later on?"

"I don't know, I don't know..." he began whispering, his hand brushing the unpleasant questions aside.

The hoarse, jangling whistle of a locomotive was heard. This extraneous, cold sound of everyday prose made Lubyantseva rouse herself.

"I haven't the time... it's time to go!" she said, getting up quickly. "The train's coming... Andrei's on his way! He's got to have dinner."

Sofya Petrovna turned her glowing face towards the embankment. First the locomotive crawled slowly by, and after it appeared the coaches. It was not the suburban passenger train, as Lubyantseva had thought, but a goods train. One after another in a long line, like the days of a human life, the coaches trailed across the white background of the church, and there seemed to be no end to them!

But then finally the train did come to an end and the last coach, with its lanterns and conductor, disappeared behind the greenery. Sofya Petrovna turned abruptly and, without looking at Ilyin, set off quickly back down the cutting. She was already in control of herself. Red with shame, insulted not by Ilyin, no, but by her own pusillanimity, the shamelessness with which she, moral and upright, had allowed this other man to hug her knees, she was now thinking of only one thing, how to reach her dacha, her family, quickly. The barrister could barely keep up with her. Turning from the cutting onto a narrow path, she glanced around at him so quickly that she saw only the sand on his knees, and waved a hand at him for him to leave her alone.

After running home, Sofya Petrovna stood motionless in her room for about five minutes, gazing now at the window, now at her writing desk...

"You're vile!" she scolded herself. "Vile!"

To needle herself, she called to mind in every detail, concealing nothing, how she had been against Ilyin's advances all these days, but had been *drawn* to go and have things out with him; moreover, when he had been sprawled at her feet she had felt unusual delight. She called everything to mind, without sparing herself, and now, choking with shame, she would have been glad to give herself slap after slap in the face.

"Poor Andrei," she thought, trying, at the memory of her husband, to lend her face the tenderest expression possible. "Varya, my poor little girl, doesn't know the kind of mother she has! Forgive me, my dears! I love you very much... very much!"

And wanting to prove to herself that she was still a good wife and mother, that corruption had not yet affected those "fundamentals" of hers, of which she had spoken to Ilyin, Sofya Petrovna ran to the kitchen and there started shouting at the cook because she had not yet laid the table for Andrei Ilyich. She tried to imagine her husband's weary, hungry appearance, expressed out loud her pity for him, and personally laid the table for him, something she had never done before. Then she found her daughter Varya, picked her up and hugged her ardently; the little girl seemed to her heavy and cold, but she did not want to admit this to herself, and set about explaining to her how good, honest and kind her father was.

And yet, when Andrei Ilyich arrived soon after, she barely said hello to him. The flood of false feelings had already passed, without having proved a thing to her, and having merely irritated and angered her with their falsehood. She sat by the window, suffering and angry. Only in misfortune can people understand how hard it is to be the master of one's feelings and thoughts. Sofya Petrovna would say later on that inside her there was "a muddle, which it was just as difficult to sort out as it was to count fast-flying sparrows". From the fact, for example, that she took no pleasure in her husband's arrival and disliked the way he behaved at dinner, she suddenly concluded that stirring within her was hatred for her husband.

Andrei Ilyich, languid from hunger and weariness, fell upon the salami while waiting for his soup to be served, and ate it greedily, chewing noisily with his temples moving.

"Good Lord," thought Sofya Petrovna, "I love and respect him, but... why does he chew so horribly?"

There was disorder in her thoughts no less than in her feelings. Lubyantseva, like anyone inexperienced in struggling with unpleasant thoughts, tried with all her might to think about her misfortune, and the harder she tried, the more did Ilyin, the sand on his knees, the fluffy clouds and the train stand out in relief in her imagination...

"And why was I so stupid as to go today?" she agonized. "And surely I'm not the sort that can't vouch for herself?"

Fear has magnifying eyes. As Andrei Ilyich was finishing the last course, she was already filled with resolution: tell her husband everything and flee from danger!

"I need to have a serious talk with you, Andrei," she began after dinner, as her husband was taking off his frock coat and boots to lie down for a rest.

"Well?"

"Let's go away from here."

"Hm... and go where? It's too soon to go back to town."

"No, and go travelling, or something of the sort..."

"Go travelling," muttered the notary, stretching. "I dream of doing that myself, but where will we get the money, and who will I leave in charge of the office?"

And after some thought he added:

"You're right, you're bored. Go yourself, if you like!"

Sofya Petrovna agreed to this, but realized straight away that Ilyin would be glad of the opportunity and would go with her in the same train, in the same carriage... She pondered, and she looked at her husband, full but still languid. Her gaze for some reason fixed upon his feet, miniature, almost feminine, in striped socks; from both socks there were threads sticking out at the toes...

Behind the lowered blind a bumblebee was buzzing and beating against the window pane. Sofya Petrovna gazed at the threads, listened to the bumblebee and imagined herself travelling... Day and night, Ilyin sits *vis-à-vis*,* never taking his eyes off her, angry at his feebleness and pale from spiritual pain. He calls himself a depraved kid, he scolds her, tears his hair out, but, after waiting for darkness, and seizing the moments when the passengers fall asleep or get out at a station, he drops to his knees before her and squeezes her legs, like then by the bench...

She suddenly caught herself daydreaming...

"Listen, I won't go alone!" she said. "You must come with me!"

"It's fantasy, Sofochka!" sighed Lubyantsev, "You have to be serious and wish only for what's possible."

"You'll come when you find out!" thought Sofya Petrovna.

Having decided to leave, come what may, she felt herself out of danger; little by little her thoughts got back into order, she cheered up and even permitted herself to think about it all; however much you think or dream, you're going all the same! Little by little, while her husband was asleep, evening was coming on... She sat in the drawing room playing the piano. The animation of the evening beyond the windows, the sounds of music and, most importantly, the thought that she was a clever thing who had dealt with misfortune, cheered her up completely. Other women in her position, her calm conscience told her, would probably not have held out and would have gone spinning like a whirlwind, whereas she had all but burnt up in shame, had suffered and was now fleeing from danger that might not even exist! Her virtue and resolution so moved her, she even glanced at herself in the mirror two or three times.

When it was dark, guests came. The men sat down in the dining room to play cards, and the ladies occupied the drawing room and terrace. Last of all to appear was Ilyin. He was gloomy, sullen and seemingly ill. Having sat down in the corner of a sofa, he did not get up the entire evening. Normally cheerful and talkative, on this occasion he was silent all the time, frowning and scratching around his eyes. When obliged to reply to someone's question, he would force a smile with his upper lip alone and give a curt, bad-tempered reply. He cracked half a dozen jokes, but his witticisms came out harsh and rude. It seemed to Sofya Petrovna that he was close to hysteria. Only now, sitting at the piano, did she clearly recognize for the first time that this unhappy man was in no mood for joking, that he was sick at heart and beside himself with anguish. For her sake he was ruining the best days of his career and youth, he was spending the last of his money on a dacha, he had abandoned his mother and sisters to the mercy of fate, but most importantly, he was becoming exhausted in his torturous struggle with himself. Out of simple, everyday philanthropy she ought to be treated seriously...

She recognized all this clearly, to the point where her heart ached, and if at that moment she had gone over to Ilyin and said to him "no!", there would have been a power in her voice it would have been hard to disobey. But she did not go over and did not say it, nor did she even think of it... A young nature's pettiness and egotism never seem to have proclaimed themselves so powerfully in her as on that evening. She recognized Ilyin was unhappy, that he was sitting on the sofa like a cat on hot bricks, and she felt pain on his behalf, but at the same time the presence of a man who loved her to the point of suffering filled her soul with triumph, with a sense of her own power. She felt her youth, beauty, unassailability and – a good thing she'd decided to leave! – that evening she gave herself free rein. She flirted, chuckled incessantly, sang with particular feeling and inspiration. Everything made her merry, and she found everything amusing. The memory of the incident at the bench and the watching sentry made her laugh. She was amused by the guests, Ilyin's rude witticisms, the pin on his tie which she had never seen before. The pin was in the form of a red snake with little diamond eyes; this snake seemed to her so amusing she would have been prepared to smother it in kisses.

Sofya Petrovna sang romances with nervous energy and a kind of half-drunken recklessness, and, as though teasing another's grief, she chose sad, melancholic ones with talk of lost hopes, the past, old age… "And old age is looming yet closer and closer…" she sang. But what was old age to her?

"Something not quite right seems to be happening to me…" she occasionally thought through the laughter and singing.

The guests dispersed at twelve o'clock. Last to leave was Ilyin. Sofya Petrovna still had sufficient recklessness to see him as far as the bottom step of the terrace. She had felt the urge to inform him she was leaving with her husband, and to see what effect this news would have on him.

The moon was hiding behind the clouds, but it was so light that Sofya Petrovna could see the wind playing with the skirts of his coat and the drapes on the terrace. It was also possible to see how pale Ilyin was and how he curled his upper lip in an effort to smile…

"Sonya, Sonichka… my dear woman!" he began murmuring, preventing her from speaking. "My sweet, my lovely!"

In a paroxysm of tenderness, with tears in his voice, he showered her with words of endearment, each more tender than the one before, already addressing her as intimately as a wife or a lover. Unexpectedly for her, he suddenly put one arm around her waist, and with the other hand took her by the elbow.

"My dear, my delight…" he began whispering, kissing her on the back of her neck, "be sincere, come back with me now!"

She slipped out of his embrace and raised her head to fly into a rage and express her indignation, but she could not manage indignation, and all of her much vaunted virtue and purity sufficed only to utter the phrase all ordinary women do in such circumstances:

"You're out of your mind!"

"Truly, let's go!" Ilyin continued. "I'm convinced now, just as then, at the bench, that you, Sonya, are just as powerless as I… It'll be a bad lookout for you too! You love me, and now you're arguing fruitlessly with your conscience…"

Seeing she was walking away from him, he seized her by her lacy sleeve and quickly finished what he was saying:

"If not today, then tomorrow, but you will have to concede! So why this waste of time? My dear, sweet Sonya, sentence has been passed, so why put off carrying it out? Why deceive yourself?"

Sofya Petrovna tore herself away from him and slipped back through the door. Returning to the drawing room, she mechanically closed the piano, gazed for a long time at the vignette on the sheet music, and then sat down. She could neither stand, nor think... After her excitement and recklessness, there remained in her only a terrible weakness, plus lassitude and boredom. Her conscience whispered to her that during the evening gone by she had behaved badly, stupidly, like a crazy girl, that she had just been in a clinch on the terrace, and she could even now feel a sort of awkwardness in her waist and by her elbow. There was not a soul in the drawing room and just one candle was burning. Lubyantseva sat on the round stool by the piano, not stirring, waiting for something. And as though exploiting her extreme exhaustion and the darkness, a painful, insuperable desire began to take hold of her. Like a boa constrictor it bound her limbs and soul, it grew with every second, and it no longer threatened, as previously, but stood clear before her in all its nakedness.

She sat for half an hour without stirring and without preventing herself from thinking about Ilyin, then got up lazily and trudged into the bedroom. Andrei Ilyich was already in bed. She sat down by the open window and surrendered herself to the desire. There was no longer any "muddle" in her head, all her feelings and thoughts were clustered in accord around one clear aim. She began to make an effort to struggle, but gave it up as hopeless straight away... She now realized how strong and implacable was the enemy. To struggle with it, strength and fortitude were needed, but her birth, upbringing and life had given her nothing she might lean on.

"Immoral! Vile!" she chided herself for her feebleness. "So is this the way you are?"

Her outraged probity was so indignant about this feebleness that she called herself absolutely all the abusive words she knew, and told herself a lot of hurtful, humiliating truths. Thus she said to herself that she had never been moral, and had not fallen before only because there had been no pretext, and that her day-long struggle had been an amusement and a comedy...

"Let's say I did struggle," she thought, "but what sort of struggle was that? Even women who are for sale struggle before selling themselves, but they sell themselves all the same. That's a fine struggle: like milk, in a single day it's gone sour! In a single day!"

She found herself guilty of being drawn to leave the house not by feeling, not by the person of Ilyin, but by the sensations awaiting her in the future... An errant dacha mistress, of whom there are many!

"When a ba-aby chick's mother wa-as killed," sang somebody outside the window in a husky tenor.

"If I'm going, then it's time," thought Sofya Petrovna. Her heart suddenly started thumping terribly hard.

"Andrei!" she all but shouted. "Listen, are we... are we going? Yes?"

"Yes... I've already told you: go yourself!"

"But listen..." she said, "if you don't come with me, you risk losing me! I think I'm... in love!"

"Who with?" asked Andrei Ilyich.

"You ought not to care who with!" shouted Sofya Petrovna.

Andrei Ilyich sat up, dangled his legs over the side of the bed and looked in surprise at the dark figure of his wife.

"Fantasy!" he yawned.

He could not believe it, but he was nonetheless afraid. After some thought, and having asked his wife several unimportant questions, he stated his view on the family and on infidelity... he talked listlessly for about ten minutes and then lay down. His moralizing had no success. There are many views in this world, and a good half of them belong to people who have never been in any trouble!

Despite the late hour, people from the dachas were still moving about outside the windows. Sofya Petrovna threw on a light cloak, stood for a moment and had a think... She still had sufficient resolution to say to her sleepy husband:

"Are you asleep? I'm going to take a stroll... Do you want to come with me?"

This was her last hope. Getting no reply, she went outside. It was windy and fresh. She noticed neither the wind, nor the darkness, but walked and walked... An irresistible force was driving her on, and it seemed as if, should she stop, she would be given a push in the back.

"Immoral!" she muttered mechanically. "Vile!"

She was choking, burning with shame, her legs could barely support her, but the thing that was pushing her onwards was stronger than her shame, and her reason, and her fear...

An Event

I T IS MORNING. Breaking into the nursery through the icy lace that covers the window panes is bright sunlight. Vanya, a boy of about six with close-cropped hair and a nose like a button, and his sister Nina, a four-year-old girl, curly-haired, chubby and short for her age, wake up and gaze angrily at one another through the bars of their cots.

"Ooh, you shameless things!" grumbles their nanny. "Good people have already finished their tea, but you can't get the sleep out of your eyes..."

The sun's rays are amusing themselves on the rug, on the walls, on the hem of their nanny's skirt, and they seem to be inviting the children to play with them, but the children fail to notice them. They have woken up in a bad mood. Nina pouts her lips, pulls a sour face and starts whining:

"Te-e-ea! Nanny, te-e-ea!"

Vanya wrinkles his brow and wonders what he can find fault with, so as to start bawling. He has already begun blinking and opened his mouth, but at that moment his mama's voice comes from the drawing room:

"Don't forget to give the cat some milk, she's got her kittens now!"

Vanya and Nina stretch out their faces and gaze at one another in bewilderment, then both at once they cry out, jump from their cots and, filling the air with piercing squeals, they run bare-footed, in just their nightshirts, into the kitchen.

"The cat's had her kittens!" they cry. "The cat's had her kittens!"

In the kitchen, under the bench, stands a small crate, the one in which Stepan lugs the coke around when lighting a fire in a fireplace. Looking out from the crate is the cat. Her little grey face expresses extreme exhaustion, her green eyes with the narrow black pupils gaze out, languid and sentimental... It is clear from her face that the one thing lacking for complete happiness is the presence in the crate of "him", the father of her children, to whom she gave herself so selflessly! She wants to miaow, and opens her mouth wide, but from her throat comes only a rasping... What *can* be heard is the squeaking of the kittens.

The children squat down in front of the crate and, not stirring, with bated breath, gaze at the cat... They are surprised, astonished, and fail to hear the grumbling of their nanny, who has chased after them. Shining in the eyes of both of them is the most sincere joy.

In the upbringing and lives of children, domestic pets play a barely perceptible, but undoubtedly beneficial role. Which of us cannot remember tough but generous mutts, scrounging lapdogs, birds dying in captivity, dim but haughty turkeys, meek old granny cats who forgave us when, for fun, we trod on their tails and caused them excruciating pain? It even seems to me sometimes that the patience, loyalty, magnanimity and sincerity that are inherent in our domestic creatures have a much more powerful and positive effect on the mind of a child than the long lectures of some Karl Karlovich, dry and pale, or the vague ramblings of a governess, trying to demonstrate to children that water is made up of oxygen and hydrogen.

"They're so little!" says Nina, wide-eyed and bursting into merry laughter. "They look like mouses!"

"One, two, three..." counts Vanya. "Three kittens. So, one for me, one for you, and one for someone else."

"Prrr... prrr..." purrs the new mother, flattered by the attention. "Prrr."

Done gazing at the kittens, the children pick them up from under the cat and start squeezing them in their hands, and then, not content with this, they put them into the hems of their nightshirts and run into the reception rooms.

"Mama, the cat's had her kittens!" they cry.

Their mother is sitting in the drawing room with some unfamiliar gentleman. Seeing the children unwashed, undressed, with their hems pulled up, she is embarrassed, and her eyes become stern.

"Lower your nightshirts, you shameless things!" she says. "Go away, or else I shall punish you."

But the children notice neither their mother's threats nor the presence of a stranger. They put the kittens down on the rug and set up a deafening squealing. The new mother walks around beside them, miaowing imploringly. When, after a little while, the children are dragged off to the nursery, dressed, made to say their prayers and given some tea, they are filled with a passionate desire to rid themselves of these prosaic obligations as quickly as they can and run back to the kitchen.

The usual activities and games retreat far into the background.

With their coming into the world, the kittens eclipse everything else and appear as living news and the topic of the day. If Vanya or Nina were offered a *pood** of sweets each or a thousand ten-copeck coins per kitten, they would reject such an exchange without the slightest hesitation. Right through until lunch, despite the heated protests of their nanny and the cook, they sit by the crate in the kitchen and busy themselves with the kittens. Their faces are serious, focused, and express concern. They are worried not only by the present, but also by the future of the kittens. They have made up their minds that one kitten will stay at home with the old cat so as to comfort its mother, another will go to the dacha, and the third will live in the cellar, where there are lots and lots of rats.

"But why don't they look?" asks Nina, bewildered. "They've got blind eyes, like beggars have."

This question is bothering Vanya too. He undertakes to open one kitten's eyes, spends a long time puffing and breathing hard, but his operation remains unsuccessful. He is not a little bothered too by the fact that the kittens stubbornly refuse the meat and milk they are offered. All that is put before their little faces is eaten by their grey mummy.

"Come on, let's build some little houses for the kittens," suggests Vanya. "They'll all live in different houses and the cat'll go and visit them…"

Cardboard hatboxes are set up in different corners of the kitchen. The kittens take up residence inside them. But this separation of the family proves premature: the cat, retaining the imploring and sentimental expression on her face, goes around to all the boxes and carries her children back to their former place.

"The cat's their mother," remarks Vanya, "but who's their father?"

"Yes, who's their father?" repeats Nina.

"They can't be without a father."

Vanya and Nina spend a long time deciding who is to be the kittens' father, and in the end their choice falls upon the big, dark-red horse with the missing tail that is lying in the storeroom under the stairs, seeing out its days with the other discarded toys. It is dragged out of the storeroom and stood beside the crate.

"Watch out, now!" it is threatened. "Stay here and see they behave properly."

All this is said and done in the most serious way and with an expression of concern on the children's faces. Vanya and Nina do not want to know any world other than the crate with the kittens. Their joy knows no bounds. But they are to go through some difficult, excruciating moments.

Just before dinner, Vanya is sitting in his father's study and gazing dreamily at the desk. By the lamp, on some headed notepaper, a kitten is turning to and fro. Vanya is following its movements and poking now a pencil, now a matchstick into its little face... Suddenly, as if from nowhere, his father appears beside the desk.

"What's this?" Vanya hears his angry voice.

"It's... it's a little kitten, Papa..."

"I'll give you a little kitten! Look what you've done, you good-for-nothing brat! You've made a mess of all my paper!"

To Vanya's great surprise, his papa does not share his liking for kittens, and instead of going into raptures and rejoicing, he gives Vanya's ear a tug and cries:

"Stepan, get rid of this filth!"

There is a scene at dinner too... During the main course the diners suddenly hear a squeak. The cause begins to be investigated, and a kitten is found underneath Nina's pinafore.

"Ninka, leave the table!" her father says angrily. "Throw the kittens out into the cesspit this minute! I will not have this filth in the house!..."

Vanya and Nina are horrified, Death in the cesspit, besides its cruelty, threatens in addition to deprive the cat and the wooden horse of their children, to lay waste the crate, to destroy their plans for the future, that splendid future when one cat will comfort its old mother, another will live at the dacha and the third will catch rats in the cellar... The children start crying and begging for the kittens to be spared. Their father agrees, but on condition that the children do not dare go to the kitchen or touch the kittens.

After dinner, Vanya and Nina mooch about in all the reception rooms, pining. The ban on going to the kitchen has plunged them into despondency. They refuse sweetmeats, throw tantrums and are rude to their mother. When Uncle Petrusha comes in the evening, they take him aside and complain to him about their father wanting to throw the kittens into the cesspit.

"Uncle Petrusha," they say to their uncle, "tell Mama to have the kittens put in the nursery. Do tell her!"

"Well, well... all right!" their uncle brushes them off. "Very well!"

Uncle Petrusha is usually not alone when he comes. With him there is Nero too, a big, black mutt of Danish breed, lop-eared and with a tail as hard as a rod. This mutt is silent, gloomy and filled with a sense of his own dignity. He does not pay the children the slightest attention and, pacing by them, hits them with his tail, just as he does the chairs. The children hate him with all their souls, but on this occasion they find practical considerations take precedence over feeling.

"You know what, Nina," says Vanya, wide-eyed, "let Nero be the father instead of the horse! The horse is dead, but he's alive, isn't he?"

All evening they wait for the moment when their papa settles down to play *vint** and they can take Nero into the kitchen unnoticed... And finally Papa does sit down to his cards, while Mama is busy with the samovar and cannot see the children... The happy moment arrives.

"Come on!" Vanya whispers to his sister.

But at this point in comes Stepan and announces with a laugh:

"Mistress, Nero's eaten the kittens!"

Nina and Vanya turn pale and gaze at Stepan in horror.

"Honest to God…" laughs the servant. "Went up to the crate and scoffed 'em."

It seems to the children that all the people in the house will be frantic and will go for the villain Nero. But the people stay calmly in their seats and merely wonder at the appetite of the enormous dog. Papa and Mama laugh… Nero walks around by the table, wagging his tail and smugly licking his chops. The only one bothered is the cat. With her tail stretched out, she goes from room to room, throwing suspicious glances at people and miaowing plaintively.

"Children, it's already gone nine o'clock! Time for bed!" Mama calls.

Vanya and Nina go to bed, they cry and spend a long time thinking about the aggrieved cat and the cruel, brazen, unpunished Nero.

Agafya

DURING MY STAY in the District of S., I often found myself spending time at the Dubovo allotments with the man in charge, Savva Stukach, otherwise simply Savka. Those allotments were my favourite place for so-called "general" fishing, when, on leaving the house, you don't know the day or the hour at which you'll return, you take every single bit of fishing tackle with you and you stock up with provisions. Strictly speaking, I wasn't as interested in the fishing as in just serenely loafing around, eating at the wrong times, chatting with Savka and having lengthy face-to-face encounters with the quiet summer nights. Savka was a lad of about twenty-five, strapping, handsome, hard as flint. He was reputed to be a reasonable and sensible man, he was literate and rarely drank vodka, but as a workman, this young, strong man wasn't worth a copeck. Flowing alongside the power in his muscles, as strong as rope, there was serious, invincible indolence. Like everyone else, he lived in the village, in his own hut, and had the use of his share of land, but he didn't plough, didn't sow and didn't have any trade. His old mother begged at every door, and he himself lived like a free bird in the sky: he didn't know in the morning what he'd be eating at noon. It wasn't that he lacked will, energy or pity for his mother: that was just the way it was, there was no sense of desire for labour and no consciousness of its use... Absolutely wafting from his entire figure came serenity and an innate, almost artistic passion for living without purpose, any old how. And when Savka's young, healthy body did feel physiologically drawn to muscular work, the lad would devote himself for a short while to some free but foolish profession such as the sharpening of utterly redundant pegs, or running races with the peasant women. His favourite position was focused immobility. He was capable of standing on one spot for hours on end without stirring, gazing at a single point in space. He would move when so inspired, but then only when the opportunity presented itself to make some rapid, impulsive movement: to grab a running dog by the tail, to rip off a peasant woman's shawl, to leap over a wide pit. It goes without saying that, in the light of such miserliness of movement, Savka was as poor as a church mouse and lived worse than any landless peasant. With the passage of time, rent arrears were bound to mount up and, healthy and young, he was sent by the *mir** to do an old man's job as watchman and scarecrow at the communal allotments. No matter how he was mocked about his premature old age, he didn't give two hoots. This job, quiet, and convenient for motionless contemplation, was perfectly suited to his nature.

I happened to be with this Savka one fine evening in May. I remember I was lying on a torn, threadbare travelling rug almost right beside a wattle shelter, from which came the rich and sultry smell of dried grasses. I'd put my arm under my head and was gazing out ahead of me. By my feet lay a wooden pitchfork. Beyond it, the black blob of Savka's little dog, Kutka, caught the eye, and no more than a couple of *sazhens* from Kutka the ground fell away abruptly as the steep bank of a little river. Lying down, I couldn't see the river. I saw only the tops of the willow bushes crowding on the near bank and the edge of the opposite one, winding, as though someone had been taking bites out of it. Far beyond the bank, on a dark knoll, huddling up to one another like frightened young partridges, were the huts of the village in which my Savka lived. Beyond the knoll the glow of evening was burning out. There remained just one pale band of purple, and even that had begun to be covered by little clouds, as coals are by ash.

To the right of the allotments, whispering quietly and occasionally quivering when the wind unexpectedly sprang up, was a dark grove of alders, and to the left stretched a boundless field. Where, in the darkness, the eye could no longer distinguish the field from the sky, a little light was twinkling brightly. At some distance from me sat Savka. With his legs crossed beneath him like a Turk's and his head hanging, he was gazing pensively at Kutka. Our hooks with live bait had already been in the river for a long time, and there was nothing left for us to do but simply devote ourselves to the relaxation of which Savka, who never tired himself and was forever relaxing, was so fond. The glow had not yet gone out completely, but the summer's night was already enveloping nature in its pampering, soporific caress.

Everything was coming to a standstill in that initial deep sleep, only in the grove was some nocturnal bird, unfamiliar to me, uttering in a long-drawn-out and lazy way a lengthy, articulated sound, reminiscent of the phrase: "Did you see Ni-ki-ta?" and answering itself immediately: "I did, I did, I did!"

"Why is it the nightingales aren't singing today?" I asked Savka.

He turned to me slowly. His features were large, but clear, expressive and soft, like a woman's. Then he glanced with his meek, pensive eyes at the grove and the willow bushes, slowly pulled a tin whistle from his pocket, put it into his mouth and began cheeping like a hen nightingale. And at once, as if in reply to his cheeping, a corncrake started craking on the opposite bank.

"There's a nightingale for you..." Savka grinned. "Crake-crake! Crake-crake! As though it's jerking on a hook, but I bet it thinks that's singing too, you know."

"I like that bird..." I said. "Did you know? During its migration, the corncrake doesn't fly, it runs along the ground. It only flies across rivers and seas, otherwise it's all done on foot."

"How about that, the dog..." muttered Savka, looking with respect in the direction of the crying corncrake.

Knowing what a lover Savka was of listening, I told him everything I knew about the corncrake from books on hunting. From the corncrake I moved on imperceptibly to migration. Savka listened to me attentively, unblinking, and all the while smiling in pleasure.

"And which country is more home for the birds?" he asked. "Ours or the one there?"

"Ours, of course. The bird is both born itself and breeds its young here, this is its homeland, and it goes there only to avoid freezing to death."

"That's curious!" Savka said, stretching. "Whatever you talk about, all of it's curious. A bird, for example, or a man... or take this stone – everything has its own mentality!... Oh dear, if

I'd but known you were coming, master, I wouldn't have told a woman to come here today... There's one asked to come today..."

"Ah, you do as you wish, I shan't get in your way!" I said. "I can go and sleep in the grove..."

"What do you mean? It wouldn't kill her to come tomorrow... If only she'd sit down here and listen to the conversation, but she'll only start whining, you know. You can't have a proper talk with her here."

"Is it Darya you're expecting?" I asked after a short silence.

"No... It was a new one asked today... Agafya Strelchikha..."*

Savka pronounced this in his usual, dispassionate, rather muffled voice, as though he were talking about tobacco or porridge, but I sat up quickly in surprise. I knew Agafya Strelchikha... She was a still very young peasant lass of nineteen or twenty, who had no more than a year before married a railway pointsman, a manly young lad. She lived in the village, and her husband came from the line to spend every night with her.

"All these episodes of yours with women are going to end badly, my friend!" I sighed.

"Well, so be it..."

But after a little thought Savka added:

"I've told the women, but they don't listen... They couldn't care less, the idiots!"

Silence fell... The darkness, in the meantime, was growing ever denser, and objects were losing their contours. The band beyond the knoll had already died away completely, while the stars were becoming ever brighter, more radiant... The melancholically monotonous chirring of grasshoppers, the craking of the corn-crake and the cry of a quail didn't disturb the nocturnal quiet, but rather, on the contrary, added still more to its monotony. It seemed to be not the birds, not the insects quietly calling and bewitching our hearing, but the stars, gazing upon us from the sky...

First to break the silence was Savka. He shifted his eyes slowly from black Kutka to me and said:

"I can see you're bored, master. Let's have supper."

And without waiting for my agreement, he crawled on his stomach into the wattle shelter and rummaged around there, at

AGAFYA

which the entire thing started trembling like a single leaf; then he crawled back and set down in front of me my vodka and an earthenware dish. In the dish were some baked eggs, some rye flat cakes made with pig fat, some pieces of black bread and something else besides... We had a drink from a crooked little glass that couldn't stand up, and set about the food... Coarse grey salt, dirty, fatty flat cakes, eggs as tough as rubber, and yet how good it all tasted!

"You lead a bachelor's life, but you have such a lot of different things," I said, indicating the dish. "Where do you get them from?"

"Women bring them..." Savka mumbled.

"And why ever do they bring you them?"

"Don't know... out of pity..."

Not just the menu, but Savka's clothing too bore traces of women's "pity". Thus that evening I noticed he was wearing a new worsted sash and a bright-crimson ribbon from which there hung, on his dirty neck, a little copper cross. I knew the fair sex's weakness for Savka and knew how unwillingly he spoke of it, and for that reason didn't continue my interrogation. And what's more, it wasn't the time for talking... Kutka, who had been rubbing around us and waiting patiently to be given something, suddenly pricked up his ears and began growling. A distant, intermittent splashing of water could be heard.

"There's someone crossing the ford..." said Savka.

Two or three minutes later, Kutka started growling again and emitted a sound like a cough.

"Shush!" his master snapped at him.

Timid footsteps began to be heard indistinctly in the darkness, and from the grove there appeared the silhouette of a woman. I recognized her, even in spite of the fact that it was dark – it was Agafya Strelchikha. She approached us tentatively, stopped and fought to catch her breath. She was probably puffing not so much from the walk as from fear and the unpleasant feeling anyone experiences when crossing a ford in the night-time. On seeing two people beside the wattle shelter instead of one, she let out a feeble cry and took a step backwards.

"Ah, it's you!" said Savka, stuffing a flat cake into his mouth.

"It's me... me, sir," she mumbled, dropping a bundle of something onto the ground and looking askance at me. "Yakov said to say hello and told me to give you... there's something in there..."

"Oh, why lie: Yakov!" grinned Savka. "There's no reason to lie, the gentleman knows why you've come! Sit down, be our guest."

Agafya threw me a sidelong glance and irresolutely sat down.

"I was already thinking you wouldn't be coming today," said Savka after a lengthy silence. "Why just sit there? Eat! Or give you some vodka to drink, should I?"

"The idea!" said Agafya. "Found himself some sort of drunkard..."

"Have a drink... It'll warm your heart up... Well!"

Savka handed Agafya the crooked little glass. She drank the vodka slowly, but had nothing to eat with it, and merely exhaled loudly.

"She's brought something..." continued Savka, untying the bundle and giving his voice a condescendingly jokey tone. "A woman can't manage without bringing something. Ah, a pie and potatoes... They live well!" he sighed, turning to face me. "They're the only ones in all the village who still have potatoes left from the winter!"

I couldn't see Agafya's face in the gloom, but from the movement of her shoulders and head she seemed to me not to take her eyes off Savka's face. So as not to play gooseberry, I decided to go for a stroll and stood up. But at that moment a nightingale in the grove suddenly sang two lower contralto notes. Half a minute later he let out a high, fine trill, and having thus tried out his voice, he began to sing. Savka leapt up and listened intently.

"That's yesterday's one!" he said. "Just hang on!.."

And darting off, he ran noiselessly towards the grove.

"So what's he to you?" I cried in his wake. "Leave him alone!"

Savka flapped an arm at me not to shout and vanished in the darkness. When he wanted, Savka was both a splendid huntsman and fisherman, but here too his talents were wasted just as pointlessly as his strength. He was too lazy to be exemplary, and devoted all his passion as a huntsman to idle tricks. Thus he would have to catch nightingales with his bare hands, shoot pike with small shot, and would sometimes stand by the river for hours on end, trying for all he was worth to catch a little fish with a big hook.

Left with me, Agafya gave a cough and drew the palm of her hand across her forehead several times... She was already getting tipsy from the vodka she'd drunk.

"How are things, Agafya?" I asked her after a lengthy silence, when it already felt awkward to stay silent.

"Fine, thank you... Don't you tell anyone, master..." she suddenly added in a whisper.

"Enough said," I reassured her. "How fearless you are, though, Agasha... What if Yakov finds out?"

"He won't..."

"No, but what if?"

"No... I'll be home before him. He's on the line now, and he'll come back once he's seen the mail train off, and you can hear the train passing from here..."

Agafya drew her hand across her forehead again and looked in the direction in which Savka had gone. The nightingale was singing. Some nocturnal bird flew by very low, just above the ground, and noticing us, it gave a start, and with a rustle of its wings flew off to the other side of the river.

Soon the nightingale fell quiet, but Savka didn't come back. Agafya stood up, took a few restless steps, and then sat down again.

"What ever is he doing?" she said, unable to contain herself. "I mean, the train isn't coming tomorrow! I need to leave now!"

"Savka!" I cried. "Savka!"

I wasn't answered even by an echo. Agafya started shifting restlessly and again stood up.

"It's time I went!" she said in a worried voice. "The train'll be here any time! I know when the trains run!"

The poor young lass wasn't wrong. Not a quarter of an hour had passed before a distant noise was heard.

Agafya fixed a long gaze on the grove and began moving her hands about impatiently.

"Well, where on earth is he?" she began, with a nervous laugh. "Where the devil has he got to? I'm leaving! I swear I am, master!"

Meanwhile, the noise was becoming ever more distinct. The rumbling of the wheels could already be distinguished from the heavy sighs of the locomotive. Now the whistle could be heard, and the train crossed the bridge with a muffled rumble... another minute and everything fell quiet.

"I'll wait one more minute..." sighed Agafya, resolutely sitting down. "So be it, I'll wait!"

Finally Savka appeared in the darkness. His bare feet were stepping noiselessly over the friable earth of the allotments, and he was quietly singing something.

"That's luck for you, isn't it, for Heaven's sake!" he laughed merrily. "I'd just, you know, like, gone up to the bush, and just started to take aim with my hand, and he goes and shuts up! Oh, you son of a bitch! I waited and waited for him to start singing again, then just gave it up as a bad job..."

Savka toppled awkwardly onto the ground beside Agafya and, to keep his balance, took hold of her waist with both hands.

"And what are you frowning about, as if your mother wasn't your mum?" he asked.

For all his soft heart and guilelessness, Savka despised women. He treated them offhandedly, haughtily, and even stooped to contemptuous mockery of their feelings for him. God knows, perhaps this offhanded, contemptuous treatment was actually one of the reasons for the powerful, irresistible fascination he held for the village's Dulcineas.* He was handsome and well proportioned, and even when he was looking at the women he despised there was always a light of gentle affection shining in his eyes; but that fascination can't be explained by physical qualities alone. Besides his fortunate appearance and distinctive manner, one has to think that women were also influenced by Savka's touching role as a universally acknowledged failure and unfortunate exile from his own family hut to the allotments.

"Come on, tell the gentleman why you've come here!" Savka continued, still holding Agafya by the waist. "Come on, tell him, wife of your husband! Ho-ho... Shall we have some more vodka, Agasha my friend?"

I rose and, making my way between the vegetable beds, set off down the side of the allotments. The dark beds looked like big, flattened graves. Wafting from them was the smell of turned earth and the delicate dampness of plants that have begun to be covered in dew. To the left, the little red light was still shining. It blinked affably and seemed to be smiling.

I heard happy laughter. It was Agafya laughing.

"And the train?" I thought. "The train came a long time ago."

After waiting a while, I returned to the shelter. Savka was sitting motionless like a Turk and quietly, barely audibly, singing some song made up of nothing but monosyllabic words, something like: "Well, well, my, my... you and I..." Agafya, intoxicated by the vodka, Savka's contemptuous affection and the closeness of the night, was lying on the ground beside him and pressing her face spasmodically against his knee. She had got so carried away by her feelings that she didn't even notice my arrival.

"Agasha, the train came a long time ago, you know!" I said.

"It's time, time you went," Savka picked up on my thought and gave his head a shake. "What are you sprawling around here for? Shameless you are!"

Agafya roused herself, drew her head away from his knee, glanced at me, then pressed herself back up against him once more.

"It's high time!" I said.

Agafya began to stir and half-rose onto one knee... She was in torment... For half a minute her entire figure, as far as I could make it out through the darkness, expressed conflict and vacillation. There was a moment when, as if coming to, she stretched out her torso to rise to her feet, but at that point some invincible and implacable force pushed at her whole body, and she fell back against Savka.

"To hell with him!" she said with a wild laugh from her chest, and audible in that laugh were reckless resolution, powerlessness and pain.

I wandered quietly into the grove, and from there went down to the river where our fishing tackle was. The river was sleeping. Some kind of soft, double flower on a long stem touched my cheek gently, like a child who wants to let you know he's not asleep.

Having nothing better to do, I groped for one of the fishing lines and pulled on it. It tensed slightly, then sagged – nothing had been caught... The other bank and the village couldn't be seen. There was a glimpse of a light in one hut, but it soon went out. I fumbled about on the bank and found a hollow I had spotted during the day, then settled down in it as if in an armchair. I sat for a long time... I saw the stars begin to grow hazy and lose their radiance, and the way a light breath of chill air swept over the earth and touched the leaves of the waking willows...

"A-ga-fya!..." someone's muffled voice carried from the village. "Agafya!"

It was her husband, back and alarmed, searching through the village for his wife. And audible from the allotments at that moment was unrestrained laughter: the wife had forgotten herself, got drunk and was trying with a few hours' happiness to make up for the torment that awaited her on the morrow.

I fell asleep...

When I woke up, Savka was sitting beside me and lightly shaking my shoulder. The river, the grove, both banks, green and washed, the village and the field – all was flooded in bright morning light. Through the slender trunks of the trees the rays of the newly risen sun beat against my back.

"So is this the way you fish?" grinned Savka. "Come on, get up!"

I got up, stretched pleasurably, and my awakened breast began greedily drinking in the moist, fragrant air.

"Has Agasha gone?" I asked.

"There she is," said Savka, pointing me in the direction where the ford was.

I looked and saw Agafya. Lifting the hem of her dress a little, dishevelled, and with her scarf slipping down off her head, she was crossing the river. Her legs could barely move...

"The cat knows well whose butter she ate!" muttered Savka, narrowing his eyes at her. "She's going with her tail between her legs... Mischievous, these women, like cats, and cowardly, like rabbits... Didn't leave yesterday when she was told to, the idiot! She'll catch it now, and the *volost* will have me flogged again because of the women..."

Agafya stepped onto the bank and set off across the field towards the village. At first she strode quite boldly, but agitation and terror soon told: she turned fearfully, stopped and caught her breath.

"There you are, she's scared!" grinned Savka sadly, gazing at the bright-green stripe that stretched through the dewy grass behind Agafya. "Doesn't want to go! Her husband's already been standing waiting for her for an hour... Have you seen him?"

Savka said the final words with a smile, but my stomach turned cold. In the village, on the road by the last hut, stood Yakov, staring straight at his wife coming back to him. He didn't stir, he was as motionless as a pillar. What was he thinking, looking at her? What words was he preparing for their meeting? Agafya stood for a while, looked back once more, as though expecting help from us, then set off. Never before had I seen anyone walk like that, neither drunk, nor sober. It was as if her husband's gaze were making Agafya contort herself. Now she would be walking in a zigzag, then just marking time, bending her knees and spreading her arms, next backing away. After going about a hundred paces, she looked back once more and sat down.

"You might at least hide behind a bush..." I said to Savka. "Suppose her husband sees you..."

"He knows who Agashka's coming from anyway... Women don't come to the allotments at night to fetch cabbage – everyone knows that."

I glanced at Savka's face. It was pale, and bore the lines of squeamish pity that people feel when they see animals being tormented.

"Fun for the cat, tears for the mouse..." he sighed.

Agafya suddenly leapt up, shook her head and stepped off boldly in the direction of her husband. She had evidently summoned all her strength and made up her mind.

Enemies

TOWARDS TEN O'CLOCK on a dark September evening, the Zemstvo doctor Kirilov's only son, six-year-old Andrei, died of diphtheria. As the doctor's wife sank to her knees before the dead child's little bed and was seized by the first paroxysm of grief, the doorbell rang out abruptly in the hall.

On account of the diphtheria, all the servants had been sent away from the house that morning. Kirilov went to open the door himself, just as he was, without his frock coat and in an unbuttoned waistcoat, wiping neither his wet face, nor his hands, burnt by carbolic. It was dark in the hall, and all that could be discerned of the man who came in was his medium height, white muffler and large, extremely pale face, so pale that the appearance of this face seemed to make the hall get lighter…

"Is the doctor in?" the visitor asked quickly.

"I'm at home," Kirilov replied. "What do you want?"

"Ah, it's you? I'm very glad!" said the man in delight, and he began searching in the darkness for the doctor's hand, found it, and squeezed it firmly in both of his own. "Very… very glad! You and I have met!… I'm Abogin… I had the pleasure of seeing you in the summer at Gnuchev's. I'm very glad I've found you in… For God's sake be so good as to come with me at once… My wife has fallen seriously ill… And I have the carriage with me…"

It was evident from the man's voice and movements that he was in a state of great excitement. As though frightened by a fire or a mad dog, he could barely check his rapid breathing, he spoke quickly, in a quavering voice, and there was something unfeignedly sincere, childishly faint-hearted in his speech. Like all who are frightened and stunned, he spoke in short, broken phrases and used a lot of superfluous and quite inappropriate words.

"I was afraid of not finding you in," he continued. "In the time it's taken to get to you, my soul's quite worn out with suffering…

Put your things on and let's go, for God's sake… This is how it happened. Papchinsky comes to visit me – Alexander Semyonovich, whom you know… We had a talk… then sat down to have tea; suddenly my wife cries out, clutches at her heart, and slumps against the back of her chair. We carried her off to bed, and… I've both rubbed her temples with liquid ammonia, and sprinkled her with water… she's lying like a corpse… I'm afraid it's an aneurysm… Let's go… Her father died of an aneurysm too…"

Kirilov listened and remained silent, as though he did not understand Russian.

When Abogin again referred to Papchinsky and to his wife's father, and again began searching for his hand in the darkness, the doctor shook his head and, drawling every word out apathetically, said:

"I'm sorry, I can't come… Some five minutes ago my… son died…"

"Really?" Abogin whispered, taking a step back. "Good Lord, what an evil hour for me to have come! What an astonishingly unfortunate day… Astonishingly! What a coincidence… as if on purpose!"

Abogin took hold of the door handle and hung his head in thought. He was evidently wavering and did not know what to do: leave, or continue with his request of the doctor.

"Listen," he said fervently, grasping Kirilov by the sleeve, "I understand your position very well! God's my witness, I'm ashamed of trying to grab your attention at such a time, but what am I to do? Judge for yourself, who can I go to? There's no other doctor here apart from you, is there? Let's go, for God's sake! I'm not asking for myself… It's not me who's ill!"

Silence fell. Kirilov turned his back on Abogin, stood still, then slowly walked out of the hall into the reception room. Judging by his uncertain, mechanical gait, and the care with which he adjusted the fluffy shade on the unlit lamp in the reception room and then looked inside a thick book lying on the table, at this point in time he had no intentions, no desires, was thinking of nothing, and probably no longer remembered there was a stranger standing in his hall. The twilight and the quiet of the reception room had evidently intensified his crazed state. Walking from the reception room to his study, he lifted his right foot higher than necessary and searched with his hands for the doorposts, and at this point a sort of bewilderment could be sensed in his figure as a whole, as if he had found himself in a strange apartment, or else had got drunk for the first time in his life, and was now giving himself up in bewilderment to his new sensation. Along one wall of the study, across the cases of books, there stretched a broad band of light; this light, along with the strong, stuffy smell of carbolic and ether, was coming from the slightly open door that led from the study to the bedroom... The doctor sank into the armchair in front of the desk; he gazed drowsily for a minute at his books with the light on them, then rose and went into the bedroom.

Here, in the bedroom, reigned a deathly peace. Everything to the last detail spoke eloquently of the storm recently endured, of exhaustion, and everything was resting. A candle standing on a stool in a tight crowd of phials, boxes and jars, and a large lamp on a chest of drawers lit the whole room brightly. On a bed, right by the window, lay a boy with open eyes and a strangled expression on his face. He did not move, but his open eyes seemed with each moment to be growing ever darker and retreating inside his skull. Kneeling before the bed with her hands laid on his torso and her face hidden in the folds of the bedding was his mother. Like the boy, she did not stir, but how much living movement could be sensed in the curves of her body and her hands! She pressed against the bed with the whole of her being, with force and avidity, as if she feared to disturb the peaceful and comfortable pose she had finally found for her exhausted body. Blankets, cloths, basins, the puddles on the floor, the brushes and spoons scattered everywhere, a large white bottle of lime water, the very air, stifling and heavy, all stood still and seemed sunk in peace.

The doctor stopped beside his wife, put his hands into his trouser pockets and, tilting his head to one side, directed his gaze at his son. His face expressed indifference, and only from the dewdrops shining on his beard was it evident he had recently been crying...

That repellent horror of which people think when death is spoken of was absent from the bedroom. In the general stupor, in the pose of the mother, in the indifference of the doctor's face lay something that was attractive, that touched the heart, namely, the subtle, barely perceptible beauty of human grief, which people will not soon learn to understand and describe, and which music alone seems able to convey. Beauty could be sensed in the gloomy quiet too; Kirilov and his wife were silent, they did not cry, as if, besides the weight of the loss, they were conscious too of all the lyricism of their position: just as once, in its time, their youth had passed, so now, along with this boy, passing away for ever into eternity was their right to have children too! The doctor is forty-four, he is already grey and looks like an old man; his faded, sick wife is thirty-five. Andrei was not just their only one, but their last one too.

In contrast to his wife, the doctor was one of those natures which at moments of spiritual pain feel a need for movement. After standing beside his wife for five minutes or so, he went through, lifting his right foot high, from the bedroom into a small room, half filled by a large, wide sofa; from here he went through into the kitchen. After wandering about for a while by the stove and the cook's bed, he stooped and went out through a little door into the hall.

Here he again saw the white muffler and the pale face.

"At last!" sighed Abogin, taking hold of the door handle. "Let's go, please!"

The doctor gave a start, looked at him and remembered...

"Listen, I've already told you, haven't I, that I can't come!" he said, stirring into life. "What a strange thing!"

"Doctor, I'm not made of stone, I understand your position very well and I sympathize with you!" said Abogin in an imploring voice, putting a hand up to his muffler. "But I'm not asking for myself, am I?... My wife is dying! If you'd heard that cry, seen her face, you'd understand my insistence! Good Lord, and I thought you'd gone to put your things on! Doctor, time is of the essence! Let's go, I beg you!"

"I cannot come!" said Kirilov, slowly and deliberately, and strode into the reception room.

Abogin went after him and grabbed him by the sleeve.

"You've had a terrible loss, I understand, but after all, I'm not asking you to treat toothache, not to give an expert opinion, but to save a human life!" he continued to implore like a beggar. "That life is above any personal loss! Why, I'm asking for courage, for an act of heroism! In the name of philanthropy!"

"Philanthropy cuts both ways," said Kirilov irritably. "In the name of that same philanthropy I ask you not to take me away. And what a strange thing, honestly! I can barely stand upright, and you're trying to scare me with philanthropy. I'm good for nothing just now... I won't come, not for anything, and who would I leave with my wife? No, no..."

Kirilov began waving his hands and backed away.

"And... and don't ask me!" he continued in a scared voice. "I'm sorry... According to Volume XIII of the law, I'm duty-bound to come, and you have the right to drag me by the scruff of the neck... Do, if you wish, but... I'm no good... I'm in no state even to talk... I'm sorry..."

"You're wrong to speak to me in that tone, Doctor," said Abogin, taking the doctor by the sleeve again. "To hell with it, Volume XIII! I have no right at all to constrain your free will. If you want, come, if you don't, have it your way, only it's not to your free will I'm appealing, but to your feelings. A young woman is dying! You say your son's just died; who then, if not you, is to understand my horror?"

Abogin's voice was trembling in agitation; in that tremor and in its tone there was much more persuasiveness than in the words. Abogin was sincere, but it is a remarkable thing that, whatever phrases he uttered, they all came out stilted, soulless, inappropriately florid, and even seemed insulting both to the air of the doctor's apartment, and to the woman who was somewhere dying. Even he himself could sense this, and for that reason, afraid of being misunderstood, he tried for all he was worth to impart softness and tenderness to his voice, so as to succeed, if not by dint of the words, then at least by sincerity of tone. In general, a phrase, however beautiful and profound it might be, acts only upon those who are indifferent, and is not always capable of satisfying those who are happy or unhappy; that is why the supreme expression of happiness or unhappiness is most often silence; those who are in love understand each other better when they are silent; and an ardent, passionate speech made over a grave touches only strangers, while to the widow and the children of the deceased it seems cold and worthless.

Kirilov stood in silence. When Abogin had uttered a few more phrases about a doctor's lofty calling, about self-sacrifice, etc., the doctor asked gloomily:

"Is it a long way to go?"

"Something like thirteen or fourteen versts. I've got excellent horses, Doctor! I give you my word of honour that I'll have you there and back in one hour. Just one hour!"

These last words acted upon the doctor more powerfully than the references to philanthropy or a doctor's calling. He had a think, and said with a sigh:

"Very well, let's go!"

He set off quickly, already with a sure step, for his study and returned a little later in a long frock coat. Taking little pattering steps beside him and shuffling his feet, the gladdened Abogin helped him on with his coat, and together they went out of the house.

Outside it was dark, but brighter than in the hall. Clearly outlined now in the darkness was the tall, rather stooping figure of the doctor with a long, narrow beard and an aquiline nose. Visible now, besides Abogin's pale face, were his large head and little student's hat, barely covering his crown. His muffler showed white only from the front, while at the back it was hidden beneath long hair.

"Believe me, I shall know how to appreciate your magnanimity," Abogin murmured, helping the doctor into the carriage. "We'll get there promptly. And you, Luka, dear chap, go as fast as you can! Please!"

The coachman drove quickly. At first there stretched a row of unprepossessing buildings standing the length of the hospital yard; it was dark everywhere, only in the depths of the yard was there a bright light from somebody's window breaking through a garden fence, and the three windows of the top floor of the hospital block seemed paler than the air as well. Then the carriage drove into dense darkness; here there was a smell of fungal dampness, and the rustling of trees could be heard; crows, woken up by the noise of the carriage, began stirring in the foliage and raised an anxious, doleful cry, as if they knew that the doctor's son had died and Abogin's wife was ill. But then individual trees and bushes began flashing by; there was the gloomy glint of a pond on which big black shadows were sleeping – and the carriage began bowling over a smooth plain. The cry of the crows, far behind, was already indistinct, and soon it ceased altogether.

Kirilov and Abogin were silent for almost the entire journey. Only once did Abogin heave a deep sigh and mutter:

"What an agonizing state! Never do you love your dear ones as much as when you risk losing them."

And when the carriage was quietly crossing a river, Kirilov suddenly started up, as though the splashing of the water had startled him, and began shifting about.

"Listen, let me go," he said miserably. "I'll come to you later. If I could just send my assistant to my wife. I mean, she's alone!"

Abogin was silent. Rocking and banging against stones, the carriage drove over a sandy bank and again went bowling along. Kirilov began fidgeting in anguish and looked around him. To the rear, through the meagre light of the stars, could be seen the road and the riverside willows disappearing in the darkness. To the right lay a plain, just as even and boundless as the sky; there were dim lights burning on it here and there in the distance, probably on the peat bogs. To the left, parallel to the road, stretched a hill, made curly by little bushes, and motionless above the hill hung the half-moon, red, slightly obscured by mist and surrounded by little clouds which seemed to be examining it from all sides and keeping watch so it did not leave.

In all nature something hopeless and sick could be felt; the earth, like a fallen woman who sits alone in a dark room and tries not to think about the past, was racked by memories of the spring and summer, and was waiting apathetically for the inevitable winter. Wherever you looked, everywhere nature seemed like a

dark, boundlessly deep and cold pit, from which not Kirilov, nor
Abogin, nor the red half moon could escape...

The closer the carriage was to the objective, the more impatient
Abogin became. He shifted about, leapt up, peered ahead over
the coachman's shoulder. And when the carriage finally stopped
by the porch, prettily draped with striped canvas, and when he
looked at the lighted first-floor windows, his breathing could be
heard to quiver.

"If anything happens... I shan't survive it," he said, going into
the hall with the doctor and rubbing his hands in agitation. "But
there's no sound of turmoil, so it's all right for the moment," he
added, listening intently to the silence.

In the hall there was no sound of either voices or footsteps,
and, despite the bright lighting, the whole house seemed to
be asleep. The doctor and Abogin, who had up to this point
been in the dark, were now able to make one another out. The
doctor was tall, rather stooped, untidily dressed and had an
unattractive face. There was something unpleasantly abrupt,
unfriendly and severe expressed in his lips, thick like a Negro's,
his aquiline nose and inert, indifferent gaze. His unkempt head
and sunken temples, the premature grey in his long, narrow
beard with the chin showing through, the pale-grey colour of
his skin and his careless, awkward manners, the callousness of it
all brought to mind hardship endured, adversity and weariness
with life and people. Looking at his dry figure as a whole, it
was hard to believe that this man had a wife or that he might
cry over a child. Abogin, though, was something different. He
was a thick-set, solid, fair-haired man with a big head and
large but soft facial features, dressed elegantly in the very latest
fashion. In his bearing, in his tightly buttoned frock coat, in his
mane and his face one could sense something noble, leonine;
he walked with his head held up straight and his chest stuck
out, he spoke in a pleasant baritone, and shining through the
manner in which he took off his muffler or tidied the hair
on his head was a refined, almost feminine elegance. Even his
pallor and the childish terror with which, from time to time,
while taking off his things, he looked up at the staircase, did

not spoil his bearing nor lessen the satiety, health and aplomb which his entire figure breathed.

"There's no one about and nothing to be heard," he said, going up the stairs. "There's no turmoil. Let's hope to God!"

He led the doctor through the hall into a large room where there was the dark shape of a black grand piano and a chandelier in a white cover; from there they both went through into a small, very cosy and pretty drawing room, filled with a pleasant, pink semi-darkness.

"Well, you sit here, Doctor," said Abogin, "and I'll... just be a moment. I'll go and take a look and give warning."

Kirilov was left on his own. The luxury of the drawing room, the pleasant semi-darkness and his very presence in another man's unfamiliar house, all of which had the character of an adventure, evidently failed to move him. He sat in an armchair and examined his hands, burnt by carbolic. Only cursorily did he see a red lampshade and a cello case, and, with a sidelong glance in the direction of a ticking clock, he noticed a stuffed wolf, just as solid and sated as Abogin himself.

It was quiet. Somewhere far off in the next rooms someone uttered a loud "ah!" sound, a glass door, probably of a cupboard, jangled, and everything fell quiet once more. After waiting five minutes or so, Kirilov stopped inspecting his hands and raised his eyes to the door through which Abogin had disappeared.

At the threshold of that door stood Abogin, but not the one who had left the room. The expression of satiety and refined elegance had vanished from him, and his face, his hands and his pose were distorted by a repulsive expression, perhaps of horror, or perhaps of agonizing physical pain. His nose, lips, moustache, all of his features were moving and seemed to be trying to tear themselves from his face, and it was as if his eyes were laughing with pain...

Abogin took long, heavy strides into the middle of the drawing room, bent over, groaned and shook his fists.

"She deceived me!" he cried, with a strong emphasis on the syllable *ceived*. "She deceived me! She's gone! She fell ill and sent me off for a doctor just to run away with that buffoon Papchinsky! My God!"

Taking heavy strides towards the doctor, Abogin stretched out his soft white fists towards Kirilov's face and, shaking them, continued to wail:

"She's gone!! She deceived me! And why this lie?! My God! My God! Why this dirty, cheating trick, this devilish, cunning game? What have I done to her? She's gone!"

Tears spurted from his eyes. He spun on one leg and began striding around the drawing room. In his short frock coat, in his fashionably narrow trousers, in which his legs seemed too slender for his trunk, with his big head and mane, he now bore an extreme resemblance to a lion. On the doctor's indifferent face there appeared a glint of curiosity. He rose and examined Abogin.

"Forgive me, where is the woman who's sick?" he asked.

"Sick! Sick!" cried Abogin, laughing, crying and still shaking his fists. "She's not sick, she's damned! The perfidy! A trick so low, I doubt Satan himself could have thought up anything viler! She sent me off so as to run away, run away with a buffoon, an obtuse clown, a gigolo! Oh God, better she were dead! I can't bear it! I just can't bear it!"

The doctor stood up straight. His eyes began blinking and filled with tears, his narrow beard began moving right and left along with his jaw.

"Forgive me, how can this be?" he asked, looking around in curiosity. "My child is dead, my wife is in anguish, all alone in the house... I can barely stand upright, I've not slept for three nights... and what? I'm forced to act in some low comedy, to play the part of a prop! I don't... I don't understand!"

Abogin unclenched one fist, tossed a crumpled note onto the floor and trod on it, as if on an insect one wants to crush.

"And I didn't see... didn't understand!" he said through clenched teeth, shaking a fist in front of his face and with an expression that suggested someone had trodden on one of his corns. "I never noticed he was coming every day, didn't notice that today he'd come in a carriage! Why in a carriage? And I didn't see! Simpleton!"

"I don't... I don't understand!" mumbled the doctor. "I mean, what's going on? I mean, this is scoffing at a man, it's a mockery of human suffering! It's just not possible... it's the first time in my life I've seen it!"

With the dull surprise of a man who has just begun to understand he has been deeply insulted, the doctor shrugged his shoulders, threw up his hands and, not knowing what to say or do, sank in exhaustion into an armchair.

"All right, you stopped loving me, fell in love with another man, so be it, but why the deceit, why this ignoble, treacherous stunt?" said Abogin in a plaintive voice. "Why? What's it for? What have I done to you? Listen, Doctor," he said ardently, going over to Kirilov. "You've been the involuntary witness of my misfortune, and I shan't begin to conceal the truth from you. I swear to you that I loved that woman, loved her devoutly, like a slave! I sacrificed everything for her: I quarrelled with my family, gave up work and music, forgave her what I couldn't have forgiven my mother or sister... Not once did I look at her askance... I gave her no cause whatsoever! So what was this lie for? I don't demand love, but why this foul deceit? If you don't love me, then say so directly and honestly, particularly as you know my views on that score..."

With tears in his eyes and his whole body trembling, Abogin sincerely poured his soul out to the doctor. He spoke ardently, pressing both hands to his heart, revealed his family secrets without the slightest hesitation and even seemed to be glad that those secrets had finally burst out from his breast into the open. Had he spoken thus for an hour or two, had he finished pouring out his soul, he would undoubtedly have felt relieved. Who knows, had the doctor heard him out, shown him some friendly sympathy, perhaps he would have become reconciled to his grief, as often happens, without protest, without doing anything unnecessary and silly... But things happened differently. While Abogin was speaking, the insulted doctor changed markedly. The indifference and surprise in his face gave way, little by little, to an expression of bitter resentment, indignation and rage. His features became even more abrupt, callous and unpleasant. When Abogin held up in front of Kirilov's eyes a photograph of a young woman with a face that was pretty, but dry and inexpressive, like a nun's, and asked whether, looking at that face, it was possible to suppose that it was capable of telling a lie, the doctor suddenly leapt up with flashing eyes and, rapping every word out rudely, said:

"Why are you telling me all this? I don't want to listen! I don't want to!" he shouted and banged his fist on the table. "I don't need your banal secrets, damn them! Don't you dare talk to me of this banality! Or do you think I've not yet been insulted enough? That I'm a flunkey who can be insulted to the bitter end? Yes?"

Abogin backed away from Kirilov and stared at him in astonishment.

"Why did you bring me here?" the doctor continued, his beard shaking. "If you marry for want of anything better to do, and live your life in the same way, acting out melodramas, what's that got to do with me? What do I have in common with your love affairs? Leave me in peace! Practise the noble shaking of fists, strike a pose with humane ideas, play," the doctor threw a sidelong glance at the cello case, "play your double basses and trombones, fatten yourselves up like capons, but don't you dare scoff at a man! If you don't know how to respect him, then at least spare him your attention!"

"Forgive me, what does all this mean?" asked Abogin, flushing red.

"What it means is that it's low and vile to play with people like this! I'm a doctor, and you consider doctors, and working people generally, who don't smell of perfume and prostitution, your flunkeys and *mauvais ton*;* well, you do that, but nobody has given you the right to turn a man who's suffering into a prop!"

"How dare you say that to me?" Abogin asked quietly, and again his face began twitching, and on this occasion clearly with rage.

"No, how did you dare bring me here, knowing I was grieving, to listen to banalities?" cried the doctor, banging his fist on the table again. "Who gave you the right to mock another's grief this way?"

"You're out of your mind!" cried Abogin. "Where's your magnanimity! I'm deeply unhappy myself, and... and..."

"Unhappy," the doctor smirked disdainfully. "Leave that word alone – it doesn't concern you. Skivers who can't find any money against a promissory note call themselves unfortunate too. A capon whose excess fat weighs heavy, he's unhappy too. Worthless people!"

"Sir, you forget yourself!" screamed Abogin. "For such words…
people get beaten! Do you understand?"

Abogin delved hurriedly into a side-pocket, pulled his wallet out
of it and, taking out two banknotes, tossed them onto the table.

"That's for you for your visit!" he said, his nostrils flaring.
"You're paid for!"

"Don't you dare offer me money!" the doctor cried, and swept
the notes off the table and onto the floor. "You don't pay for an
insult with money!"

Abogin and the doctor stood face to face, and continued in their
rage to hurl unwarranted insults at each other. Probably never in
their lives, not even when delirious, had they said so many unjust,
cruel and absurd things. The egotism of the unhappy was strongly
in evidence in both of them. The unhappy are egotistical, spiteful, unjust, cruel and less able to understand one another than
fools are. Unhappiness does not unite, but rather divides people,
and even where it would seem people ought to be joined by the
homogeneity of grief, many more injustices and acts of cruelty
are committed than in a relatively contented milieu.

"Be so kind as to have me taken home!" cried the doctor, gasping for breath.

Abogin rang the bell abruptly. When nobody answered his sum-
mons, he rang again and angrily tossed the bell onto the floor; it
struck a muffled blow on a rug and emitted a doleful groan, as
of one about to die. A servant appeared.

"Where have you been hiding, the devil take you?!" His master
went for him, clenching his fists. "Where were you just now? Go
and say that the barouche is to be brought round for this gentleman, and order the carriage harnessed for me! Wait!" he cried,
when the servant turned to go. "By tomorrow there's to be not
a single traitor left in the house! Everybody out! I'm hiring new
people! Vermin!"

While waiting for the vehicles, Abogin and the doctor were
silent. To the former, both the expression of satiety and the refined
elegance had already returned. He paced around the drawing
room, tossing his head elegantly and evidently pondering upon
some plan. His rage had not yet cooled, but he tried to give the

appearance of not noticing his enemy... Whereas the doctor stood, holding on to the edge of the table with one hand and looking at Abogin with the deep, somewhat cynical and unattractive disdain of which only grief and adversity are capable, when they see before them satiety and elegance.

When, a little later, the doctor got into the barouche and drove off, his eyes still continued to look disdainful. It was dark, much darker than an hour before. The red half-moon had already gone behind the hill, and the clouds that had been guarding it lay in dark patches about the stars. A carriage with red lights came rattling along the road and overtook the doctor. This was Abogin going to protest and do silly things...

For the whole journey the doctor thought not about his wife, not about Andrei, but about Abogin and the people who lived in the house he had just left. His thoughts were unfair and inhumanly cruel. He condemned Abogin, and his wife, and Papchinsky, and all those living in pink semi-darkness and smelling of perfume, and for the whole journey he hated and despised them until his heart ached. And a firm conviction about those people was formed in his mind.

Time will pass, and Kirilov's grief will pass, but that conviction, unfair and unworthy of the human heart, will not, and will remain in the doctor's mind to the very grave.

A Nightmare

ON RETURNING from St Petersburg to his Borisovo, the first thing that Permanent Member of the Office for Peasants' Affairs Kunin – a young man of about thirty – did was send a rider to Sinkovo to fetch Father Yakov Smirnov, who was the priest there.

Some five hours later, Father Yakov appeared.

"Very pleased to meet you!" Kunin greeted him in the hall. "I've been living and working here for a year now, so I think it's time we were acquainted. Welcome! But... how young you are, though!" said Kunin in surprise. "How old are you?"

"Twenty-eight, sir..." said Father Yakov, shaking the proffered hand limply and for some unknown reason blushing.

Kunin led his guest into his study and set about examining him.

"What an ungainly, womanish face!" he thought.

Indeed, in Father Yakov's face there was a very great deal that was "womanish": the snub nose, the bright-red cheeks and the big, grey-blue eyes with sparse, barely perceptible eyebrows. His long ginger hair, dry and smooth, fell onto his shoulders like straight sticks. His moustache was still only just beginning to form into a genuine man's one, and his little beard was the type of good-for-nothing one that gets called for some reason amongst seminarists "a tickling": quite thin and very transparent, it cannot be smoothed or combed, it can only perhaps be plucked at. All this meagre growth sat unevenly, in little clumps, as though, having taken it into his head to disguise himself as a priest and begun to stick on a beard, Father Yakov had been interrupted halfway through. He wore a cassock the colour of weak chicory coffee with big patches on both elbows.

"A strange fellow," thought Kunin, looking at the skirts of his cassock, bespattered with mud. "He comes to a house for the first time and can't dress a little more decently."

"Sit down, Father," he began, in a manner more familiar than cordial, moving an armchair up to the desk. "Do sit down, please!"

Father Yakov coughed into his fist, lowered himself awkwardly onto the edge of the armchair and rested the palms of his hands on his knees. Undersized, narrow-chested, with a sweaty and flushed face, he had made the most unpleasant initial impression on Kunin. Kunin could not possibly have thought previously that there were such unimpressive and pitiful-looking priests in Rus,* and in Father Yakov's pose, in the way he kept his palms on his knees and sat on the chair's very edge, he saw an absence of dignity, and even obsequiousness.

"I invited you, Father, on a matter of business..." Kunin began, reclining against the back of his chair. "To my lot has fallen the pleasant duty of helping you in a useful enterprise of yours... The thing is that, upon returning from St Petersburg, I found on my desk a letter from the Marshal. Yegor Dmitriyevich proposes I take the parish school you have opening in Sinkovo into my trusteeship. I'm very happy, Father, with all my heart... Even more: I'm delighted to accept this proposal!"

Kunin rose and began walking around the study.

"Of course, both Yegor Dmitriyevich and, I expect, you are aware that I don't have very great means at my disposal. My estate is mortgaged, and I live exclusively on my Permanent Member's salary. You can't therefore count on any great help, but I shall do everything in my power... And when are you thinking of opening the school, Father?"

"When there's the money..." replied Father Yakov.

"Do you have any means at your disposal now?"

"Hardly any, sir... The peasants resolved at their assembly to pay thirty kopeks per male soul annually, but that's only a promise, after all! And to set things up initially at least about two hundred roubles are needed..."

"Hm, yes... Unfortunately, I don't have that sum just now..." sighed Kunin. "I spent myself out completely during my trip and... even owe some money. Let's join forces and think of something."

Kunin started thinking out loud. He stated his ideas and kept an eye on Father Yakov's face, searching it for approval or agreement.

But the face was impassive, motionless, and expressed nothing but shy timidity and disquiet. Looking at him, one might have thought that Kunin was talking about such abstruse things that Father Yakov could not comprehend, was listening only out of tactfulness and was afraid, moreover, of being found guilty of incomprehension.

"Evidently not a very bright fellow..." thought Kunin. "Immoderately timid and rather stupid."

Father Yakov became animated, even smiling, only when a servant entered the study, bringing in on a tray two glasses of tea and a dish of pretzels. He took his glass and set about drinking at once.

"Should we write to the Bishop?" Kunin continued to ponder out loud. "After all, strictly speaking, it wasn't the Zemstvo, nor us, but the higher ecclesiastical authorities that raised the question of parish schools. Really, they ought to show us the means too. I seem to recall reading that a certain sum was even allocated in that respect. Do you know anything?"

Father Yakov had become so absorbed in his tea-drinking that he did not reply to this question at once. He raised his grey-blue eyes to look at Kunin, had a think and, as if remembering his question, gave a negative shake of the head. Spread from ear to ear across his plain face was an expression of pleasure and the most commonplace, prosaic appetite. As he drank, he savoured every mouthful. Having drunk it all to the very last drop, he put his glass down on the desk, then picked the glass back up, examined the bottom of it and then put it down again. The expression of pleasure slipped from his face... Next Kunin saw his guest take a pretzel from the dish, bite a little piece off it, then turn it round and round in his hands before quickly putting it into his pocket.

"Well, now that's not at all priestly!" thought Kunin, shrugging his shoulders fastidiously. "What is it, the clergyman's greed or childishness?"

After giving his guest another glass of tea to drink and seeing him out as far as the hall, Kunin lay down on the sofa and surrendered himself completely to the unpleasant feeling that Father Yakov's visit had brought upon him.

"What a strange, queer person!" he thought. "Dirty, scruffy, coarse, stupid and probably a drunk... My God, and that's a priest, a spiritual father! That's a teacher of the people! I can imagine how much irony there must be in the voice of the deacon exclaiming to him before every Liturgy: 'Bless me, Master!' A fine Master! A Master who has not a drop of dignity, who's ill-bred, hiding rusks in his pockets like a schoolboy... Pah! Good Lord, where were the Bishop's eyes when he ordained that man? What do they take the people for, if they give them such teachers? We need men here who are..."

And Kunin fell into thought about how Russian priests ought to be...

"If I, for example, were a clergyman... An educated clergyman who loves his work can do a lot... I'd have had the school open long ago. And sermons? If a clergyman's sincere and inspired by love for his work, what wonderful, rousing sermons he can deliver!"

Kunin closed his eyes and began composing a sermon in his head. A little later he was sitting at the desk and quickly jotting it down.

"I'll give it to that ginger fellow, let him read it out in church..." he thought.

The next Sunday morning, Kunin was driving to Sinkovo to have done with the question of the school and at the same time to get acquainted with the church of which he was considered a parishioner. Despite it being a time when the roads are bad, the morning was magnificent. The sun shone brightly, and its rays cut into the white sheets of snow where, here and there, it still lay. At its parting with the earth, the snow sparkled like diamonds, making it painful to look at, while beside it the young winter crop was in haste to turn green. Rooks were drifting in dignified fashion above the earth. A flying rook would descend to the earth, and before standing firmly on its feet, would hop up and down several times...

The wooden church that Kunin drove up to was ramshackle and grey; the little columns at the porch, once painted white, had now completely lost their paint and resembled two ugly shafts. The icon above the door looked like a single dark stain. But this poverty touched and moved Kunin. Lowering his eyes modestly, he entered the church and stopped by the door. The service as yet had only just begun. The old sexton, bent double, was reciting the hours in a muffled, indecipherable tenor. Officiating without a deacon, Father Yakov was walking through the church with a censer. Had it not been for the humility with which Kunin had been suffused on entering the poverty-stricken church, at the sight of Father Yakov he would certainly have smiled. The undersized priest was wearing a creased chasuble, ever so long and made of some kind of threadbare, yellow material. The bottom edge of the chasuble trailed across the ground.

The church was not full. On looking at the parishioners, Kunin was struck to begin with by one strange fact: he saw only old people and children... Where ever were those of working age? Where were youth and manliness? But after standing for a while and peering rather more intently at the old people's faces, Kunin saw that he had taken young people for old. However, he attached no particular significance to this little optical illusion.

Inside, the church was just as ramshackle and grey as on the outside. There was not a single spot on the iconostasis or the brown walls that had not been darkened or scratched by time. There were a lot of windows, but the overall colouring seemed grey, and so there was twilight inside the church.

"For anyone pure in heart, this is a good place to pray..." thought Kunin. "Whereas in Rome, at St Peter's, it's the grandeur that's striking, it's this humbleness and simplicity that are touching here."

But his prayerful mood vanished into thin air when Father Yakov entered the sanctuary and began the Liturgy. Because of his tender years, having become a priest straight out of the seminary, Father Yakov had not yet had time to adopt a definitive manner for conducting a service. When reciting, it was as if he were choosing which voice to settle on, a high tenor or a thin low bass; he bowed inexpertly, walked too quickly, opened and closed the holy doors jerkily... The old sexton, evidently sick and deaf, could not hear the final words of his prayers properly, which meant little misunderstandings were not to be avoided. Father Yakov would not have managed to finish reciting what he needed

to before the sexton would already be singing his part, or else
Father Yakov would have long finished, but the old man would
be stretching his ear in the direction of the sanctuary, silent and
listening intently, until someone tugged at his robe. The old man
had a muffled, sickly voice, short-winded, quavering and hissing...
To crown the lowliness, the sexton was accompanied in the singing by a very small boy, whose head was barely visible behind the
handrail of the choir place. The boy sang in a high, shrill treble,
and seemed to be trying not to hit the right notes. Kunin stood for
a while listening, then went outside for a smoke. He was already
disenchanted and gazed with all but hostility at the grey church.

"They complain of a decline in religious feeling amongst the
people..." he sighed. "No wonder! They should plant a whole lot
more priests like that here!"

Kunin subsequently went into the church two or three times
more, but each time he felt powerfully drawn out into the fresh
air. He waited until the end of the Liturgy, and then set off to
visit Father Yakov. On the outside, the priest's house was no
different from the peasants' huts, except that the straw on the
roof lay more evenly and there was the whiteness of curtains at
the windows. Father Yakov led Kunin into a small, light room
with an earthen floor and walls covered with cheap wallpaper;
despite certain attempts at luxury, such as framed photographs
and a clock with scissors fastened to the weight, the furnish-
ings were striking in their meagreness. Looking at the furniture,
one might have thought Father Yakov had gone from house to
house and collected it bit by bit: in one place he had been given
a round table on three legs, in another a stool, in a third a chair
with an extremely bent back, in a fourth a chair with a straight
back but a sagging seat, while in a fifth, in a fit of generosity,
he had been given some semblance of a sofa with a flat back
and a latticed seat. This semblance had been painted a dark-red
colour and smelt strongly of the paint. Initially Kunin meant
to sit down on one of the chairs, but thought about it and sat
down on the stool.

"Is that the first time you've been to our church?" asked Father
Yakov, hanging his hat on a large, ugly nail.

"Yes, the first. Now then, Father... Before we get down to business, give me some tea, my soul's gone quite dry, you know."

Father Yakov started blinking, gulped and went behind a partition. There was the sound of whispering...

"That must be his wife..." thought Kunin. "It'd be interesting to see what sort of wife this ginger fellow has..."

A little later, red and sweaty, Father Yakov came out from behind the partition and, forcing a smile, sat down opposite Kunin on the edge of the sofa.

"The samovar'll go on right away," he said, not looking at his guest.

"Good Lord, they haven't put the samovar on yet!" Kunin thought to himself, horrified. "So now you'll have to wait!"

"I've brought you," he said, "the draft of a letter that I've written to the Bishop. I'll read it after the tea... Maybe you'll find something to add..."

"Very well, sir."

Silence fell. Father Yakov threw a fearful sidelong glance towards the partition, tidied his hair and blew his nose.

"Wonderful weather, sir..." he said.

"Yes. By the way, I read something interesting yesterday... The Volsk Zemstvo resolved to hand all its schools over to the clergy. That's typical."

Kunin rose, started pacing over the earthen floor and began expressing his views.

"It's all very well," he said, "as long as the clergy live up to their calling and are clearly conscious of their tasks. To my misfortune, I know some priests who, in their level of intellectual maturity and moral qualities, are unfit to be army clerks, let alone priests. And you must agree, a bad teacher will do a school much less harm than a bad priest."

Kunin glanced at Father Yakov. He sat bent over, deep in thought about something, and was evidently not listening to his guest.

"Yasha, come here!" a woman's voice was heard from behind the partition.

Father Yakov roused himself and went behind the partition. Again the whispering began.

Kunin felt a twinge of longing for tea.

"No, I'll never get any tea here!" he thought, looking at the clock. "And I don't seem to be an entirely welcome guest here either. My host hasn't deigned to say a single word to me, just sits there dumbly blinking."

Kunin picked up his hat, waited for Father Yakov and then took his leave of him.

"A morning completely wasted!" he fumed on his way back. "The dullard! The oaf! He's as interested in the school as I am in last year's snow! No, I won't get anywhere with him! He and I won't achieve a thing! If the Marshal knew the sort of priest they have here, he'd be in no hurry to go to any trouble about the school. You need to do something about a good priest first, and only then about the school!"

By now Kunin all but hated Father Yakov. This man, his pitiful, ludicrous figure in the long, creased chasuble, his womanish face, his manner of conducting a service, his way of life and clerkly, bashful deference insulted the tiny little bit of religious feeling that still remained in Kunin's breast, glimmering gently alongside the rest of his nanny's fairy tales. And the coldness and inattention with which he had greeted Kunin's sincere, ardent concern for his very own work was hard for Kunin's self-esteem to bear...

In the evening of that same day Kunin walked around his rooms for a long time thinking, then sat down resolutely at the desk and wrote a letter to the Bishop. Having asked for money for the school and a blessing, he incidentally, sincerely, filially, set forth his opinion of the Sinkovo priest. "He is young," he wrote, "insufficiently mature intellectually, seems to lead an intemperate life, and entirely fails to satisfy the demands which have taken shape over centuries amongst the Russian people in respect of their pastors." When he had written this letter, Kunin breathed a sigh of relief and went to bed, conscious of having done a good deed.

On Monday morning, while he was still lying in bed, he had the arrival of Father Yakov announced to him. He did not feel like getting up, and he ordered it be said he was not at home. On Tuesday he left for a congress and, returning on Saturday, he learnt from the servants that, in his absence, Father Yakov had been coming daily.

"Well I never, he did like my pretzels!" thought Kunin.

On Sunday, as evening was approaching, Father Yakov appeared. On this occasion not just the skirts of his cassock, but even his hat was spattered with mud. Just as on his first visit, he was red and sweaty, and he sat down, just as then, on the edge of the armchair. Kunin decided not to start a conversation about the school, not to cast pearls.

"I've brought you a little list of school textbooks, Pavel Mikhailovich..." Father Yakov began.

"Thank you."

But all the indications were that Father Yakov had come not because of the little list. His entire figure expressed great embarrassment, but at the same time there was resolution written on his face, as in a man on whom an idea had suddenly dawned. He was bursting to say something important, extremely necessary, and was striving now to overcome his timidity.

"Why on earth is he silent?" Kunin fumed. "He's made himself comfortable here! But I've got no time to be bothered with him!"

In order somehow or other to assuage the awkwardness of his position and to conceal the struggle taking place within him, the priest began smiling unnaturally, and this smile, protracted, forced through sweat and facial colouring and out of keeping with the fixed stare of his blue-grey eyes, made Kunin turn away. He began to feel disgusted.

"Excuse me, Father, I have to go..." he said.

Father Yakov roused himself, like a sleepy man who has been slapped, and, without ceasing to smile, he started wrapping the skirts of his cassock around himself in embarrassment. For all his aversion for this man, Kunin suddenly felt sorry for him, and he had the urge to mollify his cruelty.

"Do come another time, Father..." he said, "and on parting I have a request for you... I got inspired here one time, you know, and wrote two sermons... I'll give them to you for your consideration... If they're suitable, you might give them."

"Very well, sir..." said Father Yakov, putting the palm of his hand over Kunin's sermons, which were lying on the desk. "I'll take them, sir..."

After standing for a while vacillating, and still wrapping his cassock around himself, he suddenly stopped his unnatural smiling and resolutely raised his head.

"Pavel Mikhailovich," he said, evidently trying to speak loudly and distinctly.

"What can I do for you?"

"I've heard that you've been pleased to, er... dismiss your clerk and... and are now looking for a new one..."

"Yes... And do you have someone to recommend?"

"You see, I... I... Could you give the position to... to me?"

"You're surely not giving up the priesthood?" asked Kunin in amazement.

"No, no," said Father Yakov quickly, for some reason turning pale and trembling all over. "God forbid! If you're in doubt, then there's no need, no need. I just thought in spare moments, kind of... to increase my earnings... There's no need, don't trouble yourself!"

"Hm... earnings... But I mean, I pay the clerk only twenty roubles a month!"

"Lord, I'd even take ten!" whispered Father Yakov, looking around. "Even ten's enough! You're... you're amazed, and everybody is. The greedy priest, grasping, what does he do with his money? I can feel it myself too, that I'm greedy... and I chastise, condemn myself... I'm ashamed to look people in the eye... In all honesty, Pavel Mikhailovich... may the true God be my witness before you..."

Father Yakov drew a deep breath and continued:

"On the way here I prepared an entire confession for you, but... I've forgotten it all, and now I can't find the words. I get a hundred and fifty roubles a year from the parish, and everyone... wonders what I do with the money... But I'll explain everything to you in all honesty... Forty roubles a year I pay in fees to the ecclesiastical college for my brother Pyotr. He's there with all found, but paper and pens are down to me..."

"Oh dear, I believe you, I believe you! Why all this, now?" Kunin started waving his hand, feeling a terrible weight as a result of this, his guest's candour, and not knowing how to escape the tearful gleam of his eyes.

"Then, sir, I haven't repaid everything to the consistory for my position yet. Two hundred roubles were assigned for me to pay for my position, with me repaying ten a month... So now you judge, what's left? And besides that I have to pay Father Avramy, don't I, at least three roubles a month anyway?"

"What Father Avramy?"

"Father Avramy who was the priest in Sinkovo before me. He was relieved of the position for... being weak, but, I mean, he lives in Sinkovo even now! Where is he to go? Who's going to feed him? He may be old but, I mean, he needs a corner of his own, and bread, and clothing! I can't allow him, with his office, to go begging for alms! I mean, the sin will be mine, if anything happens! My sin! He's... in debt to everyone, and the sin will be mine, won't it, for not paying on his behalf!"

Father Yakov burst into motion and, gazing madly at the floor, started pacing from corner to corner.

"My God! My God!" he began muttering, now raising his arms, now lowering them. "Save us, Lord, and have mercy! So why did you have to take such an office upon yourself if you're a sceptic and have no strength? There's no end to my despair! Save me, Heavenly Queen!"

"Calm yourself, Father!" said Kunin.

"I'm worn out with hunger, Pavel Mikhailovich!" Father Yakov continued. "Be generous and excuse me, but I no longer have any strength left... I know, if I were to ask, humiliate myself, then everyone would help, but... I can't! I'm ashamed! How can I think of asking of peasants? You work here and you can see for yourself... Whose hand could be raised to ask of a beggar? And ask of anyone rather richer, of the landowners, I can't! Pride! I'm ashamed!"

Father Yakov flapped his arm, and nervously started scratching his head with both hands.

"I'm ashamed! God, how ashamed! A proud man, I can't bear people seeing my poverty. When you visited me, I mean, there was no tea at all, Pavel Mikhailovich! There wasn't a speck of it, but you know, pride prevented me from confiding in you! I'm ashamed of my clothes, these patches here... I'm ashamed of my chasubles, my hunger... And is pride seemly for a priest?"

Father Yakov stopped in the middle of the study and, as if not noticing Kunin's presence, began deliberating with himself.

"Well, let's say I can bear the hunger, and the disgrace, but after all, Lord, I've got a wife as well! I mean, I took her from a good home! She's delicate and unaccustomed to working, she's used to tea, and to white bread, and to sheets... She used to play the piano at her parents'... She's young, not even twenty yet... I expect she'd like to get dressed up, and amuse herself and go out visiting... But with me she's... worse off than any cook, it's shameful to show it in public. My God, my God! The only pleasures she has are when I bring some apples from a visit, or some little pretzel...

Again Father Yakov began scratching his head with both hands.

"And what we end up with isn't love, but pity... I can't see her without compassion! And the sort of thing, Lord, that goes on in the world. Such things go on, that if you wrote to the newspapers, people wouldn't believe it... And when will there be an end to it all?"

"Come, come, Father!" Kunin all but cried out, alarmed by Father Yakov's tone. "Why look at life so gloomily?"

"Be generous and excuse me, Pavel Mikhailovich..." Father Yakov mumbled, like a drunkard. "Excuse me, it's all... idle talk, don't you pay any attention... It's just that I blame myself and will continue to do so... I will!"

Father Yakov looked around and began whispering:

"Once in the early morning I'm going from Sinkovo to Luchkovo; I look, and there's some woman standing on the bank and doing something... I go up closer and can't believe my eyes... It's terrible! It's the wife of the doctor, Ivan Sergeyich, sitting and rinsing her linen... The doctor's wife, who's a graduate from an institute! So for people not to see, she aimed to get up good and early and walk a verst out of the village... Insuperable pride! When she saw I was nearby and had spotted her poverty, she went quite red... I was dumbstruck, scared, and I run over to her, I want to help her, but she hides her linen from me, afraid I might see her torn nightshirts..."

"This is all rather unbelievable somehow," said Kunin, sitting down and gazing almost in horror at Father Yakov's pale face.

"Precisely, unbelievable! Never, Pavel Mikhailovich, has there been an instance of doctors' wives rinsing their linen in the river! It doesn't happen in any country! I, as a pastor and spiritual father, shouldn't let her get to that point, but what can I do? What? I myself even try to get free treatment from her husband! Quite rightly you've been so good as to determine that all this is unbelievable! You can't believe your eyes! During the Liturgy, you know, you can glance out from the sanctuary, and when you see your congregation, hungry Avramy and your wife, and when you remember the doctor's wife, the way her hands had gone blue from the cold water, then, would you believe it, you can drift off and stand there like a fool, insensible, until the sacristan calls out to you... It's terrible!"

Again Father Yakov started walking around and waving his arms.

"Oh, Lord Jesus! Holy saints! I can't even conduct the services... You talk to me about the school and, like a dummy, I can't understand a thing and think only about food... Even before the holy altar... Anyway... what ever am I doing?" Father Yakov suddenly thought. "You have to go. Forgive me, sir, I was just, I mean... excuse me..."

Kunin silently shook Father Yakov's hand, saw him out as far as the hall and, returning to his study, stopped in front of the window. He saw Father Yakov leave the building, pull his wide-brimmed, rust-coloured hat down low on his brow and, quietly, hanging his head, as though ashamed of his candour, set off down the road.

"His horse is nowhere to be seen," thought Kunin.

That all these days the priest had been coming to see him on foot was something Kunin was afraid to contemplate: it was seven or eight versts to Sinkovo, and the road was a veritable quagmire. Next Kunin saw the coachman Andrei and the boy Paramon run up to Father Yakov, jumping over puddles and spattering him with mud, to get his blessing. Father Yakov took off his hat and slowly blessed Andrei, and then blessed the boy and patted him on the head.

Kunin drew his hand over his eyes, and it seemed to him that his hand was wet as a result. He moved away from the window and looked with lacklustre eyes around the room in which he could still hear a timid, strangulated voice... He glanced at the desk... Fortunately, in his haste, Father Yakov had forgotten to take Kunin's sermons with him... he leapt over to them, ripped them to pieces and tossed them with repugnance under the desk.

"And I didn't know!" he groaned, falling onto the divan. "I, who've already been working here for more than a year as a Permanent Member, an honorary Justice of the Peace, a member of the College Council! A blind doll, a fop! Quickly, to their aid! Quickly!"

He tossed and turned agonizingly, squeezed his temples and strained his mind.

"I'll be getting my salary of two hundred roubles on the 20th... On a plausible pretext I'll press them on him and the doctor's wife... I'll summon him to conduct a prayer service, and for the doctor I'll have a fictitious illness... In that way I shan't insult their pride. And I'll help Avramy..."

He calculated his money on his fingers and was afraid to admit to himself that those two hundred roubles would barely suffice for him to pay the steward, the servants and the peasant who brought the meat... Against his will, he was obliged to recall the not-so-distant past, when his father's wealth was being unwisely used up, when, still a twenty-year-old milksop, he was presenting prostitutes with expensive fans, paying Kuzma the cabman ten roubles a day, taking gifts to actresses out of vanity. Ah, how useful all those squandered one-, three- and ten-rouble notes would have been now!

"Father Avramy eats on only three roubles a month," thought Kunin. "For a rouble the priest's wife can get herself a nightshirt made and the doctor's wife hire a washerwoman. But I'll still help! I'll definitely help!"

At this point Kunin suddenly remembered the denunciation he had written to the Bishop, and he was utterly contorted, as if by a blast of unexpected cold. This memory filled his entire soul with a sense of oppressive shame before himself and before invisible truth...

Thus there began, and came to an end, a sincere attempt at useful activity by one of those well-intentioned but excessively sated and unthinking men.

On Easter Eve

I was standing on one bank of the Goltva and waiting for the ferry from the other bank. In normal times the Goltva is a middling sort of minor river, taciturn and pensive, glinting meekly from behind dense reeds, but before me now stretched an entire lake. The spreading waters of spring had overstepped both banks and flooded a large part of both shorelines, seizing allotments, hayfields and marshes, so that it was no rarity to encounter on the water's surface solitary protruding poplars or bushes looking like stern crags in the darkness.

The weather seemed to me magnificent. It was dark, but I could nonetheless see trees, and water, and people... The world was illumined by stars, which were scattered thickly all over the sky. I don't remember another time when I had seen so many stars. There was literally nowhere to poke a finger in between them. There were large ones here, like a goose's egg, and little ones the size of hempseed... For the sake of a festive parade they had come out into the sky, each and every one, great and small alike, washed, renewed, joyous, and each and every one was shifting its rays about gently. The sky was reflected in the water; the stars bathed in the dark depths and trembled with the light ripples. The air was warm and quiet... Far away, on the other bank, in impenetrable dark, there burned a few, scattered, bright-red lights...

Two steps away from me was the dark silhouette of a peasant in a tall hat with a thick, knotty stick.

"What a long time and no ferry, though!" I said.

"And it *is* time it was here," the silhouette answered me.

"Are you waiting for the ferry too?"

"No, not really..." the peasant yawned, "I'm waiting for the luminations. I would go but, to be honest, I haven't got the five kopeks for the ferry."

"I'll give you five kopeks."

"No, I thank you humbly... Better if, with those five kopeks, you light a candle for me there in the monastery... That'll be more curious, and I'll just go on standing over here. Good Heavens, no ferry! Like it had sunk without trace!"

The peasant went right up to the water, took hold of the rope with his hand and cried:

"Ieronim! Ieron-i-im!"

As if in answer to his cry, there came from the other bank the long-drawn-out chime of a large bell. The chime was rich and deep, as if from the thickest string of a double bass: it seemed as if the darkness itself had gasped. And immediately a cannon shot was heard. It rolled away in the darkness and ended up somewhere far behind my back. The peasant took his hat off and crossed himself.

"Christ is risen!" he said.

The waves from the first chime had not had time to die away in the air before another was heard, then immediately after it a third, and the darkness was filled with incessant, resonant booming. New lights lit up around the red ones, and all together they began moving and restlessly flickering.

"Ieron-i-im!" came a muffled, long-drawn-out cry.

"They're shouting from the other bank," said the peasant. "So there's no ferry there either. Our Ieronim's gone to sleep."

The lights and the velvet chiming of the bell were alluring... I'd already begun to lose patience and to worry, but then, finally, peering into the dark distance, I saw the silhouette of something very like a gibbet. It was the long-awaited ferry. It moved with such slowness that, had it not been for the gradual delineation of its contours, it might have been thought it was standing still, or else going towards the other bank.

"Hurry up! Ieronim!" cried my peasant. "There's a gentleman waiting!"

The ferry crept up to the bank and, creaking, stopped with a jolt. Upon it, holding on to the rope, stood a tall man in a monk's cassock and a little conical hat.

"Why so long?" I asked, leaping onto the ferry.

"In the name of Christ, forgive me," Ieronim replied quietly. "Is there no one else?"

"No..."

Ieronim took hold of the rope with both hands, bent himself into a question mark and let out a croak. The ferry creaked and gave a jolt. The silhouette of the peasant in the tall hat slowly began to move away from me – so the ferry had set off. Ieronim soon straightened up and started working with one hand. We were silent, and looked at the bank towards which we were going. There, the "lumination" the peasant had been waiting for had already begun. Right by the water, tar barrels were blazing in enormous bonfires. Their reflections, crimson, like the rising moon, crept towards us in long, wide stripes. The burning barrels illumined their own smoke and the long human shadows that were dancing by the fire; but further to the sides and behind them, from where the velvet chimes were carrying, there was still that same impenetrable, black gloom. Suddenly, cutting through the darkness, a rocket soared up in a golden band towards the sky; it described an arc, and then, as if smashing against the sky, disintegrated with a crack into sparks. From the bank could be heard a rumble like a distant hurrah.

"How beautiful!" I said.

"You can't even say how beautiful!" sighed Ieronim. "Such a night, sir! Another time you'd pay no attention to rockets, but today you rejoice at all sorts of vanity. Where would you be from yourself?"

I said where I was from.

"Yes, sir... a joyous day today..." Ieronim continued in the weak, sighing tenor that convalescents speak in. "Heaven rejoices, and the earth, and the nether regions. All God's creatures celebrate. Only tell me, good sir, why is it that even in great joy a man can't forget his woes?"

It seemed to me that this unexpected question was meant to provoke me into one of those "extra-lengthy" salutary conversations that idle, bored monks so enjoy. I wasn't disposed to do a lot of talking, and so I simply asked:

"And what woes do you have, Father?"

"Normally the same as everyone else, Your Honour, good sir, but this day a particular woe has occurred in the monastery:

during the Liturgy itself, while the parables were being read, the hierodeacon Nikolai died…"

"Well, that's God's will!" I said, affecting a monkish tone. "Everyone has to die. In my view, you should even rejoice… They say anyone who dies just before or at Easter is certain to enter the Kingdom of Heaven."

"That's true."

We fell silent. The silhouette of the peasant in the tall hat had merged with the outlines of the bank. The tar barrels were flaring up more and more.

"Scripture clearly indicates the vanity of woe, and so too does contemplation," Ieronim broke the silence, "but why then does your soul grieve and not want to listen to reason? Why is it you feel like crying bitterly?"

Ieronim shrugged his shoulders, turned towards me and began speaking quickly:

"If it was me that had died, or someone else, perhaps it wouldn't be noticed, but it's Nikolai that's died! Not someone else, but Nikolai! It's hard even to believe that he's no longer in the world! Here I stand on the ferry and I keep thinking that at any moment he'll make himself heard from the bank. So that I didn't feel frightened on the ferry, he always came onto the bank and called to me. He used to get out of bed at night especially to do it. What a kind soul! God, how kind and merciful! Some people don't even have a mother such as that Nikolai was for me! Lord, save his soul!"

Ieronim took hold of the rope, but immediately turned to me again.

"And what a clear mind, Your Honour!" he said in a sing-song voice. "What a sweet and melodious tongue! Just like the way they're about to sing during matins: 'O, beloved! O, Thy voice most sweet!' Besides all the other human qualities, he also had within him an exceptional gift!"

"What gift?" I asked.

The monk examined me and, as though reassured that I could be entrusted with secrets, he gave a cheerful laugh.

"He had a gift for writing akathists…"* he said. "A miracle, sir, pure and simple! You'll be amazed if I explain it to you! Our

Father Abbot comes from Moscow, the Father Superior graduated from the Kazan Academy, and we have some clever monk-priests too, and elders, but well I never, there's not one of them, is there, knows how to write, but Nikolai, a simple monk, a hierodeacon, he never studied anywhere and wasn't even anything to look at, but he could write! A miracle! A genuine miracle!"

Ieronim threw up his hands and, completely forgetting about the rope, continued with enthusiasm:

"The Father Superior has difficulty composing sermons; when he was writing the history of the monastery, he gave all the brethren a hard time and went into town a dozen times, whereas Nikolai wrote akathists! Akathists! That's not a sermon or a history!"

"So akathists are difficult to write, then?"

"They're a great difficulty…" Ieronim shook his head. "You'll get nothing done there with either wisdom or holiness, if God hasn't given you the gift. Monks with no understanding reason that all you need to get it done is to know the life of the saint you're writing to and conform to other akathists. But that's wrong, sir. Of course it's true, anyone writing an akathist should know the saint's life to an extraordinary degree, to the last tiny little point. Well, and you have to conform to other akathists, like where to begin and what to write about. To give you an example, everywhere the first *kondak* begins with 'selected' or 'chosen' one… You always have to begin the first *ikos** with an angel. In the akathist to Sweetest Jesus, if you're interested, it begins like this: 'Creator of angels, and Lord of hosts', and the akathist to the Most Holy Mother of God: 'A prince of angels from the heavens was sent'; to Nikolai the Wonder-worker: 'An angel in form, an earthly being by nature', and so on. Everywhere it begins with an angel. Of course, it can't be done without conforming, but you know, the main thing isn't the saint's life, it's not the corresponding with something else, it's the beauty and the sweetness. Everything should be graceful, brief and circumstantial. In every little line there should be softness, gentleness and tenderness, there shouldn't be a single word that's coarse, harsh or inappropriate. You have to write in such a way that a worshipper might rejoice and cry in his heart, yet quake in his mind and come to be all a-tremble. In the akathist to the Mother of God there are the words: 'Rejoice, heights unattainable for human thought; Rejoice, depths unseeable for angels' eyes!' In another part of the same akathist it says: 'Rejoice, beautiful-fruit-bearing tree, from it do the faithful feed, Rejoice, sweet-leafy-shade-giving tree, beneath it do multitudes shelter!'"

As though frightened by something or feeling ashamed, Ieronim covered his face with the palms of his hands and shook his head.

"Beautiful-fruit-bearing tree... sweet-leafy-shade-giving tree..." he murmured. "The way he'd find such words! Such an ability for the Lord to give! For brevity he'd fit a lot of words and ideas into one word, and how fluent and circumstantial he has it all come out! 'A light-bestowing lampion for men...' it says in the akathist to Sweetest Jesus. Light-bestowing! There's no such word either in conversation, or in books, but he invented it, didn't he, he found it in his mind! Besides fluency and magniloquence, sir, you need to have every wee line adorned in various ways as well, so that there are flowers, and lightning, and wind, and sun, and every object of the visible world. And every exclamation has to be compiled in such a way that it should be nice and smooth, and quite easy on the ear. 'Rejoice, lily of paradisean blossoming!' it says in the akathist to Nikolai the Wonder-worker. It doesn't say simply 'lily of paradise', but 'lily of paradisean blossoming!' It's smoother like that and sweeter for the ear. And that's just the way Nikolai wrote! Like that to the letter! I can't even express to you how he wrote!"

"Yes, in that case it's a pity that he's dead," I said. "However, Father, let's go, or else we'll be late..."

Ieronim suddenly remembered himself and ran to the rope. On the bank they had started ringing the chimes on all of the bells. The procession with the icons was evidently already under way by the monastery, because the entire dark expanse beyond the tar barrels was now strewn with moving lights.

"Did Nikolai publish his akathists?" I asked Ieronim.

"Publish them where?" he sighed. "And it would have been strange to publish them. Why? No one in our monastery is interested in that. They don't like it. They knew that Nikolai wrote, but paid it no attention. No one respects new writings nowadays, sir!"

"Are they prejudiced against them?"

"Exactly. Had Nikolai been an elder, then perhaps the brethren would have quite likely shown some curiosity, but he wasn't yet even forty, you know. There were those who laughed and even considered his writing a sin."

"So why did he write?"

"Well, mostly for his own solace. Out of all the brethren, I was the only one to read his akathists. I'd go to him quietly so the others didn't see, and he was glad I was interested. He'd embrace me, pat me on the head, call me by affectionate names like a little child. He'd shut the cell door, sit me down next to him, and we'd get reading…"

Ieronim left the rope and came over to me.

"He and I were sort of friends," he whispered, gazing at me with shining eyes. "Wherever he went, I went too. If I'm not there, he misses me. And he loved me more than anyone, and all because his akathists made me cry. It's touching to remember it! I'm just the same as an orphan now, or a widow. You know, the people in our monastery are all good, kind, devout, but… in no one is there any softness or delicacy, they're just like low-born people. Everyone talks in a loud voice, when they walk they stamp their feet, they're noisy, they cough, whereas Nikolai always spoke quietly, gently, and if he noticed anyone was asleep or praying, he'd pass by like a fly or a mosquito. His face was tender, sympathetic…"

Ieronim heaved a deep sigh and took hold of the rope. We were already nearing the bank. Straight from the darkness and the quiet of the river we were floating gradually into an enchanted kingdom, full of suffocating smoke, splintering light and din. By the tar barrels, as could already be clearly seen, people were moving. The fire's flickering imparted a strange, almost fantastical expression to their red faces and figures. Amidst the heads and faces there were occasional glimpses of the faces of horses, motionless, as though cast in red copper.

"They're about to start singing the Easter canon…" said Ieronim, "but there's no Nikolai, no one to get to the heart of it… For him there was no sweeter writing than that canon. He used to get to the heart of every word! When you're there, sir, you get to the heart of what's sung: it takes your breath away!"

"Won't you be in the church, then?"

"I can't be, sir... I've got to do the ferrying..."

"But won't you be relieved?"

"I don't know... I should have been relieved before nine o'clock, but as you can see, I haven't been!... Though I must admit, I'd like to go to church..."

"Are you a monk?"

"Yes, sir... that is, I'm a novice."

The ferry bumped into the bank and stopped. I slipped Ieronim five kopeks for bringing me, and jumped onto dry land. A cart with a boy and a sleeping peasant woman immediately drove creaking onto the ferry. Ieronim, faintly tinged by the light of the fires, applied himself to the rope, bent himself over and got the ferry moving...

I took several steps through mud, but thereafter I was to walk along a soft, freshly trodden path. This path, leading to the dark, cavernous monastery gates, went through clouds of smoke, and through a disordered crowd of people, unharnessed horses, carts and britzkas. All of it was creaking, snorting and laughing, and flickering across it all were a crimson light and the undulating shadows made by the smoke... Absolute chaos! And amid all this jostling they still found the space to load a small cannon and to sell spice cakes!

On the other side of the wall, inside the church railings, there was no less bustle, but greater decorum and order were being observed. Here there was the smell of juniper and incense. There was loud talking, but no laughter or snorting was to be heard. People were huddling together by the gravestones and crosses with Easter cakes and bundles. Many of them had evidently come from far afield to have their Easter cakes blessed, and now they were weary. Young novices ran over the slabs of cast iron which lay in a line from the gates to the door of the church, bustling and with a resonant stamping of boots. On the bell tower too there was activity and shouting.

"What a restless night!" I thought. "How splendid!"

There was the urge to see restlessness and sleeplessness in all of nature, starting with the nocturnal dark and ending with the iron slabs, the crosses on the graves and the trees beneath which people were bustling. But nowhere did excitement and restlessness make themselves felt so powerfully as inside the church. Taking place at the entrance was an unremitting struggle between the flood tide and the ebb. Some were going in, others coming out, but soon returning again to stand for a while and then start moving once more. People are scurrying about from place to place, loitering and seemingly looking for something. A wave goes from the entrance and runs through the entire church, disturbing even the front rows, where solid and weighty people are stood. Concentrated prayer is quite out of the question. There are no prayers whatsoever, but there is a sort of sheer joy, childishly uncontrolled and seeking an excuse just to break out and vent itself in movement of any kind, be it only shameless loafing and jostling.

The same extraordinary movement is also strikingly obvious in the Easter celebration itself. The holy doors are wide open in all of the chapels, in the air by the chandelier float dense clouds of incense smoke; wherever you look, everywhere there are lights, brilliance, the crackling of candles... No readings are due; bustling, cheerful singing is incessant until the very end; after each song in the canon the clergy change their chasubles and come out to cense, and this is repeated almost every ten minutes.

I had not had time to find a place before the surge of a wave from the front threw me back again. In front of me passed a tall, thickset deacon with a long red candle; hurrying behind him with a censer was the grey-haired Abbot in a gold mitre. When they were out of sight, the crowd pushed me back again to where I had been before. But not ten minutes had passed before there was the surge of another wave, and again the deacon appeared. Behind him this time came the Father Superior, that same one who, according to Ieronim, had been writing a history of the monastery.

Merging with the crowd and infected by the universal joyous excitement, I felt unbearably sorry for Ieronim. Why wasn't he relieved? Why didn't someone less sensitive and less impressionable go on the ferry?

"Cast thy eyes about thee, Zion, and see..." they were singing in the choir place, "for thy children have come to thee like a divine light from the west and the north, and from the sea and the east..."

I looked at people's faces. On all there was a lively expression of celebration, but not a single person was listening carefully or getting to the heart of what was being sung, and no one was "having their breath taken away". Why wouldn't they relieve Ieronim? I could imagine Ieronim standing humbly by a wall somewhere, stooped and avidly catching the beauty of a sacred phrase. Everything that was now slipping by the ears of the people standing near me he would have drunk in greedily with his sensitive soul, he would have been intoxicated to the point of raptures, to the point of his breath being taken away, and in the entire church there would have been no man happier than he. But he was going back and forth over the dark river now, grieving for his dead brother and friend.

There was the surge of a wave from behind. A plump, smiling monk, playing with his rosary and turning to look back, was squeezing past me sideways, clearing the path for some lady in a hat and fur-lined velvet coat. In the wake of the lady, carrying a chair above our heads, there hastened one of the monastery's lay brothers.

I left the church. I wanted to see the dead Nikolai, the unknown writer of akathists. I took a turn beside a railing where a row of monks' cells stretched along the wall, had a look inside several windows and, seeing nothing, went back again. Now I don't regret not seeing Nikolai; God knows, perhaps, having seen him, I would have lost the image which my imagination now draws for me. This likeable, poetic man, who used to go out at night to exchange cries with Ieronim and who sprinkled his akathists with flowers, stars and rays of sunshine, misunderstood and lonely, I picture as timid and pale, with soft, meek, sad features. Shining in his eyes, along with intelligence, there should be gentleness and that barely contained, childish tendency to enthusiasm, such as I had heard in Ieronim's voice when he was quoting to me from the akathists.

When we left the church after the Liturgy, it was no longer night. The morning was beginning. The stars had gone out and the sky was grey-blue and sullen. The slabs of cast iron, the gravestones and the buds on the trees were coated in dew. In the air was a sharp sense of freshness. Beyond the railings there was no longer that animation I had seen in the night. The horses and people seemed weary, sleepy, they were barely moving, and of the tar barrels there remained only little piles of black ash. When a man is weary and wants to sleep, it seems to him that nature is experiencing that same state too. It seemed to me that the trees and the young grass were asleep. It seemed that even the bells were ringing less loudly and merrily than in the night. The restlessness was over, and of the excitement there remained only a pleasant languor, a thirst for sleep and warmth.

Now I could see the river with both of its banks. Above it, like hills, there drifted now here, now there, a light mist. Wafting from the water was coldness and severity. When I jumped onto the ferry, somebody's britzka and a couple of dozen men and women were already standing on it. The rope, damp and, as it seemed to me, sleepy, stretched far away across the wide river and in places disappeared in the white mist.

"Christ is risen! Is there no one else?" asked a quiet voice.

I recognized it as Ieronim's voice. Now the nocturnal darkness no longer prevented me from making the monk out. He was a tall, narrow-shouldered man of about thirty-five with large, rounded features, with half-closed, lazily gazing eyes and an unkempt, little pointed beard. He had an unusually sad and weary air.

"Haven't you been relieved yet?" I said in surprise.

"Me, sir?" he queried, turning his frozen, dew-covered face towards me and smiling. "There's no one to relieve me now until it's quite morning. Everyone'll be going to the Father Abbot's now, sir, to break their fast."

He and some little peasant in a red fur hat that looked like the lime-wood pails they sell honey in, applied themselves to the rope, croaked in unison, and the ferry got going.

We moved off, disturbing on the way the lazily lifting mist. Everyone was silent. Ieronim worked mechanically with one hand. For a long time he let his meek, lacklustre eyes wander over us, then he fixed his gaze upon the pink, black-browed face of a young merchant's wife, who was standing beside me on the ferry and silently huddling herself up against the mist that was embracing her. He did not take his eyes off her face for the duration of the entire journey.

In that protracted gaze there was little that was manly. It seems to me that Ieronim was searching in the woman's face for the soft and tender features of his departed friend.

Note on the Text

This translation is based on the Russian texts of the stories found in volumes 4, 5 and 6 of the complete edition of Anton Chekhov's works and letters in 20 volumes published in Moscow in 1944–51. These texts of the stories were, in their turn, taken from volume 3 of the collected edition of Chekhov's works published in 1901 by A.F. Marks. Variations between these two sets of texts and those found in the original 1887 collection *In the Twilight* are mostly insignificant, especially in translation, where differences in spelling and punctuation, for example, are of little or no relevance. Some brief excisions were, however, made by Chekhov in, for example, 'A Nightmare', 'Misfortune' and 'On the Road'. All sixteen stories had been published in periodicals before Chekhov collected them for publication in book form and, in a few instances, the author made more significant amendments to the stories before their inclusion in the 1887 collection. These consisted mostly of excisions, particularly in the case of 'Agafya', but also in, for example, 'The Witch' and 'Misfortune'. The translations offered here thus reflect Chekhov's final preferred versions of the sixteen stories. Full details of the variations in the different Russian texts can be found in the excellent edition *V sumerkakh. Ocherki i rasskazy*, prepared by G.P Berdnikov and A.L. Grishunin for the Literary Monuments series and published by Nauka in Moscow in 1986 to mark the centenary of Chekhov's original volume. This edition was of great help in the preparation of this translation.

Notes

p. 3, *with no recollection of his kin*: A pre-revolutionary legal term applied to tramps with no passport, often fugitives from penal servitude anxious to conceal their past.

p. 3, *Old Believer priests*: "Old Believers" was the name given to those traditionalists who split from the Russian Orthodox Church after the schism of the seventeenth century.

p. 4, *the Parable of the Prodigal Son*: See Luke 15:11–32.

p. 4, *five sazhens*: A *sazhen* was a Russian measure of length equivalent to approximately two metres.

p. 6, *six versts*: A *verst* was a Russian measure of length approximately equivalent to a kilometre.

p. 12, *comme il faut*: "Correct" (French).

p. 13, *britzka*: There is an inconsistency in the original, followed in this translation, as the britzka subsequently becomes a wagon.

p. 13, *arshin*: An *arshin* was a Russian measure of length equivalent to approximately seventy centimetres.

p. 17, *Zemstvo*: An elected district or provincial assembly with certain administrative powers established during the reforms of the 1860s.

p. 19, *Princess Tarakanova*: "Princess Tarakanova" – her true name is unknown – claimed to be the daughter of the Empress Elizabeth and her lover, Count Razumovsky, and thus the rightful ruler of Russia after the assassination of Peter III; captured in Italy and imprisoned by Catherine the Great in 1775, she died in St Petersburg's Peter and Paul Fortress that same year. A popular painting of 1864 by Konstantin Flavitsky (1830–66) depicts her in her cell with floodwater and prison rats at her feet.

p. 31, *Votre père vous appelle, allez vite*: "Your father is calling you, go quickly" (French).

p. 42, *the Prophet Daniel and the Three Youths... Alexei's Day*: Church festivals celebrated on 30th December and 30th March (New Style) respectively

p. 42, *during the Saviours*: More correctly known as the Dormition Fast, lasting from 14th to 28th August (New Style); three holy days associated with Christ at this harvest period have the popular names of the Honey Saviour, the Apple Saviour and the Nut Saviour, hence the popular name for the period of fasting.

p. 42, *the Ten Martyrs of Crete*: A church festival celebrated on 5th January (New Style).

p. 44, *Dyadkovo*: There is an inconsistency in the original, followed in this translation, as the place name is subsequently given as Dyadkino.

p. 44, *the Book of Needs*: A volume of texts of services and prayers intended to cater for all the needs of the parish.

p. 45, *the long, flat sword... the bed of Holofernes*: In the Book of Judith, the eponymous heroine decapitates the lustful Assyrian general to save her hometown of Bethulia from capture. The episode has been depicted by numerous artists including Botticelli, Mantegna, Caravaggio and, perhaps the best known in Russia, since the work features in the Hermitage collection, Giorgione.

p. 46, *one service here for the summer Nikola and one for the winter Nikola*: St Nicholas is celebrated on two days in the Russian church calendar, 22nd May and 19th December (both New Style).

p. 46, *Forgiveness Sunday*: The last day of Shrovetide, when people by tradition ask forgiveness of one another for any wrongs they may have done with a view to receiving God's forgiveness too.

p. 59, *the volosts*: A *volost* was an administrative unit consisting of a number of neighbouring villages.

p. 59, *the holy fool*: Known in the western tradition as "a fool for Christ", a holy fool is usually an ascetic who behaves in a deliberately unconventional manner with a view to distancing himself from prevailing social norms: such figures have often been greatly revered in Russia.

p. 60, *nach Hause*: "To the house" (German).

p. 69, *was reading Byron's Cain*: The mystery of 1821 by George Gordon, Lord Byron (1788–1824), dealing with the biblical theme of fratricide, was published in two different Russian translations in 1881 and 1883.

p. 77, *everything that hath breath*: See Psalms 150:6.

p. 78, *ici*: "Here" (French).

p. 82, *the Mother of God Who Shows the Way*: The name refers to a type of icon representing the Virgin Mary holding the Christ child in her left arm while pointing to Him with her right hand as the way to salvation.

p. 82, *the northerly deacon's door*: On either side of the Holy gates, situated in the centre of the iconostasis, are smaller doors, known as deacons' doors, through which the clergy can pass into the sanctuary.

p. 84, *the Lord... forgave a harlot*: See John 8:3–11.

p. 84, *the Venerable Mariya of Egypt*: Born around 344, she led a dissolute early life, but repented and became a hermit, dying around 421. She is now considered the patron of penitents.

p. 85, *a bowl of boiled wheat and honey*: A dish traditionally served in remembrance of the dead.

p. 86, *Esau's lentils, the punishment of Sodom, and the calamities of the little boy Joseph*: See Genesis 25:29–34, Genesis 19 and Genesis 37.

p. 88, *A little golden cloudlet spent the night/On the breast of one giant of a crag...*: The opening lines of the poem 'The Crag' (1841) by Mikhail Lermontov (1814–41).

p. 89, *the elder Serafim, next Shah Nasr-Ed-Din*: Serafim of Sarov, born Prokhor Moshnin (1759–1833), a hermit who became one of the most venerated of Russian saints; and Nasr-Ed-Din (1829–96), the Shah of Persia from 1848.

p. 93, *salto mortale*: "Somersault" (Italian), literally "mortal leap".

p. 95, *Joshua, who stopped the sun, and my mother, who in the name of the Prophet Elijah rejected lightning conductors*: See Joshua 10:13; Elijah was known to be able to bring down fire from the sky (see, for example, 1 Kings 18:38 and 2 Kings 1:12), and identification with the pagan god of thunder helped make him a figure of particular veneration in Russia.

p. 96, *at the Don Institute*: The Don Institute for Noble Girls was the first secondary education establishment for female pupils in the region when it opened in 1853.

p. 96, *the women's courses*: Higher education courses for women were established in Moscow, Kazan and Kiev in the 1870s and, most famously, in the form of the so-called Bestuzhev courses in St Petersburg in 1878.

p. 96, *black partitions... I went to the people*: References to the movement of the 1870s and 1880s known as Populism, which saw idealistic young members of the left-wing intelligentsia devoting themselves to the Russian peasantry, "going to the people", with very mixed results. In 1879 the populist movement Land and Freedom divided into the more radical People's Will and the short-lived Black Partition, which was also the name given to its journal.

p. 97, *I've been a Slavophile, plaguing Aksakov with letters*: The Slavophiles were those members of the Russian intelligentsia who saw Russia as distinct in its intrinsic nature and optimum path of development from Western Europe (championed by the so-called Westernizers). Two of the Slavophile movement's leading lights were the brothers Konstantin and Ivan Sergeyevich Aksakov (1817–60 and 1823–86 respectively).

p. 97, *the rejection of property... non-resistance to evil*: Elements at this time of the ethical and religious teaching of Leo Tolstoy (1828–1910).

p. 97, *zierlich-manierlich*: "In a dainty and well-mannered way" (German).

p. 102, *some man... holding a large red star on a pole*: The group in the inn are carol-singers, who would traditionally go from house to house with their star of Bethlehem in the hope of receiving presents in return for their songs.

p. 102, *Hey, you... who brought such ill*: It is uncertain who is being referred to in this Ukrainian Christmas song, possibly Herod, possibly Judas, possibly the Wandering Jew.

p. 113, *vis-à-vis*: "Opposite" (French).

p. 121, *pood*: A Russian unit of weight equivalent to approxi mately sixteen kilograms.

p. 123, *vint*: A card game similar to whist or bridge.

p. 126, *the mir*: The Russian village community that was entitled to decide some minor village matters at its meetings.

p. 128, *Agafya Strelchikha*: This is not Agafya's true surname, but a nickname based on the fact that her husband is a railway pointsman (in Russian a *strelochnik*).

p. 132, *the village's Dulcineas*: A reference to eponymous hero Don Quixote's beloved peasant woman Dulcinea in the novel (1605–15) by Miguel de Cervantes Saavedra (1547–1616).

p. 147, *mauvais ton*: "In bad taste" (French).

p. 151, *Rus*: The historical name for pre-modern Russia, used in more recent times to emphasize features of old Russian tradition.

p. 168, *akathists*: In the Orthodox Church, an akathist is a hymn to a holy event or a saint or member of the Trinity.

p. 169, *kondak... ikos*: The *kondak* and *ikos* are the different movements in an akathist.

Extra Material

on

Anton Chekhov's

In the Twilight

Anton Chekhov's Life

Anton Pavlovich Chekhov was born in Taganrog, on the Sea of Azov in southern Russia, on 29th January 1860. He was the third child of Pavel Yegorovich Chekhov and his wife Yevgenia Yakovlevna. He had four brothers – Alexander (born in 1855), Nikolai (1858), Ivan (1861) and Mikhail (1865) – and one sister, Marya, who was born in 1863. Anton's father, the owner of a small shop, was a devout Christian who administered brutal floggings to his children almost on a daily basis. Anton remembered these with bitterness throughout his life, and possibly as a result was always sceptical of organized religion. The shop – a grocery and general-supplies store which sold such goods as lamp oil, tea, coffee, seeds, flour and sugar – was kept by the children during their father's absence. The father also required his children to go with him to church at least once a day. He set up a liturgical choir which practised in his shop, and demanded that his children – whether they had school work to do or not, or whether they had been in the shop all day – should join the rehearsals to provide the higher voice parts.

Chekhov described his home town as filthy and tedious, and *Education and* the people as drunk, idle, lazy and illiterate. At first, Pavel tried *Childhood* to provide his children with an education by enrolling the two he considered the brightest, Nikolai and Anton, in one of the schools for the descendants of the Greek merchants who had once settled in Taganrog. These provided a more "classical" education than their Russian equivalents, and their standard of teaching was held in high regard. However, the experience was not a successful one, since most of the other pupils spoke Greek among themselves, of which the Chekhovs did not know a single word. Eventually, in 1868, Anton was enrolled in one of the town's Russian high schools. The courses at the Russian school included Church Slavonic, Latin and Greek, and if the entire curriculum was successfully completed, entry to a university was guaranteed. Unfortunately, as the shop was making less and less money, the school fees were often unpaid and lessons were missed. The teaching was generally mediocre, but the religious education teacher, Father Pokrovsky, encouraged his pupils to read the Russian classics and such foreign authors as Shakespeare, Swift and Goethe. Pavel also paid for private French and music lessons for his children.

Every summer the family would travel through the steppe by cart some fifty miles to an estate where their paternal grandfather was chief steward. The impressions gathered on these journeys, and the people encountered, had a profound impact on the young Anton, and later provided material for one of his greatest stories, 'The Steppe'.

At the age of thirteen, Anton went to the theatre for the first time, to see Offenbach's operetta *La Belle Hélène* at the Taganrog theatre. He was enchanted by the spectacle, and went as often as time and money allowed, seeing not only the Russian classics, but also foreign pieces such as *Hamlet* in Russian translation. In his early teens, he even created his own theatrical company with his school friends to act out the Russian classics.

Adversity In 1875 Anton was severely ill with peritonitis. The high-school doctor tended him with great care, and he resolved to join the medical profession one day. That same year, his brothers Alexander and Nikolai, fed up with the beatings they received at home, decided to move to Moscow to work and study, ignoring their father's admonitions and threats. Anton now bore the entire brunt of Pavel's brutality. To complicate things further, the family shop ran into severe financial difficulties, and was eventually declared bankrupt. The children were withdrawn from school, and Pavel fled to Moscow, leaving his wife and family to face the creditors. In the end, everybody abandoned the old residence, with the exception of Anton, who remained behind with the new owner.

Although he was now free of his father's bullying and the hardship of having to go to church and work in the shop, Anton had to find other employment in order to pay his rent and bills, and to resume his school studies. Accordingly, at the age of fifteen, he took up tutoring, continuing voraciously to read books of Russian and foreign literature, philosophy and science, in the town library.

In 1877, during a summer holiday, he undertook the seven-hundred-mile journey to Moscow to see his family, and found them all living in one room and sleeping on a single mattress on the floor. His father was not at all abashed by his failures: he continued to be dogmatically religious and to beat the younger children regularly. On his return to Taganrog, Anton attempted to earn a little additional income by sending sketches and anecdotes to several of Moscow's humorous magazines, but they were all turned down.

The young Chekhov unabatedly pursued his studies, and in June 1879 he passed the Taganrog High School exams with distinction, and in the autumn he moved to Moscow to study medicine. The family still lived in one room, and Alexander and Nikolai were well on the way to becoming alcoholics. Anton, instead of finding his own lodgings, decided to support not only himself, but his entire family, and try to re-educate them. After a hard day spent in lectures, tutorials and in the laboratories, he would write more sketches for humorous and satirical magazines, and an increasing number of these were now accepted: by the early 1880s, over a hundred had been printed. Anton used a series of pseudonyms (the most usual being "Antosha Chekhonte") for these productions, which he later called "rubbish". He also visited the Moscow theatres and concert halls on numerous occasions, and in 1880 sent the renowned Maly Theatre a play he had recently written. Only a rough draft of the piece – which was rejected by the Maly and published for the first time in 1920, under the title *Platonov* – has survived. Unless Chekhov had polished and pruned his lost final version considerably, the play would have lasted around seven hours. Despite its poor construction and verbosity, *Platonov* already shows some of the themes and characters present in Chekhov's mature works, such as rural boredom and weak-willed, supine intellectuals dreaming of a better future while not doing anything to bring it about.

As well as humorous sketches and stories, Chekhov wrote brief résumés of legal court proceedings and gossip from the artistic world for various Moscow journals. With the money made from these pieces he moved his family into a larger flat, and regularly invited friends to visit and talk and drink till late at night.

Studies in Moscow and Early Publications

In 1882, encouraged by his success with the Moscow papers, he started contributing to the journals of the capital St Petersburg, since payment there was better than in Moscow. He was eventually commissioned to contribute a regular column to the best-selling journal *Oskolki* ("Splinters"), providing a highly coloured picture of Moscow life with its court cases and bohemian atmosphere. He was now making over 150 roubles a month from his writing – about three times as much as his student stipend – although he managed to save very little because of the needs of his family. In 1884 Chekhov published, at his own expense, a booklet of six of his short stories, entitled *Tales of Melpomene*, which sold quite poorly.

Start of Medical Career   There was compensation for this relative literary failure: in June of that year Anton passed all his final exams in medicine and became a medical practitioner. That summer, he began to receive patients at a village outside Moscow, and even stepped in for the director of a local hospital when the latter went on his summer vacation. He was soon receiving thirty to forty patients a day, and was struck by the peasants' ill health, filth and drunkenness. He planned a major treatise entitled *A History of Medicine in Russia* but, after reading and annotating over a hundred works on the subject, he gave the subject up and returned to Moscow to set up his own medical practice.

First Signs of   Suddenly, in December 1884, when he was approaching the
Tuberculosis achievement of all his ambitions, Chekhov developed a dry cough and began to spit blood. He tried to pretend that these were not early symptoms of tuberculosis but, as a doctor, he must have had an inkling of the truth. He made no attempt to cut down his commitments in the light of his illness, but kept up the same punishing schedule of activity. By this time, Chekhov had published over three hundred items, including some of his first recognized mature works, such as 'The Daughter of Albion' and 'The Death of an Official'. Most of the stories were already, in a very understated way, depicting life's "losers" – such as the idle gentry, shopkeepers striving unsuccessfully to make a living and ignorant peasants. Now that his income had increased, Chekhov rented a summer house a few miles outside Moscow. However, although he intended to use his holiday exclusively for writing, he was inundated all day with locals who had heard he was a doctor and required medical attention.

Chekhov made a crucial step in his literary career, when in December 1885 he visited the imperial capital St Petersburg for the first time, as a guest of the editor of the renowned *St Petersburg Journal*. His stories were beginning to gain him a reputation, and he was introduced at numerous soirées to famous members of the St Petersburg literary world. He was agreeably surprised to find they knew his work and valued it highly. Here for the first time he met Alexei Suvorin, the press mogul and editor of the most influential daily of the period, *Novoye Vremya* (*New Times*). Suvorin asked Chekhov to contribute stories regularly to his paper at a far higher rate of pay than he had been receiving from other journals. Now Chekhov, while busy treating numerous patients in Moscow and helping to stem the constant typhus epidemics that broke out in the city, also began to churn out for Suvorin such embryonic masterpieces as 'The Requiem' and 'Grief' – although all were still published pseudonymously. Distinguished writers advised him to start publishing under his own name and, although his current collection *Motley Stories* had already gone to press under the Chekhonte pseudonym, Anton resolved from now on to shed his anonymity. The collection received tepid reviews, but Chekhov now had sufficient income to rent a whole house on Sadova-Kudrinskaya Street (now maintained as a museum of this early period of Chekhov's life), in an elegant district of Moscow. *Trip to St Petersburg and Meeting with Suvorin*

Chekhov's reputation as a writer was further enhanced when Suvorin published a collection of sixteen of Chekhov's short stories in 1887 – under the title *In the Twilight* – to great critical acclaim. However, Chekhov's health was deteriorating and his blood-spitting was growing worse by the day. Anton appears more and more by now to have come to regard life as a parade of "the vanity of human wishes". He channelled some of this ennui and his previous life experiences into a slightly melodramatic and overlong play, *Ivanov*, in which the eponymous hero – a typical "superfluous man" who indulges in pointless speculation while his estate goes to ruin and his capital dwindles – ends up shooting himself. *Ivanov* was premiered in November 1887 by the respected Korsh Private Theatre under Chekhov's real name – a sign of Anton's growing confidence as a writer – although it received very mixed reviews. *Literary Recognition*

However, in the spring of 1888, Chekhov's story 'The Steppe' – an impressionistic, poetical recounting of the experiences of a young boy travelling through the steppe on a cart – was published in *The Northern Herald*, again under his real name, enabling him to reach another milestone in his literary career, and prompting reviewers for the first time to talk of his genius. Although Chekhov began to travel to the Crimea for vacations, in the hope that the warm climate might aid his health, the symptoms of tuberculosis simply reappeared whenever he returned to Moscow. In October of the same year, Chekhov was awarded the prestigious Pushkin Prize for Literature for *In the Twilight*. He was now recognized as a major Russian writer, and began to state his belief to reporters that a writer's job is not to peddle any political or philosophical point of view, but to depict human life with its associated problems as objectively as possible.

Death of his Brother   A few months later, in January 1889, a revised version of *Ivanov* was staged at the Alexandrinsky Theatre in St Petersburg, arguably the most important drama theatre in Russia at the time. The new production was a huge success and received excellent reviews. However, around that time it also emerged that Anton's alcoholic brother, Nikolai, was suffering from advanced tuberculosis. When Nikolai died in June of that year, at the age of thirty, Anton must have seen this as a harbinger of his own early demise.

Chekhov was now working on a new play, *The Wood Demon*, in which, for the first time, psychological nuance replaced stage action, and the effect on the audience was achieved by atmosphere rather than by drama or the portrayal of events. However, precisely for these reasons, it was rejected by the Alexandrinsky Theatre in October of that year. Undeterred, Chekhov decided to revise it, and a new version of *The Wood Demon* was put on in Moscow in December 1889. Lambasted by the critics, it was swiftly withdrawn from the scene, to make its appearance again many years later, thoroughly rewritten, as *Uncle Vanya*.

Journey to   It was around this time that Anton Chekhov began con-
Sakhalin Island templating his journey to the prison island of Sakhalin. At the end of 1889, unexpectedly, and for no apparent reason, the twenty-nine year-old author announced his intention to leave European Russia, and to travel across Siberia to Sakhalin, the large island separating Siberia and the Pacific Ocean, following which he would write a full-scale examination of the penal colony maintained there by the Tsarist authorities. Explanations put forward by commentators both then and since include a

search by the author for fresh material for his works, a desire
to escape from the constant carping of his liberally minded
colleagues on his lack of a political line; desire to escape from
an unhappy love affair; and disappointment at the recent
failure of *The Wood Demon*. A further explanation may well
be that, as early as 1884, he had been spitting blood, and
recently, just before his journey, several friends and relations
had died of tuberculosis. Chekhov, as a doctor, must have been
aware that he too was in the early stages of the disease, and
that his lifespan would be considerably curtailed. Possibly he
wished to distance himself for several months from everything
he had known, and give himself time to think over his illness
and mortality by immersing himself in a totally alien world.
Chekhov hurled himself into a study of the geography, history,
nature and ethnography of the island, as background material
to his study of the penal settlement. The Trans-Siberian
Railway had not yet been constructed, and the journey across
Siberia, begun in April 1890, required two and a half months of
travel in sledges and carriages on abominable roads in freezing
temperatures and appalling weather. This certainly hastened
the progress of his tuberculosis and almost certainly deprived
him of a few extra years of life. He spent three months in
frantic work on the island, conducting his census of the prison
population, rummaging in archives, collecting material and
organizing book collections for the children of exiles, before
leaving in October 1890 and returning to Moscow, via Hong
Kong, Ceylon and Odessa, in December of that year.

The completion of his report on his trip to Sakhalin was *Travels in Europe*
to be hindered for almost five years by his phenomenally
busy life, as he attempted, as before, to continue his medical
practice and write at the same time. In early 1891 Chekhov, in
the company of Suvorin, travelled for the first time to western
Europe, visiting Vienna, Venice, Bologna, Florence, Rome,
Naples and finally Monaco and Paris.

Trying to cut down on the expenses he was paying out for *Move to Melikhovo*
his family in Moscow, he bought a small estate at Melikhovo, a
few miles outside Moscow, and the entire family moved there.
His father did some gardening, his mother cooked, while
Anton planted hundreds of fruit trees, shrubs and flowers.
Chekhov's concerns for nature have a surprisingly modern
ecological ring: he once said that if he had not been a writer
he would have become a gardener.

Although his brothers had their own lives in Moscow and only spent holidays at Melikhovo, Anton's sister Marya – who never married – lived there permanently, acting as his confidante and as his housekeeper when he had his friends and famous literary figures to stay, as he often did in large parties. Chekhov also continued to write, but was distracted, as before, by the scores of locals who came every day to receive medical treatment from him. There was no such thing as free medical assistance in those days and, if anybody seemed unable to pay, Chekhov often treated them for nothing. In 1892, there was a severe local outbreak of cholera, and Chekhov was placed in charge of relief operations. He supervised the building of emergency isolation wards in all the surrounding villages and travelled around the entire area directing the medical operations.

Ill Health   Chekhov's health was deteriorating more and more rapidly, and his relentless activity certainly did not help. He began to experience almost constant pain and, although still hosting gatherings, he gave the appearance of withdrawing increasingly into himself and growing easily tired. By the mid-1890s, his sleep was disturbed on most nights by bouts of violent coughing. Besides continuing his medical activities, looking after his estate and writing, Chekhov undertook to supervise – often with large subsidies from his own pocket – the building of schools in the local villages, where there had been none before.

Controversy around   By late 1895, Chekhov was thinking of writing for the theatre
The Seagull   again. The result was *The Seagull*, which was premiered at the Alexandrinsky Theatre in October 1896. Unfortunately the acting was so bad that the premiere was met by jeering and laughter, and received vicious reviews. Chekhov himself commented that the director did not understand the play, the actors didn't know their lines and nobody could grasp the understated style. He fled from the theatre and roamed the streets of St Petersburg until two in the morning, resolving never to write for the theatre again. Despite this initial fiasco, subsequent performances went from strength to strength, with the actors called out on stage after every performance.

Olga Knipper   By this time, it seems that Chekhov had accepted the fact that he had a mortal illness. In 1897, he returned to Italy to see whether the warmer climate would not afford his condition some respite, but as soon as he came back to Russia the coughing and blood-spitting resumed as violently as before. It was around this time that the two founders of the

Moscow Arts Theatre, Vladimir Nemirovich-Danchenko and
Konstantin Stanislavsky, asked Chekhov whether they could
stage *The Seagull*. Their aims were to replace the stylized and
unnatural devices of the classical theatre with more natural
events and dialogue, and Chekhov's play seemed ideal for
this purpose. He gave his permission, and in September 1898
went to Moscow to attend the preliminary rehearsals. It was
there that he first met the twenty-eight-year-old actress Olga
Knipper, who was going to take the leading role of Arkadina.
However, the Russian winter was making him cough blood
violently, and so he decided to follow the local doctors' advice
and travel south to the Crimea, in order to spend the winter in
a warmer climate. Accordingly, he rented a villa with a large
garden in Yalta.

When his father died in October of the same year, Chekhov *Move to the Crimea*
decided to put Melikhovo up for sale and move his mother
and Marya to the Crimea. They temporarily stayed in a large
villa near the Tatar village of Kuchukoy, but Chekhov had in
the meantime bought a plot of land at Autka, some twenty
minutes by carriage from Yalta, and he drew up a project to
have a house built there. Construction began in December.

Also in December 1898, the first performance of *The Seagull* at the Moscow Arts Theatre took place. It was a re-
sounding success, and there were now all-night queues for
tickets. Despite his extremely poor health, Chekhov was
still busy raising money for relief of the severe famine then
scourging the Russian heartlands, overseeing the building of
his new house and aiding the local branch of the Red Cross. In
addition to this, local people and aspiring writers would turn
up in droves at his villa in Yalta to receive medical treatment
or advice on their manuscripts.

In early January 1899, Chekhov signed an agreement with *Collected Works Project*
the publisher Adolf Marx to supervise the publication of a
multi-volume edition of his collected works in return for a
flat fee of 75,000 roubles and no royalties. This proved to be
an error of judgement from a financial point of view, because
by the time Chekhov had put some money towards building
his new house, ensured all the members of his family were
provided for and made various other donations, the advance
had almost disappeared.

Chekhov finally moved to Autka – where he was to spend *Romance*
the last few years of his life – in June 1899, and immediately *with Olga*

195

began to plant vegetables, flowers and fruit trees. During a short period spent in Moscow to facilitate his work for Adolf Marx, he re-established contact with the Moscow Arts Theatre and Olga Knipper. Chekhov invited the actress to Yalta on several occasions and, although her visits were brief and at first she stayed in a hotel, it was obvious that she and Chekhov were becoming very close. Apart from occasional short visits to Moscow, which cost him a great expenditure of energy and were extremely harmful to his medical condition, Chekhov now had to spend all of his time in the south. He forced himself to continue writing short stories and plays, but felt increasingly lonely and isolated and, aware that he had only a short time left to live, became even more withdrawn. It was around this time that he worked again at his early play *The Wood Demon*, reducing the dramatis personae to only nine characters, radically altering the most significant scenes and renaming it *Uncle Vanya*. This was premiered in October 1899, and it was another gigantic success. In July of the following year, Olga Knipper took time off from her busy schedule of rehearsals and performances in Moscow to visit Chekhov in Yalta. There was no longer any attempt at pretence: she stayed in his house and, although he was by now extremely ill, they became romantically involved, exchanging love letters almost every day.

By now Chekhov had drafted another new play, *Three Sisters*, and he travelled to Moscow to supervise the first few rehearsals. Olga came to his hotel every day bringing food and flowers. However, Anton felt that the play needed revision, so he returned to Yalta to work on a comprehensive rewrite. *Three Sisters* opened on 31st January 1901 and – though at first well-received, especially by the critics – it gradually grew in the public's estimation, becoming another great success.

Wedding and Honeymoon But Chekhov was feeling lonely in Yalta without Olga, and in May of that year proposed to her by letter. Olga accepted, and Chekhov immediately set off for Moscow, despite his doctors' advice to the contrary. He arranged a dinner for his friends and relatives and, while they were waiting there, he and Olga got married secretly in a small church on the outskirts of Moscow. As the participants at the dinner received a telegram with the news, the couple had already left for their honeymoon. Olga and Anton sailed down the Volga, up the Kama River and along the Belaya River to the village of Aksyonovo, where they checked into a sanatorium. At this establishment Chekhov drank four large bottles of fermented mare's milk every day, put on weight, and his condition seemed to improve somewhat. However, on their return to Yalta, Chekhov's health deteriorated again. He made his will, leaving his house in Yalta to Marya, all income from his dramatic works to Olga and large sums to his mother and his surviving brothers, to the municipality of Taganrog and to the peasant body of Melikhovo.

After a while, Olga returned to her busy schedule of rehears- *Difficult Relationship* als and performances in Moscow, and the couple continued their relationship at a distance, as they had done before their marriage, with long and frequent love letters. Chekhov managed to visit her in Moscow occasionally, but by now he was so ill that he had to return to Yalta immediately, often remaining confined to bed for long periods. Olga was tortured as to whether she should give up her acting career and nurse Anton for the time left to him. Almost unable to write, Anton now embarked laboriously on his last dramatic masterpiece, *The Cherry Orchard*. Around that time, in the spring of 1902, Olga visited Anton in Yalta after suffering a spontaneous miscarriage during a Moscow Art Theatre tour, leaving her husband with the unpleasant suspicion that she might have been unfaithful to him. In the following months, Anton nursed his wife devotedly, travelling to Moscow whenever he could to be near her. Olga's flat was on the third floor, and there was no lift. It took Anton half an hour to get up the stairs, so he practically never went out.

When *The Cherry Orchard* was finally completed in *Final Play* October 1903, Chekhov once again travelled to Moscow to attend rehearsals, despite the advice of his doctors that it would be tantamount to suicide. The play was premiered on 17th January 1904, Chekhov's forty-fourth birthday, and at the end of the performance the author was dragged on stage. There was no chair for him, and he was forced to stand listening to the interminable speeches, trying not to cough and pretending to look interested. Although the performance was a success, press reviews, as usual, were mixed, and Chekhov thought that Nemirovich-Danchenko and Stanislavsky had misunderstood the play.

Chekhov returned to Yalta knowing he would not live long *Death* enough to write another work. His health deteriorated even further, and the doctors put him on morphine, advising him to go to a sanatorium in Germany. Accordingly, in June 1904, he and Olga set off for Badenweiler, a spa in the Black Forest. The German specialists examined him and reported that they could do nothing. Soon oxygen had to be administered to him, and he became feverish and delirious. At 12.30 a.m. on 15th July 1904, he regained his mental clarity sufficiently to tell Olga to summon a doctor urgently. On the doctor's arrival, Chekhov told him, *"Ich sterbe"* ("I'm dying"). The doctor gave him a strong stimulant, and was on the point of sending for other medicines when Chekhov, knowing it was all pointless, simply asked for a bottle of champagne to be sent to the room. He poured everybody a glass, drank his off, commenting that he hadn't had champagne for ages, lay down, and died in the early hours of the morning.

Funeral   The coffin was transported back to Moscow in a filthy green carriage marked "FOR OYSTERS", and although it was met at the station by bands and a large ceremonial gathering, it turned out that this was for an eminent Russian General who had just been killed in action in Manchuria. Only a handful of people had assembled to greet Chekhov's coffin. However, as word got round Moscow that his body was being transported to the graveyard at the Novodevichy Monastery, people poured out of their homes and workplaces, forming a vast crowd both inside and outside the cemetery and causing a large amount of damage to buildings, pathways and other graves in the process. The entire tragicomic episode of Chekhov's death, transportation back to Moscow and burial could almost have featured in one of his own short stories. Chekhov was buried next to his father Pavel. His mother outlived him by fifteen years, and his sister Marya died in 1957 at the age of ninety-four. Olga Knipper survived two more years, dying in 1959 at the age of eighty-nine.

Anton Chekhov's Works

Early Writings   When Chekhov studied medicine in Moscow from 1879 to 1884, he financed his studies by writing reports of law-court proceedings for the newspapers and contributing, under a whole series of pseudonyms, hundreds of jokes, comic sketches and short stories to the numerous Russian humorous magazines and more serious journals of the time. From 1885, when he began to practise as a doctor, he concentrated far more on serious literary works, and between then and the end of his life he produced over 200 short stories, plus a score or so of dramatic pieces, ranging from monologues through one-act to full-length plays. In 1884 he also wrote his only novel, *The Hunting Party*, which was a rather wooden attempt at a detective novel.

A number of his stories between the mid-Eighties and his *Invention of a New,* journey to Sakhalin were vitiated by his attempt to propagate *"Objective" Style of* the Tolstoyan moral principles he had espoused at the time. *Writing* But even before his journey to the prison island he was realizing that laying down the law to his readers, and trying to dictate how they should read his stories, was not his job: it should be the goal of an artist to describe persons and events non-judgementally, and let the reader draw his or her own conclusions. This is attested by his letter to Suvorin in April 1890: "You reproach me for 'objectivity', calling it indifference to good and evil, and absence of ideals and ideas and so forth. You wish me, when depicting horse thieves, to state: stealing horses is bad. But surely people have known that for ages already, without me telling them so? Let them be judged by jurymen – my business is to show them as they really are. When I write, I rely totally on the reader, supposing that he himself will supply the subjective factors absent in the story." After Chekhov's return from Sakhalin, this objectivity dominated everything he wrote.

A further feature of Chekhov's storytelling, which developed throughout his career, is that he does not so much describe events taking place, but rather depicts the way that characters react to those – frequently quite insignificant – events, and the way people's lives are often transformed for better or worse by them. His dramatic works from that time also showed a development from fully displayed events and action – sometimes, in the early plays, quite melodramatic – to, in the major plays written in the last decade or so of his life, depicting the effects on people's lives of off-stage events, and the way the characters react to those events.

His style in all his later writing – especially from 1890 onwards – is lucid and economical, and there is a total absence of purple passages. The works of his final years display an increasing awareness of the need for conservation of the natural world in the face of the creeping industrialization of Russia. The breakdown of the old social order in the face of the new rising entrepreneurial class is also depicted non-judgementally; in Chekhov's last play, *The Cherry Orchard*, an old estate belonging to a long-established family of gentry is sold to a businessman, and the final scenes of the play give way to the offstage sounds of wood-chopping, as the old cherry orchard – one of the major beauties of the estate – is cut down by its new owner to be sold for timber.

Major Short Stories   It is generally accepted that Chekhov's mature story-writing may be said to date from the mid-1880s, when he began to contribute to the "thick journals". Descriptions of a small representative selection of some of the major short stories – giving an idea of Chekhov's predominant themes – can be found below.

On the Road   In 'On the Road' (1886), set in a seedy wayside inn on Christmas Eve, a man, apparently from the privileged classes, and his eight-year-old daughter are attempting to sleep in the "travellers' lounge", having been forced to take refuge from a violent storm. The little girl wakes up, and tells him how unhappy she is and that he is a wicked man. A noblewoman, also sheltering from the storm, enters and comforts the girl. The man and the woman both tell each other of the unhappiness of their lives: he is a widowed nobleman who has squandered all his money and is now on his way to a tedious job in the middle of nowhere; she is from a wealthy family, but her father and her brothers are wastrels, and she is the only one who takes care of the estate. They both part in the morning, on Christmas Day, profoundly unhappy, and without succeeding in establishing that deep inner contact with another human being which both of them obviously crave.

Enemies   Chekhov's 1887 tale 'Enemies' touches on similar themes of misery and incomprehension: a country doctor's six-year-old son has just died of diphtheria, leaving him and his wife devastated; at precisely this moment, a local landowner comes to his house to call him out to attend to his wife, who is apparently dangerously ill. Though sympathetic to the doctor's state, he is understandably full of anxiety for his wife, and insists that the doctor come. After an uncomfortable carriage journey, they arrive at the landowner's mansion to discover that the wife was never ill at all, but was simply getting rid of her husband so that she could run off with her lover. The landowner is now in a state of anger and despair, and the doctor unreasonably blames him for having dragged him out under false pretences. When the man offers him his fee, the doctor throws it in his face and storms out. The landowner also furiously drives off somewhere to assuage his anger. Neither man can even begin to penetrate the other's mental state because of their own problems. The doctor remains full of contempt and cynicism for the human race for the rest of his life.

In 1888, Chekhov's first indubitably great narrative, the novella-length 'The Steppe', was published to rapturous reviews. There is almost no plot: in blazing midsummer, a nine-year-old boy sets out on a long wagon ride, lasting several days, from his home in a small provincial town through the steppe, to stay with relatives and attend high school in a large city. The entire story consists of his impressions of the journey – of his travelling companions, the people they meet en route, the inns at which they stay, the scenery and wildlife. He finally reaches his destination, bids farewell to his travelling companions, and the story ends with him full of tears of regret at his lost home life, and foreboding at what the future in this strange new world holds for him. *The Steppe*

Another major short story by Chekhov, 'The Name-Day Party' (also translated as 'The Party'), was published in the same year as 'The Steppe'. The title refers to the fact that Russians celebrate not only their birthdays, but the day of the saint after whom they are named. It is the name day of a selfish lawyer and magistrate; his young wife, who is seven-months pregnant, has spent all day organizing a banquet in his honour and entertaining guests. Utterly exhausted, she occasionally asks him to help her, but he does very little. Finally, when all the guests have gone home, she, in extreme agony, gives birth prematurely to a still-born baby. She slips in and out of consciousness, believes she too is dying, and, despite his behaviour, she feels sorry for her husband, who will be lost without her. However, when she regains consciousness he seems to blame her for the loss of the child, and not his own selfishness leading to her utter exhaustion at such a time. *The Name-Day Party*

'A Dreary Story' (also known as 'A Tedious Story') is one of Chekhov's longer stories, originally published in 1889. In a tour de force, the twenty-nine-year-old Chekhov penetrates into the mind of a famous sixty-two-year-old professor – his interior monologue constituting the entire tale. The professor *A Dreary Story* is a world expert in his subject, fêted throughout Russia, yet has a terminal disease which means he will be dead in a few months. He has told nobody, not even his family. This professor muses over his life, and how his body is falling apart, and he wonders what the point of it all was. He would gladly give all his fame for just a few more years of warm, vibrant life. Chekhov wrote this story the year before he travelled to Sakhalin, when he was beginning to display the first symptoms of the tuberculosis which was to kill him at the age of forty-four.

The Duel   In Chekhov's 1891 story 'The Duel', a bored young civil servant has lost interest in everything in life, including his lover. When the latter's husband dies, she expects him to marry her, but he decides to borrow money and leave the town permanently instead. However, the acquaintance from whom he tries to borrow the money refuses to advance him the sum for such purposes. After a heated exchange, the civil servant challenges the acquaintance to a duel – a challenge which is taken up by a friend of the person who has refused to lend the money, disgusted at the civil servant's selfish behaviour. Both miss their shot, and the civil servant, realizing how near he has been to death, regains interest in life, marries his mistress, and all are reconciled.

Ward No. 6   In 'Ward No. 6' (1892), a well-meaning but apathetic and weak rural hospital director has a ward for the mentally disturbed as one of his responsibilities. He knows that the thuggish peasant warden regularly beats the lunatics up, but makes all kinds of excuses not to get involved. He ends up being incarcerated in his own mental ward by the ruse of an ambitious rival, and is promptly beaten by the same warden who used to call him "Your Honour", and dies soon afterwards. This is perhaps Chekhov's most transparent attack on the supine intelligentsia of his own time, whom he saw as lacking determination in the fight against social evils.

Three Years   In 1895, Chekhov published his famous story 'Three Years', in which Laptev, a young Muscovite, is nursing his seriously ill sister in a small provincial town, and feels restricted and bored. He falls in love with the daughter of her doctor and, perhaps from loneliness and the need for companionship, proposes marriage. Although she is not in love with him, she accepts, after a good deal of hesitation, because she is afraid this might be her only offer in this dull town. For the first three years this marriage – forged through a sense of isolation on one side and fear of spinsterhood on the other – is passionless and somewhat unhappy. However, after this period, they manage to achieve an equable and fulfilling relationship based on companionship.

In the 'The House with a Mansard' (1896), a talented but lazy young artist visits a rich landowning friend in the country. They go to visit the wealthy family at the title's "house with a mansard", which consists of a mother and two unmarried daughters. The artist falls in love with the younger daughter, but her tyrannical older sister sends both her and her mother abroad. The story ends some years later with the artist still wistfully wondering what has become of the younger sister. *The House with a Mansard*

In 'Peasants' (1897), Nikolai, who has lived and worked in Moscow since adolescence, and now works as a highly respected waiter at a prestigious Moscow hotel, is taken very ill and can no longer work, so he decides to return to the country village of his childhood, taking with him his wife and young daughter, who were both born in Moscow. He has warm recollections of the village, but finds that memory has deceived him. The place is filthy and squalid, and the local inhabitants all seem to be permanently blind drunk. Since anybody with any intelligence – like Nikolai himself – is sent to the city as young as possible to work and send money back to the family, the level of ignorance and stupidity is appalling. Nikolai dies, and the story ends with his wife and daughter having to become tramps and beg for a living. *Peasants*

In 1898, Chekhov published 'The Man in a Case', in which the narrator, a schoolmaster, recounts the life of a recently deceased colleague of his, Byelikov, who taught classical Greek. A figure of ridicule for his pupils and colleagues, Byelikov is described as being terrified of the modern world, walking around, even in the warmest weather, in high boots, a heavy overcoat, dark spectacles and a hat with a large brim concealing his face. The blinds are always drawn on all the windows in his house, and these are permanently shut. He threatens to report to the headmaster a young colleague who engages in the appallingly immoral and progressive activity of going for bicycle rides in the countryside. The young man pushes him, Byelikov falls down and, although not hurt, takes to his bed and dies, apparently of humiliation and oversensitivity. *The Man in a Case*

'The Lady with the Lapdog' (1899) tells the story of a bored
and cynical forty-year-old senior bank official who, trapped in a
tedious marriage in Moscow, takes a holiday by himself in Yalta.
There he meets the thirty-year-old Anna, who is also unhappily
married. They have an affair, then go back to their respective
homes. In love for possibly the first time in his life, he travels to
the provincial town where she lives, and tracks her down. They
meet in a theatre, and before her husband returns to his seat,
she promises to visit him in Moscow. The story ends with them
both realizing that their problems are only just beginning.

Sakhalin Island   As well as being a prolific writer of short fiction, Chekhov
also wrote countless articles as a journalist, and the volume-
length *Sakhalin Island* ranks as one of the most notable
examples of his investigative non-fiction. As mentioned above,
Chekhov's decision to travel to Sakhalin Island in easternmost
Siberia for three months in 1890 was motivated by several
factors, one of them being to write a comprehensive study of
the penal colonies on the island.

Chekhov toured round the entire island, visiting all the
prisons and most of the settlements, and generally spending up
to nineteen hours a day gathering material and writing up his
findings. Chekhov returned from Sakhalin at the end of 1890,
but it took him three years to write up and start publishing
the material he had collected. The first chapter was published
in the journal *Russian Thought* (*Russkaya Mysl*) in late 1893,
and subsequent material appeared regularly in this magazine
until July 1894, with no objection from the censor, until finally
the chapters from number twenty onwards were banned from
publication. Chekhov took the decision to "publish and be
damned" – accordingly the whole thing appeared in book
form, including the banned chapters, in May 1895.

The book caused enormous interest and discussion in
the press, and over the next decade a number of substantial
ameliorations were brought about in the criminals' lives.

Major Plays   Chekhov first made his name in the theatre with a series
of one-act farces, most notably *The Bear* and *Swan Song*
(both 1888). However, his first attempts at full-length plays,
Platonov (1880), *Ivanov* (1887) and *The Wood Demon* (1889)
were not entirely successful. The four plays which are now
considered to be Chekhov's masterpieces, and outstanding
works of world theatre, are *The Seagull* (1896), *Uncle Vanya*
(1899), *Three Sisters* (1901) and *The Cherry Orchard* (1904).

The central character in *The Seagull* is an unsuccessful *The Seagull* playwright, Treplev, who is in love with the actress Nina. However, she falls in love with the far more successful writer Trigorin. Out of spite and as an anti-idealist gesture, Treplev shoots a seagull and places it in front of her. Nina becomes Trigorin's mistress. Unfortunately their baby dies, Nina's career collapses, and Trigorin leaves her. However, on Treplev renewing his overtures to Nina, she tells him that she still loves Trigorin. The play ends with news being brought in that Treplev has committed suicide offstage.

The second of Chekhov's four dramatic masterpieces, *Uncle* *Uncle Vanya* *Vanya*, a comprehensive reworking of the previously unsuccessful *Wood Demon*, centres on Vanya, who has for many years tirelessly managed a professor's estate. However, the professor finally retires back to his estate with his bored and idle young wife, with whom Vanya falls in love. Vanya now realizes that the professor is a thoroughly selfish and mediocre man and becomes jealous and embittered at his own fate, believing he has sacrificed his own brilliant future. When the professor tells him that he is going to sell the estate, Vanya, incensed, fires a pistol at him at point-blank range and misses – which only serves to compound his sense of failure and frustration. The professor and his wife agree not to sell up for the time being and leave to live elsewhere. Vanya sinks back into his boring loveless life, probably for ever.

In *Three Sisters*, Olga, Masha and Irina live a boring life in *Three Sisters* their brother's house in a provincial town, remote from Moscow and Petersburg. All three remember their happy childhood in Moscow and dream of one day returning. A military unit arrives nearby, and Irina and Masha start up relationships with officers, which might offer a way out of their tedious lives. However, Irina's fiancé is killed in a duel, Masha's relationship ends when the regiment moves on, and Olga, a schoolteacher, is promoted to the post of headmistress at her school, thus forcing her to give up any hope of leaving the area. They all relapse into what they perceive to be their meaningless lives.

The Cherry Orchard, Chekhov's final masterpiece for the theatre, is a lament for the passing of old traditional Russia *The Cherry* and the encroachment of the modern world. The Ranevsky *Orchard* family estate, with its wonderful and famous cherry orchard, is no longer a viable concern. Various suggestions are made to stave off financial disaster, all of which involve cutting down

ANTON CHEKHOV · IN THE TWILIGHT

the ancient orchard. Finally the estate is auctioned off, and in the final scene, the orchard is chopped down offstage. The old landowning family move out, and in a final tragicomic scene, they forget to take an ancient manservant with them, accidentally locking him in the house and leaving him feeling abandoned.

Select Bibliography

Standard Edition:
The most authoritative Russian edition of *In the Twilight* is *V sumerkakh. Ocherki i rasskazy*, prepared by G.P Berdnikov and A.L. Grishunin for the Literary Monuments series and published by Nauka in Moscow in 1986.

Biographies:
Hingley, Ronald, *A New Life of Anton Chekhov* (Oxford: Oxford University Press, 1976)
Pritchett, V.S., *Chekhov: A Spirit Set Free* (London: Hodder & Stoughton, 1988)
Rayfield, Donald, *Anton Chekhov* (London: HarperCollins, 1997)
Simmons, Ernest, *Chekhov: A Biography* (London: Jonathan Cape, 1963)
Troyat, Henri, *Chekhov*, tr. Michael Henry Heim (New York: Dutton, 1986)

Additional Recommended Background Material:
Helman, Lillian, ed., *Selected Letters of Anton Chekhov* (1984)
Magarshack, David, *Chekhov the Dramatist*, 2nd ed. (London: Eyre Methuen,1980)
Malcolm, Janet, *Reading Chekhov: A Critical Journey* (London: Granta, 2001)
Pennington, Michael, *Are You There, Crocodile?: Inventing Anton Chekhov* (London: Oberon, 2003)

ALMA CLASSICS

ALMA CLASSICS aims to publish mainstream and lesser-known European classics in an innovative and striking way, while employing the highest editorial and production standards. By way of a unique approach the range offers much more, both visually and textually, than readers have come to expect from contemporary classics publishing.

LATEST TITLES PUBLISHED BY ALMA CLASSICS

To order any of our titles and for up-to-date information about our current and forthcoming publications, please visit our website on:

www.almaclassics.com